RIDING THE NIGHTMARE

LISA TUTTLE is an award-winning author of science fiction, fantasy and horror. Her first novel, written in collaboration with George R.R. Martin, *Windhaven*, has been in print since 1981, and was adapted by her as a graphic novel. Her most recent novels are part of a detective series with supernatural elements, set in 1890s England: *The Curious Affair of the Somnambulist and the Psychic Thief*, *The Curious Affair of the Witch at Wayside Cross*, and the third volume, *The Curious Affair of the Missing Mummies*, published in June 2023. Born and raised in Texas, she has lived in Scotland since 1990.

NEIL GAIMAN is the bestselling author and creator of books, graphic novels, short stories, film and television for all ages, including *Norse Mythology, Neverwhere, Coraline, The Graveyard Book, The Ocean at the End of the Lane, The View from the Cheap Seats*, and the *Sandman* comic series. His fiction has received Newbery, Carnegie, Hugo, Nebula, World Fantasy, and Will Eisner Awards. Neil has adapted many of his works to television series, including *Anansi Boys, Good Omens,* and *Sandman*. He is a Goodwill Ambassador for the UNHCR and he is also a Professor in the Arts at Bard College.

Lisa Tuttle

Riding the Nightmare

Introduction by
NEIL GAIMAN

VALANCOURT BOOKS

Riding the Nightmare by Lisa Tuttle
First edition 2023

Published by Valancourt Books, Richmond, Virginia
http://www.valancourtbooks.com

ISBN 978-1-954321-90-8 (hardcover)
ISBN 978-1-954321-89-2 (trade paperback)

Also available as an electronic book.

Cover by Vince Haig
Set in Bembo Book MT Pro

Contents

She Rides the Nightmare

by Neil Gaiman

Here are the twelve words that conclude the twelve stories in this volume: *pitiless, choice, alive, ending, successful, lies, ditch, it, absolute, darkness, end* and *father*.

Memory is not reliable. Well, nothing is as reliable as I would like it to be, but memory fools me always by being useful and I rely on it, and then discover what happened to be otherwise. For almost forty years I've remembered that Lisa Tuttle had a slip of paper on the wall of her study in her flat in Ortygia House,[*] in Harrow, which said that the only two true subjects for an author were sex and death. I read it there in 1985 or 1986 and I've never forgotten it. I've even quoted it to other people.

A few days ago I wrote to Lisa, knowing I would be writing this introduction, to ask who had said it. She was unsure, then replied, 'There's this used as an epigraph to Aickman's *Powers of Darkness* – from W.B. Yeats: "I am still of the opinion that only two topics can be of the least interest to a serious and studious mind – sex and the dead." I just found an old notebook I kept in 1984-85 and it has that quote from W.B. Yeats exactly – and a few pages later I copied in something else that I remember I had pinned up above my desk – "Every fear is a desire. Every desire is fear." (from "A Staffordshire Murderer" by James Fenton). And there are some ideas for stories I never wrote – maybe now I will?! – and some rather disturbing dreams.'

It seemed remarkably appropriate that Aickman's name was being invoked, because rereading all the stories in *Riding the*

[*] (*I had remembered that Ortygia was Greek and was a bird, but had misremembered the bird as a nightingale. It's a quail.*)

Nightmare, I found myself thinking of Robert Aickman. Like Aickman's stories, Lisa Tuttle's stories are never truly horror stories (although none of them will leave you unmoved and several draw blood). Aickman described his stories as 'strange stories', designed to prey on the mind, to derail your day and mood, to leave you thinking about the stories and the people in them, about what was said and what was left unsaid, for hours or for days after reading them. Like Robert Aickman, Lisa Tuttle is able to tell impossible stories which evoke dread and strangeness and the uncanny, stories that feel right while being resistant to any explanation. Unlike Aickman, Lisa writes women who feel real (Aickman's women always made me feel that they represented something, womanhood or goddesses, entrapment or sexuality, but were rarely ever allowed to be people).

Lisa Tuttle began her career as a writer of science fiction, and one story in this connection exists on the borders of science fiction, in a world in which sex and gender are fluid in ways that even Ursula Le Guin did not anticipate.

She was born, raised, and worked in Texas, moved to Harrow in England. She has lived for several decades in Scotland.

We became friends at a Milford Writers Conference in 1985, although she was a towering figure in the field (and the only person I have met ever to have refused a Nebula Award she was given), and I was a baby writer.

Lisa Tuttle is, in her human person, cheerful, sensible, and very easy to be around. She smiles often, and laughs easily. She knows many things.

Lisa Tuttle is, in her fiction-writing capacity, a killer with a handy boning knife, dangerous of eye and bleak of humour, and convincing enough in her depiction of reality and of human relationships to make her most improbable lies and her most pitiless plot twists feel both true and darkly inevitable.

There is a precision to Lisa's writing that I was already in awe of when I first met her, and an understanding of gender dynamics, of the ways that men and women relate, that described a world that I had, back then, in retrospect, no clue about, that I'm still trying to figure out.

This book is a Best Unsettling Fiction of Lisa Tuttle, I guess, for it contains stories published over a period of more than thirty years, but it would be possible to put together several other collections of the Best Unsettling Fiction of Lisa Tuttle without ever repeating a story. She has written many short stories and written them well. Still, the dozen stories in this book are certainly representative of the strange and disturbing place that Lisa Tuttle is able to take you to.

In 'Riding the Nightmare' Lisa explores the nightmare of parenthood.

'Bits and Pieces' examines what we leave behind in relationships and who we become.

'The Mezzotint' is not only a reinterpretation of a classic story, but one which you can reread with increased joy and dread.

'After the End' is the final case of a great detective.

'The Third Person' is about other people and their affairs, and how their affairs can become yours.

'The Wound' is science fiction, of a sort, only it's not. Not really. It allows one thing to change, to allow us to see other things more clearly.

'Home in the Sky' is, for me, the most Aickman story here.

'Voices in the Night' is a tale of how our lives can sometimes go to hell.

'The Hungry Hotel' is a story to get lost in.

'The Dragon's Bride' feels like a novel, albeit a short one, and a dark one.

They are stories about sex and the dead, which are, as I learned long ago, the only two topics for a serious mind. For that matter, every fear in these tales is a desire, every desire is fear.

Memory is unreliable, but these are things to take with you to the grave, or to wherever you are going to finish in the end.

NEIL GAIMAN
Woodstock, New York
March 2023

Riding the Nightmare

Twilight, *l'heure bleu*. Tess O'Neal sat on the balcony of her sixth-floor apartment and looked out at the soft, suburban sprawl of New Orleans, a blur of green trees and multicoloured houses, with the jewels of lights just winking on. It was a time of day which made her nostalgic and gently melancholy, feelings she usually enjoyed. But not now. For once she wished she were not alone with the evening.

Gordon had cancelled their date. No great disaster – he'd said they could have all day Sunday together – but the change of plan struck Tess as ominous, and she questioned him.

'Is something wrong?'

He hesitated. Maybe he was only reacting to the sharp note in her voice. 'Of course not. Jude . . . made some plans and it would spoil things if I went out. She sends her apologies.'

There was nothing odd in that. Jude was Gordon's wife and also Tess's friend, a situation they were all comfortable with. But Jude was slightly scatter-brained, and when she confused dates, it was Tess who had to take second place. Usually Tess did not mind. Now she did.

'We'll talk on Sunday,' Gordon said.

Tess didn't want to talk. She didn't want explanations. She wanted Gordon's body on hers, making her believe that nothing had changed, nothing would ever change between them.

They're in it together, she thought. Him and his wife. And I'm left out in the cold.

She looked up at the darkening sky. As blue as the nightmare's eye, she thought, and shivered. She got up and went inside, suddenly feeling too vulnerable in the open air.

She had never told Gordon about the nightmare. He admired

her as a competent, sophisticated, independent woman. How could she talk to him about childhood fears? How could she tell him that this was one childhood fear which hadn't stayed in childhood but had come after her?

As she turned to lock the sliding glass door behind her, Tess froze.

The mare's long head was there, resting on the balcony rail as if on a stable door, the long mane waving slightly in the breeze, the bluish eye fixed commandingly on her.

Tess stumbled backward and the vision, broken, vanished.

There was nothing outside that should not be, nothing but sky and city and her own dark reflection in the glass.

'Snap out of it, O'Neal,' she said aloud. Bad enough to dream the nightmare, but if she was going to start seeing it with her eyes open, she really needed help.

For a moment she thought of phoning Gordon. But what could she say? Not only would it go against the rules to phone him after he'd said they could not meet, but it would go against everything he knew and expected of her if she began babbling about a nightmare. She simply wanted his presence, the way, as a child, she had wanted her father to put his arms around her and tell her not to cry. But she was a grown woman now. She didn't need anyone else to tell her what was real and what was not; she knew that the best way to banish fears and depression was by working, not brooding.

She poured herself a Coke and settled at her desk with a stack of transcripts. She was a doctoral candidate in linguistics, working on a thesis examining the difference in language use between men and women. It was a subject of which, by now, she was thoroughly sick. She wondered sometimes if she would ever be able to speak unselfconsciously again, without monitoring her own speech patterns to edit out the stray, feminine modifiers and apologies.

The window was open. Through it, she could see the black and windy sky and there, running on the wind, was the creamy white mare with tumbling mane and rolling blue eye. Around her neck hung a shining crescent moon, the golden lunula strung on a white and scarlet cord. And Tess was on her feet, walking toward the window as if hypnotized. It was then that she became aware of herself, and knew she was dreaming, and that she must break the dream. With a great effort of will, she flung herself backwards, towards the place where she knew her bed would be, tossing her head as she strained to open her eyes.

And woke with a start to find herself still at her desk. She must have put her head down for a moment. Her watch showed it was past midnight. Tess got up, her heart beating unpleasantly fast, and glanced at the sliding glass door. That it was not the window of her dream made no difference. The window of her dream was always the bedroom window of her childhood, the scene always the same as the first time the nightmare had come for her. There was no horse outside on the balcony, or in the sky beyond. There was no horse except in her mind.

Tess went to bed, knowing the nightmare would not come again. Never twice in one night, and she had succeeded in refusing the first visit. Nevertheless, she slept badly, with confused dreams of quarrelling with Gordon as she never quarrelled with him in life, dreams in which Gordon became her father and announced his intended marriage to Jude, and Tess wept and argued and wept and woke in the morning feeling exhausted.

Gordon arrived on Sunday with champagne, flowers, and a shopping bag full of gourmet treats for an indoor picnic. He gave off a glow of happiness and well-being which at once put Tess on the defensive, for his happiness had nothing to do with her.

He kissed her and looked at her tenderly — so tenderly that her stomach turned over with dread. He was looking at her with affection and pity, she thought — not with desire.

'What is it?' she asked sharply, pulling away from him. 'What's happened?'

He was surprised. 'Nothing,' he said. Then: 'Nothing bad, I promise. But I'll tell you all about it. Why don't we have something to eat, first. I've brought —'

'I couldn't eat with something hanging over me, wondering —'

'I told you, it's nothing bad, nothing to worry about.' He frowned. 'Are you getting your period?'

'I'm *not* getting my period, I'm *not* being irrational –' She stopped and swallowed and sighed, forcing herself to relax. 'All right. I am being irrational. I've been sleeping badly. And there's this nightmare – the same nightmare I had as a kid, just before my mother died.'

'Poor baby,' he said, holding her close. He sounded protective but also amused. 'Nightmares. That doesn't sound like my Tess.'

'It's not that I'm superstitious.'

'Of course not.'

'But I've been feeling all week that something bad was about to happen, something to change my whole life. And with the nightmare – I hadn't seen it since just before my mother died. To have it come now, and then when you said we'd talk –'

'It isn't bad, I promise you. But I won't keep you in suspense. Let's just have a drink first, all right?'

'Sure.'

He turned away from her to open the champagne, and she stared at him, drinking in the details as if she might not see him again for a very long time: the curls at the back of his neck, the crisp, black beard, his gentle, rather small hands, skilled at so many things. She felt what it would be to lose him, to lose the right to touch him, never again to have him turn and smile at her.

But why think that? Why should she lose him? How could she, when he had never been 'hers' in any traditional sense, nor did she want him to be. She liked her freedom, both physical and emotional. She liked living alone, yet she wanted a lover, someone she could count on who would not make too many demands of her. In Gordon she had found precisely the mixture of distance and intimacy which she needed. It had worked well for nearly three years, so why did she imagine losing him? She trusted Gordon, believed in his honesty and love for her. She didn't think there was another woman, and she knew he hadn't grown tired of her. She didn't believe he had changed. But Jude might.

Gordon handed her a long-stemmed glass full of champagne, and after they had toasted one another, and sipped, he said, 'Jude's pregnant. She found out for sure last week.'

Tess stared at him, feeling nothing at all.

He said quickly, 'It wasn't planned. I wasn't keeping anything from you. Jude and I, we haven't even – hadn't even – discussed having children. It just never came up. But now that it's happened . . . Jude really likes the idea of having a baby, she's found, and . . .'

'Who's the father?'

She felt him withdraw. 'That's not worthy of you, Tess.'

'Why? It seems like a reasonable question, considering.'

'Considering that Jude hasn't been involved with anyone since Morty went back to New York? I thought you and Jude were friends. What do you talk about over your lunches?'

The brief, mean triumph she had felt was gone, replaced by anguish. 'Not our sex lives,' she said. 'Look, you've got an open marriage. You tell me it was an accident – I'm sorry, I didn't know you'd take it that way. I was just trying to find out what – forget I asked.'

'I will.' He began to set out the food he had brought. The champagne was harsh in her mouth as Tess watched his so-familiar, economical movements, and wanted to touch his back where the blue cloth of his shirt stretched a little too tightly.

She drew a deep breath and said, 'Congratulations. I should have said that first of all. How does it feel, knowing you're going to be a father?'

He looked around, still cautious, and then smiled. 'I'm not sure. It doesn't seem real yet. I guess I'll get used to it.'

'I guess it'll change things,' she said. 'For you and me.'

He went to her and took her in his arms. 'I don't want it to.'

'But it's bound to.'

'In practical ways, maybe. We might have less time together, but – we'll manage somehow. Jude and I were never a traditional couple, and we aren't going to be traditional parents. I'll still need you. I'm not going to stop loving you.' He said it so fiercely that she smiled, and pressed her face against his chest to hide it. 'Do you believe me? Nothing can change the way I feel about you. I love you. That's not going to change. Do you believe me?'

She didn't say anything. He forced her head up off his chest and made her look at him. 'Do you believe me?' He kissed her when she wouldn't reply, then kissed her again, more deeply, and then they were kissing passionately, and she was pulling him onto the floor, and they made love, their bodies making the promises they both wanted.

After Gordon had left that night, the nightmare came again.

Tess found herself standing beside the high, narrow bed she'd slept in as a child, facing the open window. The pale curtains billowed like sails. Outside, galloping in place like a rocking horse, moving and yet stationary, was the blue-eyed, cream-coloured mare.

With part of her mind Tess knew she could refuse this visit. She could turn her head and wrench her eyes open, and find herself, heart pounding, safe in her bed.

Instead, she let herself go into the dream. She took a step forward. She felt alert and hypersensitive, as if this were the true state of waking. She was aware of her own body as she usually never was in life or in a dream, conscious of her nakedness as the breeze from the open window caressed it and feeling the slight bounce of her breasts and the rough weave of the carpet beneath her feet as she walked towards the window.

She clambered onto the window-sill and, with total confidence leaped out, knowing that the horse would catch her.

She landed easily and securely on the mare's back, feeling the scratch and prickle of the horsehair on her inner thighs. Her arms went around the high, arched neck, and she pressed her face against it, breathing in the rough, salty, smoky scent of horse-flesh. She felt the pull and play of muscle and bone beneath her and in her legs as the mare began to gallop. Tess looked down at the horse's legs, seeing how they braced and pounded against the air. She felt a slight shock, then, for where there should have been a hoof, she saw instead five toes. Tess frowned, and leaned further as she stared through the darkness, trying to see.

But they were her own hooves divided into five toes – they had always been so since the night of her creation. The thinly-beaten gold of the lunula on its silken chain bounced against the solid muscle of her chest as she loped through the sky.

Some unquestioned instinct took her to the right house. Above it, she caught a crosswind and, tucking her forelegs in close to her chest, glided spirally down until all four feet could be firmly planted on the earth. This was a single-storey house she visited tonight. She turned her head and, at a glance, the window swung open, the screen which had covered it a moment earlier now vanished. The mare took one delicate step closer and put her head through the window into the bedroom.

The bed, with a man and woman sleeping in it, was directly beneath the window. She breathed gently upon the woman's sleeping face and then drew back her head and waited.

The woman opened her eyes and looked into the mare's blue gaze. She seemed confused but not frightened, and after a moment she sat up slowly, moving cautiously as if for fear of alarming the horse. The horse was not alarmed. She suffered the woman to stroke her nose and pat her face before she backed away, pulling her head out of the house. She had timed it perfectly. The woman came after her as if drawn on a rope, leaning out the window and making soft, affectionate noises. The mare moved as if uneasy, still backing, and then, abruptly flirtatious, offered her back, an invitation to the woman to mount.

The woman understood at once and did not hesitate. From the window ledge she slipped onto the mare's back in a smooth, fluid movement, as if she had done this every night of her life.

Feeling her rider in place, legs clasped firmly on her sides, the mare leaped skyward with more speed than grace. She felt the woman gasp as she was flung forward and felt the woman's hands knot in her mane. She was obviously an experienced rider, not one it would be easy to throw. But the mare did not wish to throw her, merely to give her a very rough ride.

High over the sleeping city galloped the nightmare, rising at impossibly steep angles, shying at invisible barriers, and now and then tucking her legs beneath her to drop like a stone. The gasps and cries from her rider soon ceased. The woman, concentrating on clinging for her life, could have had no energy to spare for fear.

Not until dawn did the nightmare return the woman, leaping through the bedroom window in defiance of logic and throwing her onto the motionless safety of her bed, beside her still-sleeping husband.

When Tess woke a few hours later she was stiff and sore, as if she had been dancing, or running, all night. She got up slowly, wincing, and aware of a much worse emotional pain waiting for her, like the anticipation of bad news. The nightmare had come for her, and this time she had gone with it – she was certain of that much. But where had it taken her? What had she done?

In the bathroom, as she waited for the shower to heat up and wracked her sleepy brain for some memory of the night before, Tess caught a glimpse in the mirror of something on her back, at waist level. She turned, presenting her back to the glass, and then craned her neck around, slowly against the stiffness, to look at her reflection.

She stared at the bloodstains. Stared and stared at the saddle of blood across her back.

She washed it off, of course, with plenty of hot water and soap, and tried not to think about it too hard. That was exactly what she had done the last time this had happened: when she was nine years old, on the morning after the night her mother had miscarried; on the morning of the day her mother had died.

All day Tess fought against the urge to phone Gordon. All day she was like a sleepwalker as she taught a class, supervised studies, stared at meaningless words in the library, and avoided telephones.

She thought, as she had thought before, that she should see a psychiatrist. But how could a psychiatrist help her? She *knew* she could not, by all the rules of reason and logic, have caused her mother's death. She knew she felt guilty because she had not wanted the little sister or brother her parents had planned, and on some level she believed that her desire, expressed in the nightmare, had been responsible for the miscarriage and thus – although unintentionally – for her mother's death. She didn't need a psychiatrist to tell her all that. She had figured it out for herself, sometime in her teens. And yet, figuring it out hadn't ended the feeling of guilt. That was why the very thought of the nightmare was so frightening to her.

If Jude is all right, she thought, if nothing has happened to her, then I'll know it was just a crazy dream – and I'll see a psychiatrist.

Gordon telephoned the next day, finally. Jude was all right, he said, although Tess had not asked. Jude was just fine. Only – she'd lost the child. But miscarriage at this early stage was apparently relatively common. The doctors said she was physically healthy and strong and would have no problem carrying another pregnancy to term. Only – although she was physically all right, Jude was pretty upset. She had taken the whole thing badly, and in a way he had never expected. She was saying some pretty strange things –

'What sort of things?' She clutched the phone as if it were his arm, trying to force him to speak.

'I need to see you, Tess. I need to talk to you. Could we meet for lunch?'

'Tomorrow?'

'Better make it Friday.'

'Just lunch?' She was pressing him as she never did, unable to hide her desperation.

'I can't leave Jude for long. She needs me now. It'll have to be just lunch. The Italian place?'

Tess felt a wave of pure hatred for Jude. She wanted to tell Gordon that she needed him just as much, or more than, his wife did; that she was in far more trouble than Jude with her mere, commonplace miscarriage.

'That's fine,' she said, and made her voice throb with sympathy as she told Gordon how sorry she was to hear about Jude. 'Let me know if there's anything at all I can do – tell her that.'

'I'll see you on Friday,' he said.

Gordon didn't waste any time on Friday. As soon as they had ordered, he came right to the point.

'This has affected Jude much more than I could have dreamed. I'd hardly come to terms with the idea that she was pregnant, and she's responding as if she'd lost an actual baby instead of only … I've told her we'll start another just as soon as we can, but she seems to think she's doomed to lose that one, too.' He had been looking into her eyes as he spoke but now he dropped his gaze to the white tablecloth. 'Maybe Jude has always been a little unstable, I don't know. Probably it's something hormonal, and she'll get back to normal soon. But whatever . . . it seems to have affected her mind. And she's got this crazy idea that the miscarriage is somehow *your* fault.' He looked up with a grimace, to see how she responded.

Tess said quietly, 'I'm sorry.'

'Maybe she's always been jealous of you on some level – no, I don't believe that. It's only now, the shock and the grief, that's made her fix on you . . . I don't know why. I'm sure she'll get over it. But right now there's no reasoning with her. She won't even consider seeing you, so don't try to call her. And . . .' he sighed deeply. 'She doesn't want me to see you, either. She wanted me to tell you, today, that it's all over.'

'Just like that.'

'Oh, Tess.' He looked at her across the table, obviously in pain.

She noticed for the first time the small lines that had appeared around his eyes. 'Tess, you know I love you. It's not that I love Jude more than I love you. I'd never agree to choose between you.'

'That's exactly what you're doing.'

'I'm not. It's not forever. But Jude is my wife – I have a responsibility to her. You've always known that. She can't cope right now, that's all. I've got to go along with her. But this isn't the real Jude – she's not acting like herself at all.'

'Of course she is,' said Tess. 'She's always been erratic and illogical and acted on emotion.'

'If you saw her, if you tried to talk to her, you'd realize. She just won't – or can't – listen to reason. But once she's had time to recover, I know she'll realize how ridiculous she was. And once she's pregnant again, she'll be back to normal, I'm certain.'

Tess realized she wasn't going to be able to eat her lunch. Her stomach was tight as a fist.

Gordon said, 'This won't last forever, I promise. But for now, we're just going to have to stop seeing each other.'

No apologies, no softening of the blow. He was speaking to her man to man, Tess thought. She wondered what he would do if she burst into tears or began shouting.

'Why are you smiling?' he asked.

'I didn't know I was. Do we have to stop all contact with each other? Do I pretend you've dropped off the face of the earth, or what?'

'I'll phone you. I'll keep in touch. And I'll let you know if anything changes – when something happens.'

Tess looked at her watch. 'I have to get back and supervise a test.'

'I'll walk you.'

'No, stay, finish your food,' she said. 'Don't get up.' She had suddenly imagined herself clinging to him on a street corner, begging him not to leave her. She didn't want to risk that, yet she could not kiss him casually, as if she would be seeing him again in a few hours or days. As she came around the table she put her hand on his face for just a moment, then left without looking back.

As a child, Tess had been mad about horses, going through the traditional girlish phase of reading, talking, drawing and dreaming of them, begging for the impossible, a horse of her own. For her ninth birthday her parents had enrolled her for riding lessons. For half a year she had been learning to ride, but after her mother's death Tess had refused to have anything more to do with horses, even had a kind of horror of them. She had only one memento from that phase of her life: the blue-glazed ceramic head of a horse. In her youth she'd kept it hidden away, but now she took pleasure in it again, in its beauty, the sweeping arch of the sculpted neck and the deep, mottled colour. It was a beautiful object, nothing like the nightmare.

Tess sat alone in her apartment sipping bourbon and Coke and gazing at the horse head, now and again lifting it to touch its coolness to her flushed cheek.

You didn't kill your mother, she told herself. Wishing the baby would not be born is not the same thing as *making* it not be born. You weren't – aren't – responsible for your dreams. And dreams don't kill.

Outside, the day blued towards night and Tess went on drinking. She felt more helpless and alone than she had ever before felt as an adult, as if the power to rule her own life had been taken from her. She was controlled, she thought, by the emotions of others: by Jude's fear, by Gordon's sense of responsibility, by her own childish guilt.

But Tess did not allow herself to sink into despair. The next morning, although hungover and sad, she knew that life must go on. She was accustomed, after all, to being alone and to taking care of herself. She knew how to shut out other thoughts while she worked, and she made an effort to schedule activities for her non-working hours so that dinner out, or a film, or drinks with friends carried her safely through the dangerous, melancholy hour of blue.

Over the next six weeks, Gordon spoke to her briefly three times. Jude seemed to be getting better, he said, but she was still adamant in her feelings towards Tess. Tess could never think of anything to say to this, and the silence stretched between them, and then Gordon stopped calling. After three months, Tess began to believe that it was truly over between them. And then Gordon came to see her.

He looked thin and unhappy. At the sight of him, Tess forgot her own misery and only wanted to comfort him. She poured him a drink and hovered over him, touching his hair shyly. He caught her hand and pulled her down beside him on the couch, and began to kiss and caress her rather clumsily. She was helping him undress her when she realized he was crying.

'Gordon! Darling, what's wrong?' She was shocked by his tears. She tried to hold him, to let him cry, but understood he didn't want that. After a minute he blew his nose and shook his head hard, repudiating the tears.

'Jude and I,' he began. Then, after a pause, 'Jude's left me.'

Tess felt a shocking sense of triumph which she repressed at once. She waited, saying nothing.

'It's been hell,' he said. 'Ever since the miscarriage. That crazy idea she had, that you were somehow responsible for it. She said it was because you didn't mind sharing me with her, but that a baby would have changed things – you would have been left out of the cosy family group. I told her you weren't like that, you weren't the jealous type, but she just laughed at me and said men didn't understand.'

She must go carefully here, Tess thought. She had to admit her responsibility, and not let Gordon blame Jude too much, but she didn't want Gordon thinking she was mad.

'Gordon,' she said. 'I *was* jealous. And very afraid that once you were a father things would change and I'd be left out in the cold.'

He dismissed her confession with a grimace and a wave of his hand. 'So what? That doesn't make any difference. Even if you'd wanted her to have a miscarriage you didn't make it happen. You couldn't. Jude seems to think that you wished it on her, like you were some kind of a witch. She's crazy, that's what it comes down to.'

'She might come back.'

'No. It's over. We talked about a trial separation and started seeing a marriage counsellor. It made it worse. All sorts of things came up, things I hadn't thought were problems. And then she found somebody else. She's with somebody else now. She may not be with him for long, but she won't be coming back.'

Tess had thought for a long time that the break-up of Gordon and Tess would inevitably lead to the break-up between Gordon and herself, and so for the next few months she was tense, full of an unexamined anxiety, waiting for this to happen. Gordon, too, was uneasy, unanchored without his wife. Unlike Tess, he did not enjoy living alone, but he made a great effort to ration his time with her, not to impose upon her. They tried to go on as they always had, ignoring the fact that Jude was no longer there to limit the time they spent together. But when Tess finished her doctorate they had to admit to the inevitability of some major, permanent change in their relationship. Tess could stay on in New Orleans, teaching English as a foreign language and scraping a living somehow, but that wasn't what she wanted. It wasn't what she had worked and studied for, and so she tried to ignore the feeling of dread that lodged in her stomach as she sent out her CV and searched in earnest for a university which might hire her. She had always known this time would come. She didn't talk about it to Gordon. Why should she? It was her life, her career, her responsibility. She would make her plans, and then she would tell him.

An offer came from a university in upstate New York. It wasn't brilliant, but it was better than she'd expected: a heavy teaching schedule, but with a chance to continue her own research.

She told Gordon about it over dinner in a Mexican restaurant.

'It sounds good, just right for you.'

'It's not perfect. And it probably won't last. I can't count on more than a year.'

'You're good. They'll see that. You'll get tenure.'

'Maybe not. And I might hate it there.'

'Don't be silly.' He looked so calm and unmoved that Tess felt herself near panic. Didn't he care? Could he really let her go so easily? She crunched down hard on a tortilla chip and almost missed his next words: '... scout around,' he was saying. 'If I can't find anything in Watertown, there must be other cities close enough that we could at least have weekends together.'

She stared, disbelieving. 'You'd quit your job? You'd move across the country just because I'm ...'

'Why not?'

'Your job?'

'I'm not in love with my job,' he said.

Tess looked into his eyes and felt herself falling. She said, 'Upstate New York is not the most exciting place.'

'They need accountants there just like everywhere else,' he said. 'I'll find a job. I'm good. Don't you believe me?' He grinned at her with that easy arrogance she'd always found paradoxically both irritating and attractive.

'If you're sure.'

'I'm sure about this: I'm not letting you go without a fight. If you don't want me, better say so now, and we can start fighting.' He grinned again, and, beneath the table, gripped her knees between his. 'But I'm going to win.'

Six months later they were living together in a small, rented house in Watertown, New York. Despite living together, they saw less of each other than they had in New Orleans. Unable to get a job locally, Gordon spent three hours every weekday travelling to and from work. He left before Tess was up, and returned, exhausted, in time for dinner, TV and bed. It was a very different life they led than the one they'd known before. They had left behind all those restaurant meals, the easy socializing in French Quarter bars, the flirtations with other people, the long, sultry evenings of doing very little in the open air. Days this far north were short, the nights long and cold. Because Tess didn't like to cook, and Gordon had time only on the weekends, they ate a lot of frozen meals, omelettes and sandwiches. They watched too much television, complaining about it and apologizing to each other. They planned to take up hobbies, learn new things and join local organizations, but when the weekends came almost always they spent the time at home, in bed, together.

Her own happiness surprised Tess. She had always believed she would feel suffocated if she lived with a man, but now whenever Gordon was away, she missed him. Being with him, whether talking, making love or simply staring like twin zombies at the flickering screen, was all she wanted outside of work. She couldn't believe that she had imagined herself content with so little for so long – to have shared Gordon with another woman without jealousy. She knew she would be jealous now, if Gordon had another lover, but she also knew she had nothing to worry about. She had changed, and so had he. When he asked her to marry him she didn't even hesitate. She knew what she wanted.

Within four months of the marriage, Tess was pregnant.

It wasn't planned, and yet it wasn't an accident, either. She had been careful for too many years to make such a simple mistake, and in Gordon's silence was his acceptance. Without a word spoken, in one shared moment, they had decided. Or at least they had decided not to decide, to leave it to fate for once. And afterwards Tess was terrified, waking in the middle of the night to brood on the mistake she was making, wondering, almost until the very last month, if she couldn't manage to have an abortion, after all.

Gordon did everything he could to make things easier for her. Since he couldn't actually have the baby for her, he devoted himself to her comfort. And except for the physical unpleasantness of being pregnant, and her middle of the night terrors,

Tess sometimes thought, as she basked in the steady glow of Gordon's attentive love, that this might be the happiest time of her life.

In the months before the baby was born they decided that Gordon's continuing to commute to work wouldn't be possible. Instead, he would set up on his own as an accountant and work from home. It might be difficult for the first few years, but Gordon had a few investments here and there, and at a pinch they could scrape by on Tess's salary. Gordon said, with his usual self-confidence, that he could make far more money self-employed than anyone ever did as an employee, and Tess believed him. Things would work out.

Her labour was long and difficult. When at last the baby was placed in her arms Tess looked down at it, feeling exhausted and detached, wondering what this little creature had to do with her. She was glad when Gordon took it away from her. Lying back against the pillows she watched her husband.

His face changed, became softer. Tess recognized that rapturous, melting expression because she had seen it occasionally, during sex. She had never seen him look at anyone else like that. She burst into tears.

Gordon was beside her immediately, pushing the baby at her. But she didn't want the baby. She only wanted Gordon, although she couldn't stop crying long enough to tell him. He held her as she held the baby, and gradually his presence calmed her. After all, the baby was *theirs*. She and Gordon belonged to each other more certainly now than ever before. No longer merely a couple, they were now a family. She knew she should be happy.

She tried to be happy, and sometimes she was, but this baby girl, called Lexi (short for Alexandra), made her feel not only love, but also fear and frustration and pain. Motherhood was not as instinctive as she had believed it would be, for Gordon was clearly better at it than she was, despite her physical equipment. Breastfeeding, which Tess had confidently expected to enjoy, was a disaster. No one had told her, and she had never dreamed, that it would *hurt*. And her suffering was in vain. Lexi didn't thrive until they put her on the bottle. Watching Gordon giving Lexi her late-night feed while she was meant to be sleeping, Tess tried not to feel left out.

It was a relief, in a way, to be able to go back to work after six weeks: back to her own interests, to her students and colleagues, doing the things she knew she was good at. But it wasn't quite the same, for she missed Lexi when she wasn't around. Always, now, she felt a worrying tug of absence. For all the problems, she couldn't wish Lexi away. She only wished that loving Lexi could be as simple and straightforward as loving Gordon. If only she could explain herself to Lexi, she thought, and Lexi explain herself to Tess – if only they shared a language.

When she said this to Gordon one evening after Lexi had been put to bed, he laughed.

'She'll be talking soon enough, and then it'll be why? Why? Why? all the time, and demanding toys and candy and clothes. Right now, life is simple. She cries when she wants to have her diaper changed, or she wants to be fed, or she wants to be burped or cuddled. Then she's happy.'

'But you have to figure out what she wants,' Tess said. 'She can't tell you – that's my point. And if you do the wrong thing, she just goes on crying and getting more and more unhappy. I'm no more complex than Lexi, really. I have the same sorts of needs. But I can tell you what I want. If I started crying now, you'd probably think I wanted my dinner. But what I really want is a cuddle.'

He looked at her tenderly, and left his chair to join her on the couch. He kissed her affectionately.

She kissed him more demandingly, but he didn't respond.

'You'll have to do better than that,' she said. 'Or I'll start crying.'

'I was thinking about dinner.'

'Forget about dinner. Why don't you check to see if my diaper needs changing?'

He laughed. Maybe he laughed too loudly, because a moment later, like a response, came Lexi's wail.

'Leave her,' said Tess. 'She'll fall back to sleep.'

They sat tensely, holding each other, waiting for this to happen. Lexi's cries became louder and more urgent.

Tess sighed. The moment had passed, anyway. 'I'll go,' she said. 'You fix dinner.'

Time alone with Gordon was what Tess missed most. Their desires, and the opportunity to make love, seldom meshed. As Lexi approached her first birthday she seemed to spend even more time awake and demanding attention. This affected not only her parents' relationship, but also Gordon's fledgling business. He was floundering, distracted by the demands of fatherhood, unable to put the time and energy he needed into building up a list of clients. Time was all he needed, Tess thought, and he must have that time. She thought it all through before approaching him about it, but she was certain he would agree with her. He would be reasonable, as he always was. She didn't expect an argument.

'Daycare!' he repeated, pronouncing it like an obscenity. 'Leave Lexi in some crummy nursery? Are you kidding?'

'Why do you think it would be crummy? I'm not proposing we look for the cheapest – of course we'll choose the best we can afford.'

'But why?'

'Because there's no way we can afford a full-time babysitter. You know that.'

'We don't need a babysitter. We've got me.'

'This is why. You're not being paid to look after Lexi, and while you're looking after her you can't make a living.'

He stared at her. She couldn't read his expression; he was miles away from her. 'I see. I've had my chance and I've failed, so now I have to get a real job.'

'No!' She clutched his hand, then lowered her voice. 'For heaven's sake, Gordon, I'm not criticizing you. And I am not saying you should go back to – I believe in you. Everything you said about being able to make a lot of money in a few years, I'm sure that's true. I know you can make a success of it. Only . . . you need time. Your work needs attention just as much as Lexi does. You can't be out meeting people or balancing their books when you have to keep breaking off to take care of her. You need to be able to commit to one thing at a time.'

'You're right,' he said in his usual, reasonable tone. He sighed, and Tess's heart lifted as he said, 'I've been thinking about it a lot, and coming to the same conclusion. Well, not quite the same. You're right, I can't get much work done when I'm looking after Lexi. Weekends aren't enough. But why do we have to pay some-one else to take care of our child? There are two of us; we can manage. We just need to be a little more flexible. We could divide up the week between us. You don't have classes on Tuesdays and Thursdays. If you stayed home then and took responsibility for the weekends, too – why are you shaking your head?'

'Just because I don't teach on Tuesdays and Thursdays doesn't mean I don't have work to do. I have to be around to supervise and advise and go to meetings, and then there's my own research. When will I ever get my book written if I don't have some time to myself? There's no shame in not being able to manage everything by ourselves. That's why daycare centres exist. We both have to make a living, and we need – '

'What about what Lexi needs?'

'She needs care and attention and she'll get plenty of that; we wouldn't deprive her of anything.'

'No, but we'd be depriving ourselves.' He was almost vibrat-ing with intensity. 'Look, one of the greatest experiences in the world is bringing up a child. Teaching her, watching her change and grow every day. I don't want to miss out on that. Maybe in a couple of years, but not now. We can manage. So what if we're not rich? There are things more important than money and careers. If you spent more time with her yourself you'd know what I mean.'

'You think I don't spend enough time with her?'

'I didn't say that.'

'But it's what you think. You think I'm selfish, or that I care more about my job than I do about her and you. It's not true. I love Lexi very much. I love her as much as you do. But I won't – I can't – let motherhood absorb me. I miss her whenever I'm away from her, but I know I can't let my whole life revolve around her daily needs. You can't hold on to her forever. Eventually she'll grow up and leave us.'

'For God's sake, she's not even a year old! You're talking like I'm going to stop her going away to college.'

'She may be a baby, but she's still a person. She has a life apart from you and me – she has to. And so do we. Both individually and as a couple. Or aren't we a couple anymore? Are we just Lexi's parents? I miss you, Gordon, I feel like – ' she stopped because if she said anything more she knew she would be crying.

'Let's go to bed,' Gordon said, not looking at her. 'Let's not argue.'

They went to bed and made love, and, for a little while, Tess felt they had reached an understanding, had confirmed the love they still had for each other.

But then the nightmare came.

Lying in bed, drowsily aware of Gordon's close, sleeping warmth, Tess heard the window fly open. When she opened her eyes she saw, as she had known she would, the familiar, bone-white head of the mare staring in at her, waiting for her.

Her heart sank. I won't move, she thought. I won't go. I will wake myself. But she struggled in vain to open her eyes, or to close them, or even to turn her head so that the creature would be out of her sight. She felt the bitter chill of the winter night flooding the bedroom, and she began to shiver. I must close the window, she thought, and as she thought that, she realized she was getting up, and walking toward the creature who had come for her.

Tess stared at the horse, recognizing the invitation in the toss of the pale head. She tried to refuse it. I don't wish anyone any harm, she thought. I love my daughter. I love my husband. I don't want you. Go away.

But she could not wake, or speak, or do anything but walk in slow, somnambulist fashion towards the window, outside of which the nightmare ran in place on the wind.

I don't want to hurt anyone – I won't! Oh, please, let me wake!

But it was her own body which carried her, despite her mental protests, to the window and onto the sill. And as she struggled against the dream, almost crying with frustration, she flung herself through the open window, into the cold night, upon the nightmare's back.

And then she was clinging desperately to the creature's neck, feeling herself slipping on its icy back, as it mounted the sky. This ride was nothing like the last one. She was terrified, and she knew she was in imminent danger of falling, if not of being thrown. Whatever she had once known of riding vanished. The muscles in her thighs ached, and the cold had numbed her fingers. She didn't think she would be able to hang on for very long, particularly not if the mare continued to leap and swerve and climb so madly. Closing her eyes, Tess tried to relax, to let instinct take over. She pressed her cheek against the mare's neck and breathed in the smell of blood. Choking back her revulsion, she struggled to sit upright, despite the pressure of the wind. Neck muscles knotted and moved within her embrace, and the mare's long head turned back, one wild eye rolling to look at her.

Tess felt herself slipping, sliding inexorably down. Unless the mare slowed her pace she would fall, she thought. She struggled to keep her grip on the creature's twisting neck, and because she still could not speak, sent one final, pleading look at the mare to ask for mercy. And just before the nightmare threw her, their eyes met, and Tess understood. Within the nightmare's eye she saw her daughter's cold, blue gaze: judgemental, selfish, pitiless.

Bits and Pieces

On the morning after Ralph left her Fay found a foot in her bed.

It was Ralph's foot, but how could he have left it behind? What did it mean? She sat on the edge of the bed holding it in her hand, examining it. It was a long, pale, narrow, rather elegant foot. At the top, where you would expect it to grow into an ankle, the foot ended in a slight, skin-covered concavity. There was no sign of blood or severed flesh or bone or scar tissue, nor were there any corns or bunions, over-long nails or dirt. Ralph was a man who looked after his feet.

Lying there in her hand it felt as alive as a motionless foot ever feels; impossible as it seemed, she believed it was real. Ralph wasn't a practical joker, and yet – a foot wasn't something you left behind without noticing. She wondered how he was managing to get around on just one foot. Was it a message? Some obscure consolation for her feeling that, losing him, she had lost a piece of herself?

He had made it clear he no longer wanted to be involved with her. His goodbye had sounded final. But maybe he would get in touch when he realized she still had something of his. Although she knew she ought to be trying to forget him, she felt oddly grateful for this unexpected gift. She wrapped the foot in a silk scarf and put it in the dresser's bottom drawer, to keep for him.

Two days later, tidying the bedroom, she found his other foot under the bed. She had to check the drawer to make sure it wasn't the same one, gone wandering. But it was still there, one right foot, and she was holding the left one. She wrapped the two of them together in the white silk scarf and put them away.

Time passed and Ralph did not get in touch. Fay knew from

friends that he was still around, and as she never heard any suggestion that he was now crippled, she began to wonder if the feet had been some sort of hallucination. She kept meaning to look in the bottom drawer, but somehow she kept forgetting.

The relationship with Ralph, while it lasted, had been a serious, deeply meaningful one for them both, she thought; she knew from the start there was no hope of that with Freddy. Fay was a responsible person who believed the act of sex should be accompanied by love and a certain degree of commitment; she detested the very idea of 'casual sex' – but she'd been six months without a man in her bed, and Freddy was irresistible.

He was warm and cuddly and friendly, the perfect teddy bear. Within minutes of meeting him she was thinking about sleeping with him – although it was the comfort and cosiness of bed he brought to mind rather than passion. As passive as a teddy bear, he would let himself be pursued. She met him with friends in a pub, and he offered to walk her home. Outside her door he hugged her. There was no kissing or groping; he just wrapped her in a warm, friendly embrace, where she clung to him longer and tighter than friendship required.

'Mmmm,' he said, appreciatively, smiling down at her, his eyes button-bright, 'I could do this all night.'

'What a good idea,' she said.

After they had made love she decided he was less a teddy bear than a cat. Like a cat in the sensual way he moved and rubbed his body against hers and responded to her touch: she could almost hear him purr. Other cat-like qualities, apparent after she had known him a little longer, were less appealing. Like a cat he was self-centred, basically lazy, and although she continued to enjoy him in bed, she did wish sometimes he would pay more attention to her pleasure instead of assuming that his was enough for them both. He seemed to expect her to be pleased no matter what time he turned up for dinner, even if he fell asleep in front of the fire immediately after. And, like many cats, he had more than one home.

Finding out about his other home – hearing that other woman's tear-clogged voice down the phone – decided her to end it. It wasn't – or so she told him – that she wanted to have him all to herself. But she wouldn't be responsible for another woman's sorrow.

He understood her feelings. He was wrong, and she was right. He was remorseful, apologetic, and quite incapable of changing. But he would miss her very much. He gave her a friendly hug before they parted, but once they started hugging it was hard to stop, and they tumbled into bed again.

That had to be the last time. She knew she could be firmer with him on the phone than in person, so she told him he was not to visit unless she first invited him. Sadly, he agreed.

And that was that. Going back into the bedroom she saw the duvet rucked up as if there was someone still in the bed. It made her shiver. If she hadn't just seen him out the door, and closed it behind him she might have thought . . . Determined to put an end to such mournful nonsense she flung the duvet aside, and there he was.

Well, part of him.

Lying on the bed was a headless, neckless, armless, legless torso. Or at least the back side of one. As with Ralph's feet there was nothing unpleasant about it, no blood or gaping wounds. If you could ignore the sheer impossibility of it, there was nothing wrong with Freddy's back at all. It looked just like the body she had been embracing a few minutes before, and felt . . .

Tentatively, she reached out and touched it. It was warm and smooth, with the firm, elastic give of live flesh. She could not resist stroking it the way she knew he liked, teasing with her nails to make the skin prickle into goosebumps, running her fingers all the way from the top of the spine to the base, and over the curve of the buttocks where the body ended.

She drew her hand back, shocked. What was this? It seemed so much like Freddy, but how could it be when she had seen him, minutes before, walking out the door, fully equipped with all his body parts? Was it possible that there was nothing, now, but air filling out his jumper and jeans?

She sat down, took hold of the torso where the shoulders ended in smooth, fleshy hollows, and heaved it over. The chest was as she remembered, babyishly pink nipples peeking out of a scumble of ginger hair, but below the flat stomach only more flatness. His genitals were missing, as utterly and completely gone as if they had never been thought of. Her stomach twisted with shock and horror although, a moment later, she had to ask herself why that particular lack should matter so much more than the absence of his head – which she had accepted remarkably calmly. After all, this wasn't the real Freddy, only some sort of partial memory of his body inexplicably made flesh.

She went over to the dresser and crouched before the bottom drawer. Yes, they were still there. They didn't appear to have decayed or faded or changed in any way. Letting the silk scarf fall away she gazed at the naked feet and realized that she felt differently about Ralph. She had been unhappy when he left, but she had also been, without admitting it even to herself, furiously angry with him. And the anger had passed. The bitterness was gone, and she felt only affection now as she caressed his feet and remembered the good times. Eventually, with a sigh that mingled fondness and regret, she wrapped them up and put them away. Then she returned to her current problem: what to do with the part Freddy had left behind.

For a moment she thought of leaving it in the bed. He'd always been *so* nice to sleep with . . . But no. She had to finish what she had begun; she couldn't continue sleeping with part of Freddy all the time when all of Freddy part of the time had not been enough for her. She would never be able to get on with her life, she would never dare bring anyone new home with her.

It would have to go in the wardrobe. The only other option was the hall closet which was cold and smelled slightly of damp. So, wrapping it in her best silken dressing gown, securing it with a tie around the waist, she stored Freddy's torso in the wardrobe behind her clothes.

Freddy phoned the next week. He didn't mention missing anything but her, and she almost told him about finding his torso in her bed. But how could she? If she told him, he'd insist on coming over to see it, and if he came over she'd be back to having an affair with him. That wasn't what she was after, was it? She hesitated, and then asked if he was still living with Matilda.

'Oh, more or less,' he said. 'Yes.'

So she didn't tell him. She tried to forget him, and hoped to meet someone else, someone who would occupy the man-sized empty space in her life.

Meanwhile, Freddy continued to phone her once a week — friendly calls, because he wanted to stay friends. After a while she realized, from comments he let drop, that he was seeing another woman; that once again he had two homes. As always, she resisted the temptation she felt to invite him over, but she felt wretchedly lonely that evening.

For the first time since she had stored it away, she took out his body. Trembling a little, ashamed of herself, she took it to bed. She so wanted someone to hold. The body felt just like Freddy, warm and solid and smooth in the same way; it even smelled like him, although now with a faint overlay of her own perfume from her clothes. She held it for a while, but the lack of arms and head was too peculiar. She found that if she lay with her back against his and tucked her legs up so she couldn't feel his missing legs, it was almost like being in bed with Freddy.

She slept well that night, better than she had for weeks. 'My teddy bear,' she murmured as she packed him away again in the morning. It was like having a secret weapon. The comfort of a warm body in bed with her at night relaxed her, and made her more self-confident. She no longer felt any need to invite Freddy over, and when he called it was easy to talk to him without getting more involved, as if they'd always been just friends. And now that she wasn't looking, there seemed to be more men around.

One of them, Paul, who worked for the same company in a different department, asked her out. Lately she had kept running into him, and he seemed to have a lot of business which took him to her part of the building, but it didn't register on her that this was no coincidence until he asked if she was doing anything that Saturday night. After that, his interest in her seemed so obvious that she couldn't imagine why she hadn't noticed earlier.

The most likely reason she hadn't noticed was that she didn't care. She felt instinctively that he wasn't her type; they had little in common. But his unexpected interest flattered her, and made him seem more attractive, and so she agreed to go out with him.

It was a mistake, she thought, uneasily, when Saturday night came around and Paul took her to a very expensive restaurant. He was not unintelligent, certainly not bad-looking, but there was something a little too glossy and humourless about him. He was interested in money, and cars, and computers – and her. He dressed well, and he knew the right things to say, but she imagined he had learned them out of a book. He was awfully single-minded, and seemed intent on seduction, which made her nervous, and she spent too much of the evening trying to think of some way of getting out of inviting him in for coffee when he took her home. It was no good; when the time came, he invited himself in.

She knew it wasn't fair to make comparisons, but Paul was the complete opposite of Freddy. Where Freddy sat back and waited calmly to be stroked, Paul kept edging closer, trying to crawl into her lap. And his hands were everywhere. From the very start of the evening he had stood and walked too close to her, and she didn't like the way he had of touching her, as if casually making a point, staking a physical claim to her.

For the next hour she fended him off. It was a wordless battle which neither of them would admit to. When he left, she lacked the energy to refuse a return match, the following weekend.

They went to the theatre, and afterward to his place – he said he wanted to show her his computer. She expected another battle, but he was a perfect gentleman. Feeling safer, she agreed to a third date, and then drank too much; the drink loosened her inhibitions, she was too tired to resist his persistent pressure, and finally took him into her bed.

The sex was not entirely a success – for her, anyway – but it would doubtless get better as they got to know each other, she thought, and she was just allowing herself a few modest fantasies about the future, concentrating on the things she thought she liked about him, when he said he had to go.

The man who had been hotly all over her was suddenly distant and cool, almost rude in his haste to leave. She tried to find excuses for him, but when he had gone, and she discovered his hands were still in her bed, she knew he did not mean to return.

The hands were nestling beneath a pillow like a couple of soft-shelled crabs. She shuddered at the sight of them, shouted and threw her shoes at them. The left hand twitched when struck, but otherwise they didn't move.

How dare he leave his hands! She didn't want anything to remember him by! She certainly hadn't been in love with him.

Fay looked around for something else to throw, and then felt ashamed of herself. Paul was a creep, but it wasn't fair to take it out on his hands. They hadn't hurt her; they had done their best to give her pleasure – they might have succeeded if she'd liked their owner more.

But she didn't like their owner – she had to admit she wasn't really sorry he wouldn't be back – so why was she stuck with his hands? She could hardly give them back. She could already guess how he would avoid her at work, and she wasn't about to add to his inflated ego by pursuing him. But it didn't seem possible to throw them out, either.

She found a shoebox to put them in – she didn't bother about wrapping them – and then put the box away out of sight on the highest shelf of the kitchen cupboard, among the cracked plates, odd saucers, and empty jars which she'd kept because they might someday be useful.

The hands made her think a little differently about what had happened. She had been in love with Ralph and also, for all her attempts to rationalize her feelings, with Freddy – she hadn't wanted either of them to go. It made a kind of sense for her to fantasize that they'd left bits of themselves behind, but that didn't apply to her feelings for Paul. She absolutely refused to believe that her subconscious was responsible for the hands in the kitchen cupboard.

So if not her subconscious, then what? Was it the bed? She stood in the bedroom and looked at it, trying to perceive some sorcery in the brand-name mattress or the pine frame. She had bought the bed for Ralph, really; he had complained so about the futon she had when they met, declaring that it was not only too short, but also bad for his back. He had told her that pine beds were good and also cheap, and although she didn't agree with his assessment of the price, she had bought one. It was the most expensive thing she owned. Was it also haunted?

She could test it, invite friends to stay . . . Would any man who made love in this bed leave a part of himself behind, or only those who made love to her? Only for the last time? But how did it know? How could it, before she herself knew a relationship was over? What if she lured Paul back – would some other body part appear when he left? Or would the hands disappear?

Once she had thought of this, she knew she had to find out. She tried to forget the idea but could not. Days passed, and Paul did not get in touch – he avoided her at work, as she had guessed he would – and she told herself to let him go. Good riddance. To pursue him would be humiliating. It wasn't even as if she were in love with him, after all.

She told herself not to be a fool, but chance and business kept taking her to his part of the building. When forced to acknowledge her his voice was polite and he did not stand too close; he spoke as if they'd never met outside working hours, as if he'd never really noticed her as a woman. She saw him, an hour later, leaning confidentially over one of the newer secretaries, his hand touching her hip.

She felt a stab of jealous frustration. No wonder she couldn't attract his attention; he had already moved on to fresh prey.

Another week went by, but she would not accept defeat. She phoned him up and invited him to dinner. He said his weekends were awfully busy just now. She suggested a weeknight. He hesitated – surprised by her persistence? Contemptuous? Flattered? – and then said he was involved with someone, actually. Despising herself, Fay said lightly that of course she understood. She said that in fact, she herself was involved in a long-standing relationship, but her fellow had been abroad for the past few months, and she got bored and lonely in the evenings. She'd enjoyed herself so much with Paul that she had hoped they'd be able to get together again sometime; that was all.

That changed the temperature. He said he was afraid he

couldn't manage dinner, but if she liked, he could drop by later one evening – maybe tomorrow, around ten?

He was on her as soon as he was through the door. She tried to fend him off with offers of drink, but he didn't seem to hear. His hands were everywhere, grabbing, fondling, probing, as undeniably real as they'd ever been.

'Wait, wait,' she said, laughing but not amused. 'Can't we . . . talk?'

He paused, holding her around the waist, and looked down at her. He was bigger than she remembered. 'We could have talked on the phone.'

'I know, but . . .'

'Is there something we need to talk about?'

'Well, no, nothing specific, but . . .'

'Did you invite me over here to talk? Did I misunderstand?'

'No.'

'All right.' His mouth came down, wet and devouring, on hers, and she gave in.

But not on the couch, she thought, a few minutes later. 'Bed,' she gasped, breaking away. 'In the bedroom.'

'Good idea.'

But it no longer seemed like a good idea to her. As she watched him strip off his clothes she thought this was probably the worst idea she'd ever had. She didn't want him in her bed again; she didn't want sex with him. How could she have thought, for even a minute, that she could have sex for such a cold-blooded, ulterior motive?

'I thought you were in a hurry,' he said. 'Get your clothes off.' Naked, he reached for her.

She backed away. 'I'm sorry, I shouldn't have called you, I'm sorry –'

'Don't apologize. It's very sexy when a woman knows what she wants and asks for it.' He'd unbuttoned her blouse and unhooked her bra earlier, and now tried to remove them. She tried to stop him, and he pinioned her wrists.

'This is a mistake, I don't want this, you have to go.'

'Like hell.'

'I'm sorry, Paul, but I mean it.'

He smiled humourlessly. 'You mean you want me to force you.'

'No!'

He pushed her down on the bed, got her skirt off despite her struggles, then ripped her tights.

'Stop it!'

'I wouldn't have thought you liked this sort of thing,' he mused.

'I don't, I'm telling the truth, I don't want to have sex, I want you to leave.' Her voice wobbled all over the place. 'Look, I'm sorry, I'm really sorry, but I can't, not now.' Tears leaked out of her eyes. 'Please. You don't understand. This isn't a game.' She was completely naked now and he was naked on top of her.

'This *is* a game,' he said calmly. 'And I do understand. You've been chasing me for weeks. I know what you want. A minute ago, you were begging me to take you to bed. Now you're embarrassed. You want me to force you. I don't want to force you, but if I have to, I will.'

'No.'

'It's up to you,' he said. 'You can give, or I can take. That simple.'

She had never thought rape could be that simple. She bit one of the arms that held her down. He slapped her hard.

'I told you,' he said. 'You can give, or I can take. It's that simple. It's your choice.'

Frightened by his strength, seeing no choice at all, she gave in.

Afterward, she was not surprised when she discovered what he had left in her bed. What else should it be? It was just what she deserved.

It was ugly, yet there was something oddly appealing in the sight of it nestling in a fold of the duvet; she was reminded of her teenage passion for collecting bean-bag creatures. She used to line them up across her bed. This could have been one of them: maybe a squashy elephant's head with a fat nose. She went on staring at it for a long time, lying on her side on the bed, emotionally numbed and physically exhausted, unable either to get up or to go to sleep. She told herself she should get rid of it, that she could take her aggressions out on it, cut it up, at least throw it, and the pair of hands, out with the rest of her unwanted garbage. But it was hard to connect this bean-bag creature with Paul and what he had done to her. She realized she had scarcely more than glimpsed his genitals; no wonder she couldn't believe this floppy creature could have had anything to do with her rape. The longer she looked at it, the less she could believe it was that horrible man's. It, too, had been abused by him. And it wasn't his now, it was hers. OK, Paul had been the catalyst, somehow, but this set of genitalia had been born from the bed and her own desire; it was an entirely new thing.

Eventually she fell asleep, still gazing at it. When she opened her eyes in the morning it was like seeing an old friend. She wouldn't get rid of it. She put it in a pillowcase and stashed the parcel among the scarves, shawls and sweaters on the shelf at the top of the wardrobe.

She decided to put the past behind her. She didn't think about Paul or Ralph or even Freddy. Although most nights she slept with Freddy's body, that was a decision made on the same basis, and with no more emotion, as whether she slept with the duvet or the electric blanket. Freddy's body wasn't Freddy's anymore; it was hers.

The only men in her life now were friends. She wasn't looking for romance, and she seldom thought about sex. If she wanted male companionship there was Christopher, a platonic friend from school, or Marcus, her next-door neighbour, or Freddy. They still talked on the phone frequently, and very occasionally met in town for a drink or a meal, but she had never invited him over since their break-up, so it was a shock one evening to answer the door and discover him standing outside.

He looked sheepish. 'I'm sorry,' he said. 'I know I should have called first, but I couldn't find a working phone, and . . . I hope you don't mind. I need somebody to talk to. Matilda's thrown me out.'

And not only Matilda, but also the latest other woman. He

poured out his woes, and she made dinner, and they drank wine and talked for hours.

'Do you have somewhere to stay?' she asked at last.

'I could go to my sister's. I stay there a lot anyway. She's got a spare room – I've even got my own key. But –' He gave her his old look, desirous but undemanding. 'Actually, Fay, I was hoping I could stay with you tonight.'

She discovered he was still irresistible.

Her last thought before she fell asleep was how strange it was to sleep with someone who had arms and legs.

In the morning she woke enough to feel him kiss her, but she didn't realize it was a kiss goodbye, for she could still feel his legs entwined with her own.

But the rest of him was gone, and probably for good this time, she discovered when she woke up completely. For a man with such a smooth-skinned body he had extremely hairy legs, she thought, sitting on the bed and staring at the unattached limbs. And for a woman who had just been used and left again, she felt awfully cheerful.

She got Ralph's feet out of the drawer – thinking how much thinner and more elegant they were than Freddy's – and, giggling to herself, pressed the right foot to the bottom of the right leg, just to see how it looked.

It looked as if it was growing there and always had been. When she tried to pull it away, it wouldn't come. She couldn't even see a join. Anyone else might have thought it was perfectly natural; it probably only looked odd to her because she knew it wasn't. When she did the same thing with the left foot and left leg, the same thing happened.

So then, feeling daring, she took Freddy's torso out of the wardrobe and laid it down on the bed just above the legs. She pushed the legs up close, so they looked as if they were growing out of the torso – and then they were. She sat it up, finding that it was as flexible and responsive as a real, live person, not at all a dead weight, and she sat on the edge of the bed beside it and looked down at its empty lap.

'Don't go away; I have just the thing for Sir,' she said.

The genitals were really the wrong size and skin-tone for Freddy's long, pale body, but they nestled gratefully into his crotch, obviously happy in their new home.

The body was happy, too. There was new life in it – not Freddy's, not Paul's, not Ralph's, but a new being created out of their old parts. She wasn't imagining it. Not propped up, it was sitting beside her, holding itself up, alert and waiting. When she leaned closer she could feel a heart beating within the chest, sending the blood coursing through a network of veins and arteries. She reached out to stroke the little elephant-head slumbering between the legs, and as she touched it, it stirred and sat up.

She was sexually excited, too, and, at the same time, horrified. There had to be something wrong with her to want to have sex with this incomplete collection of body parts. All right, it wasn't dead, so at least what she felt wasn't necrophilia, but what was it? A man without arms was merely disabled, but was a man without a head a man at all? Whatever had happened to her belief in the importance of relationships? They couldn't even communicate, except by touch, and then only at her initiative. All he could do was respond to her will. She thought of Paul's hands, how she had been groped, forced, slapped, and held down by them, and was just as glad they remained unattached, safely removed to the kitchen cupboard. Safe sex, she thought, and giggled. In response to the vibration, the body listed a little in her direction.

She got off the bed and moved away, then stood and watched it swaying indecisively. She felt a little sorry for it, being so utterly dependent on her, and that cooled her ardour. It wasn't right, she couldn't use it as a kind of live sex-aid – not as it was. She was going to have to find it a head, or forget about it.

She wrapped the body in a sheet to keep the dust off and stored it under the bed. She couldn't sleep with it anymore. In its headless state it was too disturbing. 'Don't worry,' she said, although it couldn't hear her. 'This isn't forever.'

She started her head-hunt. She knew it might take some time, but she was going to be careful; she didn't want another bad experience. It wouldn't be worth it. Something good had come out of the Paul experience, but heads – or faces, anyway – were so much harder to depersonalize. If it looked like Freddy or Paul in the face, she knew she would respond to it as Freddy or Paul, and what was the point of that? She wanted to find someone new, someone she didn't know, but also someone she liked; someone she could find attractive, go to bed with, and be parted from without the traumas of love or hate.

She hoped it wasn't an impossible paradox.

She asked friends for introductions, she signed up for classes, joined clubs, went to parties, talked to men in supermarkets and on buses, answered personal ads. And then Marcus dropped by one evening and asked if she wanted to go to a movie with him.

They had seen a lot of movies and shared a fair number of pizzas over the past two years, but although she liked him, she knew very little about him. She didn't even know for sure that he was heterosexual. She occasionally saw him with other women, but the relationships seemed to be platonic. Because he was younger than she was, delicate-looking and with a penchant for what she thought of as 'arty' clothes, because he didn't talk about sex and had never touched her, the idea of having sex with him had never crossed her mind. Now, seeing his clean-shaven, rather pretty face as if for the first time, it did.

'What a good idea,' she said.

After the movie, after the pizza and a lot of wine, after he'd said he probably should be going, Fay put her hand on his leg and suggested he stay. He seemed keen enough – if surprised – but after she got him into bed he quickly lost his erection and nothing either of them did made any difference.

'It's not your fault,' he said anxiously. It had not occurred to her that it could be. 'Oh, God, this is awful,' he went on. 'If you only knew how I've dreamed of this . . . Only I never thought, never dared to hope, that you could want me too, and now . . . you're so wonderful, and kind, and beautiful, and you deserve so much, and you must think I'm completely useless.'

'I think it's probably the wine,' she said. 'We both had too much to drink. Maybe you should go on home . . . I think we'd both sleep better in our own beds, alone.'

'Oh, God, you don't hate me, do you? You will give me another chance, won't you, Fay? Please?'

'Don't worry about it. Yes, Marcus, yes, of course I will. Now, good night.'

She found nothing in her bed afterward; she hadn't expected to. But neither did she expect the flowers that arrived the next day, and the day after that.

He took her out to dinner on Friday night – not pizza this time – and afterward, in her house, in her bed, they did what they had come together to do. She fell asleep, supremely satisfied, in his arms. In the morning he was eager to make love again, and Fay might have been interested – he had proved himself to be a very tender and skilful lover – but she was too impatient. She had only wanted him for one thing, and the sooner he left her, the sooner she would get it.

'I think you'd better go, Marcus. Let's not drag this out,' she said.

'What do you mean?'

'I mean this was a mistake, we shouldn't have made love, we're really just friends who had too much to drink, so ...'

He looked pale, even against the pale linen. 'But I love you.'

There was a time when such a statement, in such circumstances, would have made her happy, but the Fay who had loved, and expected to be loved in return, by the men she took to bed, seemed like another person now.

'But I don't love you.'

'Then why did you –'

'Look, I don't want to argue. I don't want to say something that might hurt you. I want us to be friends, that's all, the way we used to be.' She got up, since he still hadn't moved, and put on her robe.

'Are you saying you never want to see me again?'

She looked down at him. He really did have a nice face, and the pain that was on it now – that she had put there – made her look away hastily in shame. 'Of course I do. You've been a good neighbour and a good friend. I hope we can go on being that. Only ...'

She tried to remember what someone had said to her once, was it

Ralph? 'Only I can't be what you want me to be. I still care about you, of course. But I don't love you in that way. So we'd better part. You'll see it's for the best, in time. You'll find someone else.'

'You mean you will.'

Startled, she looked back at him. Wasn't that what she had said to Ralph? She couldn't think how to answer him. But Marcus was out of bed, getting dressed, and didn't seem to expect an answer.

'I'll go,' he said. 'Because you ask me to. But I meant what I said. I love you. You know where I live. If you want me . . . if you change your mind . . .'

'Yes, of course. Goodbye, Marcus, I'm sorry.'

She walked him to the door, saw him out, and locked the door behind him. Now! She scurried back to the bedroom, but halted in the doorway as she had a sudden, nasty thought. What if it hadn't worked? What if, instead of a pretty face, she found, say, another pair of feet in her bed?

Then I'll do it again, she decided, and again and again until I get my man.

She stepped forward, grasped the edge of the duvet, and threw it aside with a conjurer's flourish.

There was nothing on the bare expanse of pale blue sheet; nothing but a few stray pubic hairs.

She picked up the pillows, each in turn, and shook them. She shook out the duvet, unfastening the cover to make sure there was nothing inside. She peered beneath the bed and poked around the sheet-wrapped body, even pulled the bed away from the wall, in case something had caught behind the headboard. Finally she crawled across the bed on her belly, nose to the sheet, examining every inch.

Nothing. He had left nothing.

But why? How?

They left parts because they weren't willing to give all. The bed preserved bits and pieces of men who wanted only pieces of her time, pieces of her body, for which they could pay only with pieces of their own.

Marcus wanted more than that. He wanted, and offered, everything. But she had refused him, so now she had nothing.

No, not nothing. She crouched down and pulled the sheet-wrapped form from beneath the bed, unwrapped it and reassured herself that the headless, armless body was still warm, still alive, still male, still hers. She felt the comforting stir of sexual desire in her own body as she aroused it in his, and she vowed she would not be defeated.

It would take thought and careful planning, but surely she could make one more lover leave her?

She spent the morning making preparations, and at about lunchtime she phoned Marcus and asked him to come over that evening.

'Did you really mean it when you said you loved me?'

'Yes.'

'Because I want to ask you to do something for me, and I don't think you will.'

'Fay, anything, what is it?'

'I'll have to tell you in person.'

'I'll come over now.'

She fell into his arms when he came in, and kissed him passionately. She felt his body respond, and when she looked at his face she saw the hurt had gone and a wondering joy replaced it.

'Let's go in the bedroom,' she said. 'I'm going to tell you everything; I'm going to tell you the truth about what I want, and you won't like it, I know.'

'How can you know? How can you possibly know?' He stroked her back, smiling at her.

'Because it's not normal. It's a sexual thing.'

'Try me.'

They were in the bedroom now. She drew a deep breath. 'Can I tie you to the bed?'

'Well.' He laughed a little. 'I've never done that before, but I don't see anything wrong with it. If it makes you happy.'

'Can I do it?'

'Yes, why not.'

'Now, I mean.' Shielding the bedside cabinet with her body, she pulled out the ropes she had put there earlier. 'Lie down.'

He did as she said. 'You don't want me to undress first?'

She shook her head, busily tying him to the bedposts.

'And what do I do now?' He strained upwards against the ropes, demonstrating how little he was capable of doing.

'Now you give me your head.'

'What?'

'Other men have given me other parts; I want your head.'

It was obvious he didn't know what she meant. She tried to remember how she had planned to explain; what, exactly, she wanted him to do. Should she show him the body under the bed? Would he understand then?

'Your head,' she said again, and then she remembered the words. 'It's simple. You can give it to me, or I can take it. It's your choice.'

He still stared at her as if it wasn't simple at all. She got the knife out of the bedside cabinet, and held it so he could see. 'You give, or I take. It's your choice.'

'The Mezzotint'

*It was a rather indifferent mezzotint, and an indifferent
mezzotint is, perhaps, the worst form of engraving known.*
— M.R. James, 'The Mezzotint'

The front of the bungalow was like a crudely drawn face. The
two windows on either side were big, square eyes and the
red brick arch around the front door was a lipsticked mouth wide
open. It was a squat, ill-proportioned face, with neither nose nor
chin and a roof like a hat jammed over a low brow. The first time
she'd seen it, Mel had imagined it in a 1930s cartoon. Even then,
in love with the occupant as she was, it hadn't seemed to her a
friendly house – she'd imagined the cartoon house sneering at
Betty Boop, giving her a hard time – and today, in the gathering darkness, with half-drawn curtains over lightless windows
giving it an idiot's blank gaze, it looked even less welcoming than
usual. She had to steel herself to step into the gaping mouth of the
unlighted porch to let herself in.

No cooking smells greeted her. As she hung up her coat she
could hear the faint, insectile scuttling sound of Kieran's fingers
on the computer keyboard. She walked down the hall and opened
his office door.

He was in profile, sitting at his desk, attention fixed on the
screen as he typed, and he spoke without looking around. 'I
thought you said you'd be late?'

'It's nearly eight now,' she said, carefully noncommittal.

'Oh, right. OK, I won't be much longer.'

On the screen were lines of type, what looked like dialogue.
Curious, she stepped closer, trying to read it, but his annoyance,
vibrating like a wire in the room, stopped her. She knew he hated

her 'spying' as he called it, and they'd had far too many quarrels lately. Wanting peace, she turned away, saying, 'Shall I start dinner?'

'Just give me a few more minutes, love.' He voice was gentle.

As she was about to go out of the room, she noticed a picture hanging on the wall beside the door. It was an old engraving of a house and its grounds, by moonlight. She'd never seen it before, although it did remind her of something. It was the sort of thing Kieran used to buy at country auctions or in junk shops for a pittance and then sell on for a vastly inflated price. Before he got into website design, he'd told her, he had made his living trading in art, books and other collectibles, but since Mel had moved in with him, there'd been no time for the visits to junk shops or the trawls around country market-towns which had been a feature of their courtship. She thought of the amber necklace he'd given her two months ago; a few months before that, there'd been a beaded handbag. Was he buying again?

'Where'd you get this?' she asked.

'What?' He sounded harassed. 'Just a mo'.' He clattered away at the keys, then shut down the screen. Then, with a put-upon sigh, he swung his chair around and faced her. 'What?'

'This picture. When did you get it?'

'*That?* I've had it forever.'

'But I've never seen it before.'

'It's always been there.'

She turned to look at him: no sign of a tease, and he wasn't defensive. Yet it couldn't be true.

'Not always,' she objected.

He raised his eyebrows. 'It came with the house,' he elaborated. 'I don't know where my parents got it from. It was just there, as long as I can remember.'

'Then why did I never notice it before?'

'How should I know? Well, why should you have noticed it – it's not that interesting. Just an old mezzotint of a house ...'

The word *mezzotint* raised goosebumps.

He noticed, and grinned. 'Mezzotint doesn't mean haunted picture, my darling,' he said, rather superciliously. Kieran had ten years on Mel and quite naturally adopted the role of tutor. He'd read so many books and seemed to know so many odd and interesting things, especially about art and literature, that at first she had been grateful. But lately it seemed he only told her things she already knew, or didn't want to hear.

'Yes, I know,' she said quickly. 'I know it's a type of engraving.' Her eyes went back to it. 'But it is awfully like the mezzotint in James' story, isn't it?'

He shook his head. ' Not at all. There's no spooky figure, for one thing.'

'There wasn't one at the beginning of the story, either. It only changed later.'

'Hmm. Well, all I can tell you is that in, oh, thirty-seven years at least, that picture has not changed in any way. Although I suppose I might not have noticed if it did. I have to admit I don't spend a great deal of time looking at it. It's not a terribly *interesting* picture.' He cleared his throat. 'Look, I'm sorry I haven't got dinner ready – I didn't realize how late it was getting to be. Why don't I get us a take-away. What would you like?'

Although she was still curious about the picture, she gave it up for the moment. 'Indian,' she decided. 'You can order; you know what I like.'

'I *know* what you like,' he said with a lascivious grin.

She smiled back, not to offend.

After he'd gone out for the food, Mel went straight back to look at the strange mezzotint. The first thing she did was take it off the wall. A greyish wisp of cobweb, two or three inches long, clung there, and the rectangle of wall paint which the picture had covered was discernibly a different shade from the rest of the room. Clearly, the picture had been hanging in that same spot for years. She put it back carefully just as it had been, not even brushing away the cobweb.

So he hadn't lied. But why hadn't she ever noticed it before? After all, she had been living in this house for more than six months, and although she didn't spend much time in Kieran's office, until this moment she had been confident she could close her eyes and reliably describe the contents and layout of every

room. Back at the start of their relationship, she'd been eager
to know everything about him. On her first visits to his house
she had studied it for clues to his past and his character – she had
practically memorized it. Except for the bedroom, which she had
redecorated, nothing much had changed since she'd moved in.
Nearly all the furniture, artwork and books were his, and much
had been his parents', coming along with the two-bedroom bungalow he'd inherited from his mother.

Mel closed her eyes and summoned up memory. It showed her
nothing at all on that wall.

She opened her eyes. It was an odd place to hang a picture, just
above a light switch; she would have been afraid of driving the
nail into the electrical wiring. The heavy, black-framed engraving was wrong for the narrow space – it was too heavy and dark,
and nearly as wide as the wall itself. She knew little about Kieran's
parents – they had died before she met him – but she was surprised
that his own aesthetic sense hadn't forced him to rehang the picture, which would have been better placed in the sitting-room, or
even on the far wall of his office, swapping places with one of the
smaller, watercolour landscapes.

And why had she never seen it before? She was a visual person,
alert to her surroundings. She noticed things others did not. She
simply would not, could not have missed something that big.

She was starting to get spooked. In the M.R. James story, the
mezzotint had changed every few hours, revealing a secret crime
from the past. But it had turned up in the usual way, with a prov-
enance, sent by a well-known dealer through the mail, offered for
sale at a particular price . . . it hadn't just teleported into a room,
the way this one seemed to have done.

Should she believe Kieran, and mistrust her own memory?
Did Kieran really remember it from his childhood, or only think
he did? Was it some kind of trick?

Her heart hammering, Mel left the room, closing the door
firmly behind her. She wished she could lock it, although how
much effect a locked door would have on something which could
materialize at will, she didn't know. She was being silly. The
thought of Kieran's ridicule stopped her from barring it with

a chair: was she really afraid of a *picture*? What on earth did she think it could do to her if it got out?

She went and found Kieran's first edition of *Ghost Stories of an Antiquary* and perched on the edge of the couch in the sitting room to read 'The Mezzotint'. She'd first read the M.R. James story at the age of ten or eleven, coming across it in a mouldy-smelling paperback with a disembodied hand on the cover, a collection of horror stories bought at a jumble sale. She couldn't remember the other stories, but 'The Mezzotint' had given her nightmares. How sinister the title had seemed to her – that strange, hissing word – even after she'd read it (such was the gulp-ing, rapid, half-comprehending way she'd read at that age) she'd thought the mezzotint of the title was – not a haunted picture, but the vengeful, skeletal, robed creature who had crept across the lawn by moonlight and stolen away a child. For years she'd believed *mezzotint* was a type of monster, a word like ghoul, ghost or vampire for a terrifying supernatural being.

As she read 'The Mezzotint' again, as an adult, Mel was surprised by how unserious it was. It was narrated in a casual, conversational manner, with a lot of irrelevant chat, and jokes about golfing, university life and servants. The horror story she remembered was still there, but it was presented at a remove, in a few paragraphs, as something which had happened long ago and elsewhere to people all dead and gone. All emotion was safely distanced. The horror was only an idea, a notion to be enjoyed.

Kieran came in and saw what she had been reading. 'Still think that's *the* mezzotint?'

Mel shook her head. 'Different house.'

'Shall we go see if ours has *changed?*'

She did want to, but he was teasing, so she grinned. 'Maybe after dinner. We don't want our food to get cold.'

'Oh, yes, and it'll be that fascinating we won't be able to tear ourselves away!' he cried in a northern-accented falsetto.

'It was so different from the story I remembered,' she said once they were settled at the kitchen table with their food. 'Not as scary as I'd thought. The idea that a moving picture is scary – well, I guess, in the olden days, before cinema – '

'They had motion pictures,' Kieran objected. 'That story was written no earlier than 1900. Edison invented his kinetoscope, when was it? 1893,' he answered himself, tearing off a piece of naan.

Mel shrugged. 'OK, so they knew about movies. The mezzotint wasn't a film, anyway – it just kept changing to a different still picture. If somebody today saw it they'd be like, "How'd you do that? How does it work?" They wouldn't be *scared*.'

'That's because we have the technology, and it gets smaller and less detectable every day,' Kieran said pedantically. 'And then you read about things, or you see them in movies, and you just accept it all. Look at flat screens. Look what you can do with a good computer program. With high resolution ... but the picture quality wouldn't matter so much with an engraving, because you haven't got the colour and it doesn't have to look like real life. It would be easy to program five or six different scenes to change at regular intervals throughout the day. Then you can give somebody in a windowless office views of mountains, or the rainforest, or whatever you like,' he concluded, digging into his rogan josh.

Was that it? No, the mezzotint was just a picture, not a flat screen disguised as something else. The only thing that needed explanation was where it had come from ... or why she could not remember having seen it before today.

Their conversation moved on to other things: what she'd done at work that day, what was on TV that night. She liked to keep Kieran abreast of office gossip, to share what she did, even though he'd never met anyone she worked with. He didn't talk about his work; he said programming didn't make for conversation. He could give her the URLs and she could visit his websites if she wanted. Sometimes he told her jokes or interesting factoids he'd picked up on his internet trawls.

After the washing-up, he agreed to go back to look at the picture with her, although he professed himself baffled: 'I don't know why you're so interested in it all of a sudden.'

'Just because I never was before.'

Although he joked, she honestly *was* relieved to see no change in the picture. It still showed a medium-sized, squarish, very plain house, without the parapets or porticos of the manor house in the

James story, and with only two, rather than three, rows of plain sashed windows – none of them open. There were a few trees and bushes and a lawn in front, but no figures.

'What is the house – do you know?'

'No idea.' She thought he hesitated.

'But . . . ?'

He shrugged. 'Oh, well, when I was a kid I imagined it was the house my parents *used* to live in, before I was born. I don't know where I got that idea from; I don't remember that I ever asked them. I just remember wishing we lived there. This was such a poky little place . . . I loved the idea of two storeys, and all those rooms, with a lawn big enough to play cricket on . . .'

She turned and looked at him sharply. 'You lived *here?*'

'Yes, of course. I told you.'

'I thought your parents came here after they retired.' Although, as she spoke, she couldn't recall him actually saying so. Maybe she had just assumed, since all of their neighbours were pensioners, and this tiny, seaside bungalow, all right for a couple, had never seemed like a family home.

He shook his head. 'No, I've always lived here. This was my bedroom.'

She felt a dizzying sense of shock, of betrayal. *Always?* 'But what about – you told me you lived in Bristol, and Brighton –'

'Yes, of course. And London. As an *adult*. I never lived anywhere but here as a child. When I grew up, of course I left home. First to art college, then there was the girl in London, the job in Brighton, then after a bit I went back to London, and then a few years later Brighton again – but I've told you all this before.'

Of course. 'And then, in the end, you came back here again.' She heard the querulous tone in her voice, tried to soften it by going on, 'It seems strange, that's all, that you'd *choose* to live in a place you hated.'

'I never said I hated it.' He was annoyed now. 'It was just small for three people, that's all. I never had any privacy. It's different now. I'm grown up. Wanting to live in a house like that was a kid's fantasy. I could never afford anything that big, not in reach of London. This is big enough for two, and convenient for London and Brighton. And since I don't care about playing cricket anymore, and I know how long it takes to mow a lawn that size, I much prefer a small garden.'

'But even so – you could have sold this, bought someplace else, taken your time, shopped around . . . moving house is such a big thing . . . where were you living when your mother died?'

He stared at her. 'Right here. Looking after my mother.'

Her mouth was dry. He had never said anything about this before. She was absolutely certain he'd told her his mother had died suddenly. 'How long were you looking after her?'

He shrugged. 'Eighteen months? I don't know. More than a year, less than two. She had a stroke, about a month after my father's funeral. She recovered a bit, but she couldn't live on her own. So I had to come. I'd just been living in a rented bedsit, anyway. I let it go. So you see, there was no place to go back to. When Mum died, this *was* my home. And, as you say, moving house is a big thing.' He was watching her with close concern. 'What's this about, Melly? Do you want to move?'

She shook her head mechanically, hardly hearing him as she tried to concentrate. His role as the devoted carer, his mother's nurse – no, he'd never mentioned that before. As she remembered it, he'd been living not in a bedsit, but as the tenant/lover of a woman called Kelly. A flat in Highgate – rather a nice one – but the relationship was in trouble. So when his mother quite suddenly and unexpectedly died, leaving him her house, he hadn't thought of selling it, or invited Kelly to share it, but had taken the opportunity to end the relationship. *That's* what she remembered. Had he lied to her then? Or was he lying now?

'Because if you do, that's fine,' he went on. 'I'm not absolutely wedded to this place, whatever you may think. I'm happy to move, if that would make *you* happy. Would a joint mortgage make you feel more secure? I'm sure we could find someplace that would suit us both.' He took her in his arms and held her close, murmuring into her hair, 'I want you to be happy, Melly, I really do. I know I'm a selfish bastard sometimes, but I really do care about you. I love you. You're not like the others. I want you to stay.'

They made love later that night. Mel didn't want to, but it

had been nearly two weeks since their last time, and Kieran was making such an effort that she sensed it would be more trouble than it was worth to refuse. It went on rather longer than usual, because he was being so careful and sensitive, and in the end Mel faked an orgasm just to get him off her. He fell asleep fairly quickly after that, but she lay awake, finally free to think the things she couldn't when he was watching.

When he'd said, 'You're not like the others', presumably he'd meant the women who had come before her, the ones he had loved and left. How many had there been? Mel didn't know. When they'd first become intimate and were exchanging histories, he had mentioned various names. Only four or five of them had really mattered, he said, and he'd only lived with two. Yet details, even names, varied from time to time in his accounts. When Mel called him on inconsistencies, he flatly denied them. She could hardly argue that it was Susan, not Fiona, he'd lived with in Brighton, or that Fiona had been the bookseller and Kelly the teacher rather than vice versa. She'd never known any of them, and if his stories changed, and he seemed to be mixing them up and getting the details wrong, well, wasn't it more likely that *she* was the one with the bad memory? It made her uneasy, but surely it was unimportant what he remembered about his former lovers. They were all in the past, and had nothing to do with her.

Even if he was guilty of forgetting, or even rewriting, his past, she didn't think he lied to her. Although he had what seemed to her a fetish for privacy (she thought of the locked drawers of his desk) she had no real reason for thinking he had any dark secrets to hide. He was still sexually interested in her (it was only she who had changed in recent months) and there were no suspicious phone calls, no weekends away. Occasionally he went out in the evenings, for something computer-related. (He'd explained that most of the people he dealt with had day jobs.) Once every two or three months he might spend the whole evening out, leaving in the late afternoon, going up to London for drinks with colleagues, not getting home until well after midnight. She didn't think he was hiding an affair in those infrequent, boozy evenings.

No, if he was having an affair it had to be during the day. He worked alone at home, spending hours in front of the computer, but also finding time to do the laundry and a bit of housework or gardening; more often than not he was cooking dinner when she arrived home. Yet he did go out occasionally, to run errands or just to stretch his legs. From the mileage on the car she knew he must sometimes go farther afield than the local village and, although he hadn't told her where he'd found them, she assumed that at least a couple of the gifts he'd given her in the past year – the amber necklace, the beaded evening bag – had come from unmentioned, solitary trawls through the antique markets or second-hand shops of Brighton or some more distant country town.

If he *did* have another lover, it would have to be someone content with occasional daytime assignations, someone who would never call in the evenings, or expect to see him at the weekend. What sort of woman would put up with that, and where would Kieran have met her?

Mel turned over abruptly in the bed, sickened. Of course Kieran didn't have another lover. What was she thinking?

The mezzotint disturbed her. It was a warning. If it had truly been there all along, why hadn't she seen it before? What else had she missed about this house . . . about Kieran? For some time now she had been uneasy in the relationship. She didn't know why, she couldn't find a reason, and maybe there wasn't one, but her feelings had changed within a month or two of moving in with him. And now, she thought, self-loathing, I'm trying to find some reason to blame Kieran because *I've* changed.

The next morning, Kieran told her that he'd be out when she got home from work. He had a meeting over in Lewes, and they might go for a curry afterwards.

'You don't mind if I'm out for dinner?' He regarded her anxiously and, although he was *always* like this when he went out in the evenings by himself, concerned that she should not feel neglected, Mel felt he was watching her more closely than usual, and wondered if he sensed her disloyal pleasure at the thought of an evening without him.

'No, of course not!' she exclaimed vigorously, hoping she wasn't blushing. 'I'll be fine!'

She was rarely in the house by herself. It was an opportunity that might never come again. So, as soon as she got in from work Mel made a beeline for Kieran's office.

The title to another M.R. James story sprang to mind: 'A Warning to the Curious'. She didn't remember the plot of it, but the title seemed appropriate to the tale of Psyche and Cupid, the story of a woman who had lost her lover because she had insisted on gazing upon his hidden face.

The mezzotint still hung on the same wall. Her eyes slowly scanned the picture, searching for change, a different scene, any detail out of place, but it was unchanged from yesterday, as far as she could tell. Her heart pounded painfully hard as she gazed around the room. She was reminded of childhood games of hide-and-seek, and scarier games. She kept expecting that he would jump out at her: it was a trick, a trap . . . And what, anyway, did she expect to find? She felt guilty and frightened, but determined.

The office looked much as ever to her, untidy yet organized. Probably there were different books, pamphlets, operating instructions, CDs and diskettes scattered about in different places, but that was normal. If there were secrets here, she thought they would be in the locked drawer of his desk. He kept the key to that on the keychain that he always carried with him. If there was a spare key, she didn't know where it was.

Nevertheless, she went and sat in his chair at his desk, and tried the drawer handle, just in case. It was locked.

So that was that, she thought with relief. As she moved her hand, she jogged the computer mouse. The machine gave an electronic cough and the screen swam back to life, blossoming into colour.

She gazed at the rows of shortcut icons which would take her to his word processing program, to his diary (if he kept one), to all his e-mail files and folders. She could find out which internet sites he'd visited in the past weeks, track down what he'd been doing yesterday when she'd interrupted him. She could open work folders, personal files . . .

There was too much choice. She was still sitting, paralysed with indecision, when the screensaver came on, and suddenly, instead of looking at green tiles studded with icons, she was staring at the house from the mezzotint.

It had been done in shades of grey, like the original, but it wasn't still. Screensavers *weren't* — they needed moving pictures. Clouds slowly drifted across the night sky, revealing and then concealing the moon. A star twinkled. A bat flapped past the windows.

Mel let out a sigh and shook her head, baffled and impressed. He must have spent all day on it! She waited to see what else it would reveal, although she knew she really should walk away now. She'd have to pretend surprise when he showed it to her.

A figure appeared at the edge of the screen, running towards the house. She was surprised: instead of a skeletal figure in a robe, this was a very modern-looking man in a hooded track-suit and running shoes. It reached the door and went in, and the screen went black.

Mel frowned, leaning towards the screen. In response, it lightened again. The scene revealed now was totally different. She realized she was inside the house, in a cavernous, rather gloomy room incongruously furnished with dumpy old sofas and chairs, a TV, stereo system, overstuffed bookshelves — she recognized some of Kieran's things, even his pictures in miniature hanging on the shadowed walls, but before she could look more closely her viewpoint was rushed away, towards another door, and then down, down, down a steep, dark staircase. Even though it was only computer graphics, she felt a fearful, vertiginous rush as if she really was descending much too fast.

And then she was in the basement — or would dungeon have been a better word? The graphics were much cruder here; it was like a nasty comic, the sort for 'adult readers only'. Women's bodies, naked and leaking blood, lay twisted in awkward poses on the stone floor.

She wanted to look away, she wanted *out,* but she had to try to understand what she was being shown. She had been looking for secrets, and here they were.

Words appeared, in lurid green, flashing slightly, above each body.

Susan it said above one. (*Beaded Evening Bag*)
Over another, *Fiona*. (*Byron's Letters*)
Kelly. (*Silver ear-rings*)
Sharon. (*Amber Necklace*)
Jasmine. (*Pink Pashmina*)

She knew what it meant. Oh, yes, horribly, she knew, even though she'd never seen the pink pashmina. (Was it blood-stained? Or simply put aside for another day?)

She reached for the mouse, jiggled it, and at once the horrid dungeon scene faded away and she was back staring at the green tiles and icons of Kieran's entry screen. She was panting as if she'd had to rush up those stairs to get out. She felt dizzy and sick.

Get out, get out – she knew she had to leave the house at once, run away, although her head was swirling and her legs felt too weak to support her. But she knew what she had to do. In her mind, the bungalow and the house in the mezzotint, the house on the screen, became one. She had to get across that huge, cavernous living room – she could see herself doing it – and get to the door, which receded like a door in a nightmare.

Don't think about it – just do it!

She knew she had to move, but it was strangely difficult, a huge effort just to push herself away from the desk and Kieran's softly humming computer. She managed to swing the chair around – and there he was in the doorway, watching her, not saying a word.

She got up, knowing words were useless now, and he came in. He was between her and the door, blocking her escape.

Her eyes flew to the picture on the wall and, yes, she was there, she could see herself inside the house, a tiny figure, pushing open a window, awkwardly clambering out, then fleeing across the empty, silent, moonlit lawn, running for her life.

Yet even as she watched herself escape from one house, in another Kieran's big, blank face was coming closer and closer, looming over her: she was shrinking, or he had become as big as a house. His eyes were wide open, two windows: she could look straight in. She looked inside and saw no one. No one alive.

After the End

A new story about C. Auguste Dupin (with apologies to E.A. Poe)

I have written before about my quondam friend, the Chevalier C. Auguste Dupin, with whom I long ago resided in an ancient house in a retired and desolate street in Paris, yet never have I described the details of his final case. That it would be of great interest to a very wide readership I was never in doubt, for it involved a series of horrific murders that terrified the public and baffled the police, and without the intervention of Dupin and his superior powers of analytical thought, the killer would never have been found and brought to justice.

The victims were all young women, but there was no discernible connection between them; one was married, one affianced; one a *grisette,* another the daughter of a lawyer. They were of different classes and lived in different quarters of the city. At first, therefore, the police quite naturally assumed each had been murdered by a different man; there were no suspects, and no one came forward to inform or confess, but when yet another woman died, the public became convinced one single, bloodthirsty monster was responsible.

Dupin had already recognized the evidence, what he called the killer's *signature,* even while the police resisted the idea.

The problem was, how to find the murderer? No matter how he searched for a connection between these disparate women (or their families), Dupin could find nothing. They had lived and died in different *arrondissements,* did not attend the same church or buy their bread from the same baker. The only thing they had in common was their sex and relative youth (the eldest was twenty-four; the youngest, seventeen) and, perhaps most importantly, the fact that they did not know their killer. Dupin concluded that the man the popular press had dubbed 'the beast of Paris' was deliberately choosing his victims from the large pool of total strangers, women previously unknown to him with whom he had no traceable connection.

But who sets out to kill strangers, not in wartime, for no reason or benefit?

Only a madman. Indeed, the senseless cruelty of the crimes could be the very definition of madness. Yet, apart from that, the killer did not act like someone in the grip of insanity. He was cool and calculating. He planned his murders in advance and possessed sufficient self-control to resist drawing attention to himself. If he was mad, it was only now and then, at times of his own choosing – which surely is not madness at all, but an expression of pure evil. A better name for this monster than 'beast' would be 'devil', I thought.

By now, some of my readers will have guessed the identity of this devil, and recall the scandal that erupted when the police, acting on the results of M. Dupin's investigations, arrested one Paul Gabriel Reclus. M. Reclus was known as a respectable, wealthy, unmarried gentleman of Paris. Not himself a member of either the government or the press, he had influential friends in both, and as a result, the police found themselves obliged to release him almost immediately, with grovelling apologies. For they had no evidence against him. Although convinced by Dupin's argument, constructed out of his subtle observations, it amounted to nothing more than a delicate chain of logic. There were no witnesses to any of the murders, and nothing, not a single, solid object or piece of bloodstained clothing in the possession of M. Reclus to tie him to any one of the crimes. As he showed no signs of guilt nor inclination to confess, the police had nothing with which to convict him, nor even any obvious reason for arresting him.

Naturally, they blamed Dupin for leading them astray. The results were quite disastrous for my friend. He did not mind the mockery in the press (although some of the cartoons were particularly savage) and simply ignored those military friends of

Reclus who challenged him to duel (after all, duelling was illegal, however common it might have been among bantam cocks obsessed with their notion of honour), but the charges of slander and libel brought against him in court cost him most of his patrimony to defend. However, there was something far worse than all of that: the secret, subterranean vengeance enacted by Reclus against Dupin, about which my friend dared say nothing. For M. Reclus continued to kill innocent young women. He must have believed himself invincible, untouchable. But now for his victims he chose girls who had some connection to the one man who had revealed he knew his secret. Because Dupin led a retired and celibate existence, the connections were necessarily remote, of a sort only *he* would be sure to recognize. The first victim worked in the shop where my friend customarily bought his daily bread. The next was the wife of his butcher. Then a bookseller's daughter met her mysterious, violent end.

Dupin realized that unless he could deliver the killer to the police with irrefutable evidence of his crimes – or killed the clever madman himself – more women would die. In addition, he knew that he had little time to act, as he anticipated the killer's scheme was to implicate him in his crimes, planting clews that must eventually lead to the inevitable (although false) conclusion that *Dupin* was the murderer.

The Chevalier's analytical skills were not limited to unravelling mysteries of the past, but extended to predicting what, following a certain course of action, an individual would do next. This, he insisted, was not a matter of intuition, but of observation; it was a purely scientific exercise, and would always be successful so long as the initial observations were sufficient and correct. To me, this seemed to contradict the notion of free will, suggesting human beings were little more than mechanical objects, forced to move in a particular way once their springs had been wound, but his results were such that I could never argue. When he declared that he had worked out precisely when, where and *who* the killer would next attack, I knew he must be right, and the only problem was how to ensure that the police arrived on the scene before the girl was killed, but while Reclus' murderous intentions were clear enough that his arrest and subsequent conviction should be inevitable.

To the public, Dupin's skills could seem magical, yet he always insisted they were purely rational, and in the past, in my previous stories about M. Dupin, I have delighted in explaining the chain of reasoning that led him to feats of understanding that seemed like clairvoyance, mind-reading, or some other of those super-human skills that are sometimes displayed by people who have been mesmerised.

But I have never written about the case I might once have called 'The Devil of Paris', never given all the details of what was to be C. Auguste Dupin's last case. Yes, he solved it, but at a great cost.

Of course, it was not *his* fault the police arrived too late to save the life of Dupin's own cousin. At least they were in time to catch Reclus red-handed, and none of his influential friends were able to save him from the guillotine. In vain did I argue with my old friend that he had performed the great public service of protect-ing any number of young women from the ravages of 'the beast'; he could not get past the guilt he felt for bringing the attention of the murderer to his cousin and the other three blameless young women whose misfortune it was to be connected to men with whom he had commercial dealings. In vain did I argue he could not possibly be held to blame for the actions of that evil creature; he said he should have *known* how Reclus would take his revenge, and he should not have given the police the killer's name without the evidence they needed to arrest him.

His partial failure weighed upon his conscience, and it turned him away from the police. They had let him down as much as he had let down the last four victims of Reclus, and henceforth he would take no interest in contemporary crime or current affairs, but would instead dedicate all his mental capacities to questions of historic and philosophical matters. He instructed me never to write about his last case, and although I no longer feel bound by that injunction, neither do I wish to revisit those old days and write of his solving of the case of the beast – or devil – of Paris in the sort of detail I devoted to his earlier exploits. I merely raise the subject as a reminder to my readers, for its bearing on what would transpire later, the subject of this story.

Had I remained in Paris, I sometimes think things might have turned out differently for Dupin, but it was not to be. Even as my old friend was becoming more determinedly entrenched in his studies, retreating from the present day, I received a letter from my father, summoning me home with some urgency to help with the family business. With a feeling of profound melancholy, I bid farewell to the Chevalier, begging him not to forget me, and to write often.

I had, I think, half a dozen letters from him after my return to Baltimore, each one a superb, if not entirely comprehensible, essay on a subject of deepest obscurity, such as the origins of the Kartvelian languages; the meaning of the gigantic stone heads of Easter Island; the manner in which eels reproduce; and a new interpretation of the Mayan calendar. Apart from mentioning certain rare volumes he had been fortunate enough to acquire for his library he made little reference to the details of his quotidian life, although from the regular changes of address I understood his fortunes were continuing to decline, as he moved to ever poorer quarters.

That is, until the last letter, in which he mentioned, in a postscript, that he was about to be married, and would shortly be departing Paris for his wife's country estate. He mentioned no word of love, nor did he describe the beauty or charm of his intended, although he did inform me that the future Madame Dupin came from a family equal in age and nobility to his own, but far superior in wealth. She had also inherited a library of impressive size. I perceived at once that this was no love-match, but a practical arrangement by which M. Dupin might subsidize his bibliophilia.

Unfortunately, he neglected to include his new address, or even his fiancée's name or the location of her library. Surely he intended to inform me once he was settled into his new home, but within days of receiving that last letter, I found myself in a tricky financial situation and was forced to leave the city abruptly without leaving a forwarding address. Alas, this set an unhappy pattern for the next two years, and as I lived a vagabond existence and moved from Brooklyn to Boston, and then from Philadelphia to Poughkeepsie, I could only scour the newspapers for news from France, and quiz any recent visitors for word of him, but to no avail.

Until, at last, one day, in the pages of the *New York Herald*, I glimpsed the name of *C. Auguste Dupin* almost buried in a dense column of black type devoted to a series of shocking deaths – that series of hideous, inhuman killings dubbed by our press 'the French Wolf-Man Murders'. Although he had no connection with the police or this case (as I discovered after reading the entire article), Dupin's name was invoked by the journalist who fancied he saw some similarities to the murders in the Rue Morgue and thought the genius who had solved that strange mystery could also explain this one.

At that point, there had been two deaths, within weeks of each other, in the same region of France. One young woman had been bloodily slaughtered in a lonely forest, and the other died in her own bed. Both had their throats ripped out, apparently by some fierce beast. The girl in the forest had been presumed to have fallen prey to a wolf (very rare in that part of the country, yet presumably not quite extinct) until the second killing which, apart from the setting, seemed almost identical to the first. But how had a wolf come to enter and leave a young lady's bedroom without attracting attention? Sensationalist newspapers and superstitious public alike spoke of that creature which is a man in daylight and a wolf by night: the were-wolf, or *loup garou*.

A week later, the newspaper carried more reports from France. The police were convinced the two deaths were completely unrelated, and nor were they murders, despite misleading reports. One woman had been attacked by a wolf, which had been spotted several times in the district. The other had been killed by her own dog, turned unexpectedly savage. Although it had run away, it had been caught and destroyed.

Yet even as this story appeared in our American papers, another woman had died in a quiet country lane in a French village, her throat torn out, and in every other particular her death resembled those of the other two women. Soon enough that story reached us across the ocean, accompanied by some of the hysteria which was gripping that region of France, and full of speculation as to the true reason for these deaths.

A surgeon who had examined all three bodies announced his conviction that the culprit was a human being, not an animal, and certainly not a supernatural, skin-changing creature, but an exceptionally cunning and ruthless man who was driven to kill by some inexplicable compulsion (here he reminded questioners of the Reclus case in Paris a few years earlier) – mad in that way, but utterly rational in his ability to disguise his crimes.

It would have been better for Dr. de la Roche if he had never spoken out, for his announcement did not affect the rising hysteria about the *loup garou,* and three days later, both he and his wife were found dead in their home, their throats savaged in the same manner as seen on the other victims. When I heard that, it occurred to me that even if the police asked for his help, Dupin – now with the safety of his own wife to think about – would surely refuse. Would he be right to do so? Could anyone else solve this fearful mystery?

My mind therefore was certainly fixed on Dupin, as well as the recent terrible crimes in France, on the evening that I attended a session promising 'mesmeric revelations' in the home of Mr. D—— W—— of Elmira, New York.

Displays of mesmerism have been so popular and widespread in recent years that I think I need hardly explain the theory. The gathering at the W—— home in Elmira was small and informal, for the parlour could comfortably accommodate no more than a dozen guests. The designated somnambule was the sixteen-year-old daughter of the house, and we had been told in advance that her particular talent, when under the influence of the magnetic passes made by her father, was to become a channel, or medium, through which we might receive the voices of the dead. Particularly likely to speak were those troubled spirits who had recently passed out of the realm of the physical, their deaths so sudden that they had not yet come to terms with their new state.

Even under the rapt gaze of an audience, Miss W—— succumbed to the expected strange, sleep-like state quite rapidly. Almost at once she gasped and exclaimed in French, and then, in that same language, began to teasingly scold some gentleman who had, it seemed, taken her by surprise. The one-sided conversation that followed, at first flirtatious, became increasingly bold and salacious as the speaker began to bargain with the male stranger, offering the pleasures of her body in return for payment. I shifted uncomfortably in my seat, but noticing none of my fellow guests responding, realized I must be the only person there who understood the language.

The somnambule – or I should say, whoever spoke through her – now changed her tone. She seemed nervous, even frightened of the man she had been so intent upon wooing, and then there could be no mistaking her terror when she screamed.

At that bloodcurdling sound there was a shocked flurry throughout the stuffy parlour – one lady fainted dead away – and Mr W—— seemed about to try to wake his daughter when I stopped him. Recognizing that we'd heard evidence of a crime, I begged him to question his daughter as to the identity of the spirit.

But Miss W—— was only a conduit, and knew nothing of what transpired while she was in this state. Fortunately, the spirit was still nearby. As the only French-speaker, it fell to me to question her, and I first inquired her name.

'I am Marie Callot.'

That was the name of the third victim of the murderous 'wolf-man' of France. I felt a chill, and heard gasps and murmurs from others who also recognized her name from the papers.

How I longed for the aid of Auguste Dupin as I quizzed the victim about her attacker! Perhaps he would have made more of her slender evidence than I could. The girl had not known the man, and had scarcely seen his face in the dark lane where he encountered her. She could only say that she did not think he was a local; he had a Paris accent, and from the fine cloth and fashionable cut of his clothes, she knew he was 'quality'. No, he did not bite her throat, nor did he metamorphose into a hairy animal. She did not see what sort of knife he held, only felt its rough bite as he slashed her throat and took her life with it.

After I had translated her words for the others, Marie was allowed to depart. I asked Mr. W—— if we could summon other victims of this killer so I could question them.

He agreed to try, saying that it was best to summon the recently departed by name – and thus we called up Dr. de la Roche. I thought a man of science might have the most helpful observations to offer.

When Miss W—— began to speak, her voice had dropped by nearly an octave: 'Where am I?' growled an unfamiliar voice in French. 'Is this Heaven or Hell?'

'Neither,' said I, 'But a parlour in New York State. We speak to you by means of a medium created through mesmerism.'

'Mesmerism! Do you mean that absurd charade still keeps idiots occupied? How long have I been dead?'

'Scarcely more than a week.'

'Ah, so I am still in Limbo. And what of Dupin?'

I was quite startled to hear this name issue from the lips of the young medium. 'You refer to the Chevalier C. Auguste Dupin?'

'Certainly. When he came to my door –'

Excited, I burst out: 'When?'

'When but the last morning of my life! I was surprised, yet pleased, thinking that if he had taken an interest, the murders must be solved. And I should hear it first! I invited him inside, to take a bowl of coffee. It was still early, and my wife and I had not yet broken our fast.

'Once we were seated in the morning room he congratulated me on having solved the mystery. I assured him that I was still very much in the dark.

' "But you know," said he, "You *perceived* that the three young women were murdered, killed by a man, not attacked by wolves, dogs, or the frightful *loup garou*."

' "Yes," said I, "but not the identity of their slayer; that, like his motives, remained mysterious."

'He denied there was any mystery, and when I asked if he meant that he could identify the killer, he said, very calmly, that he could name the man and explain every detail of the three killings.'

'Astonished, I asked why he had not told the police. Was it not true they had asked for his help, and he had declined to become involved?

'Yes, he said, that was true. He had decided never to work with the police again after his last experience with them had left him agitated and disturbed. Although he had identified the killer to the police and the man had subsequently been executed for his crimes, Dupin considered he had failed to solve the case.

'I begged him to explain, and he replied that although he had discovered *who* had committed the murders, there remained unanswered the more troubling query: *why*.

'Most crimes could be explained, he told me. A man becomes a killer in a fit of passion – he goes for his knife in a jealous rage, or beats or strangles a woman who repulsed his amorous attentions, or when driven past endurance by a nagging wife. Other killers are more calculating, they kill for revenge, or to remove an obstacle in their path. What reason could there be for a rational man to deliberately choose to murder strangers almost at random?

'I replied that some killers were insane, and it was fruitless to attempt to apply reason to the actions of a madman.

'Dupin replied that it made no sense to describe *this* killer as mad. The man was both clever and rational. He knew that what he did was wrong, but he killed for a purpose, although he knew his purpose would be considered repulsive by most civilized beings, and if he was caught, he would pay for his crimes with his life. He was quite sane. He made a decision. He had no wish to die, but his desire to kill was so powerful, the reward so great, that he judged the risk of being caught was worth it.

'I stared at the great detective in astonishment, thinking he was joking, but he looked utterly serious. "Reward?" I repeated. "Explain to me, sir, what possible *reward* could there be in killing a stranger?"

'Dupin gave me a cold, distant look as he replied: "Pleasure."

' "You expect me to believe Reclus killed purely for the pleasure – the, I should say, *imaginary* pleasure of it – and yet you say he was not mad?"

' "He was not mad," argued Dupin. "He was a man of superior

intellect, and quite peculiarly refined sensibilities, able to feel sensations that would be lost on most. He told me that the pleasure of taking a life was the greatest pleasure he had ever known – it was particularly keen when the victim was a young and beautiful woman, but any death was to be savoured."

A faint sigh, a melancholy, expiring sigh, issued from the lips of the fair young medium and she wavered a little in her seat.

'I think it is time – we must not overtax her system,' said Mr W——, moving towards his daughter and raising his arms as if anxious to perform the passes that would bring her out of her mesmerized state, but I blocked him.

'Not yet,' I said urgently. 'Please – just give me a little longer!' I looked around the stuffy room, hoping one of the other guests would support me, and realized that there would be no help from them. The audience had grown bored with our incomprehensible conversation.

'Just a few more questions,' I said quickly. 'Then I will translate – you see, he is about to reveal the identity of the French were-wolf!'

This caused a satisfactory stir of interest, so I put the question to Dr. de la Roche at once: 'But what about the more recent murders. Did you ask Dupin to identify the killer?'

'Of course. He advised patience – all in good time, I think he said – and asked how I could be so certain the killer was a man and not an animal. Was it not true that, as he had read, each of the women's throats revealed the unmistakable tooth marks?'

'Indeed they did, and I may have chuckled a little as I explained that my closer examination, under a microscope, had convinced me that although the marks had been made by animal teeth, the wounds were not bites. There is a distinction, you see. After examining the pattern of the marks, I felt certain that the wounds had been inflicted by some implement, either artificially made, or the jawbone of some large, carnivorous animal, a wolf or a tiger, wielded by a human hand in such a way as to *mimic* the bite of an animal as it cut the throat.

''Yet it was not very well done if you were able to recognize its artificiality,' said Dupin, frowning.

'I assured him that it had fooled the police and would pass muster with most people, even other doctors, but that I had a great deal of experience with animal-bites. Dupin looked oddly reassured as he nodded his head. 'You are particularly observant, and very thorough in your examinations,' he said, 'A paragon among men of medicine!'

'As I was modestly denying this, Dupin reached inside his coat to reveal what he had hidden there. It was something like the curved blade of a sickle, but lined with rows of sharp teeth, some of them natural animal teeth, others manufactured from glass and steel. At first, I felt only wonder at the sight of it, for I had not yet comprehended why Dupin had come to visit me at home, so early in the morning, and I did not realize that the emotion I should have felt was fear, until I saw my own blood spurting out over the white table cloth, and knew it was far too late.

'I tried to ask him *why*, but could barely manage to gurgle as the life seeped out of my body. Yet he understood me well enough, smiling that distant, cold, inhuman smile of his as he replied, "You may call it madness, but I do not. It *is* the greatest pleasure"'

If it is true that the mesmerized can channel the voices of the dead, and if I truly spoke to the spirit of a murdered man, still I must ask, Can the dead lie? Is his story true, or could it be some nightmare experienced by the soul in limbo, no more to be believed than the mad visions that fill my own head every night?

There is no doubt in my mind that de la Roche met Dupin, for when I heard the altered voice of the medium describe his 'distant, cold, inhuman smile' I could see it myself, with my inward eye, recalling how Dupin, in the grip of his analytical passion, would become frigid and abstract, his expression vacantly staring, his voice rising to a higher tone as if (I sometimes fancied) he was possessed of a bi-part soul, his body inhabited in turn by one of two distinctly different personalities. But never did I for a moment imagine that one of those two selves might be evil incarnate; I always knew Dupin for a prodigy and a wonder, not a monster.

I broke my promise to the rest of the audience and did not satisfy their curiosity by translating the conversation I'd had with the dead French doctor. Instead, I pleaded an attack of the megrims, and staggered out of the house just as soon as young Miss W——— was restored to her natural self. The fortunate girl retained no recollection whatsoever of anything that had transpired during her trance, and no one else could enlighten her on the subject of what the Frenchman had said.

I do not want to believe that my old friend has become a killer. But I sense no trickery and can think of no reason why someone should wish to fool me, or to blacken the name of C. Auguste Dupin.

Perhaps the most terrible thing is that although I do not want to believe it, neither can I wholly disbelieve. Knowing him as I did, I can imagine how his own curiosity and reliance on rationality could have been his undoing. The lack of any *reason* for the series of murders in his last case always preyed upon his mind. However repugnant and absurd, the explanation given by Reclus for his own actions could not be dismissed. The idea of murder as a pleasure might have become a maggot in Dupin's brain, eating away at him until he was finally driven to test the matter for himself.

Once having killed ... but here my chain of reasoning breaks down, for I cannot believe that the man I knew, even at his most coldly analytical, could perform such a ghastly experiment, surely he would not murder a helpless, harmless young woman simply to *test a theory?*

Even if he killed in self-defence, or to save someone else, killing someone who deserved to die ... if, in so doing, he had tasted something of the intoxicating pleasure Reclus had promised, might he not have become addicted, driven to kill again?

But no, the idea is too repulsive. It is madness. Only a madman could conceive the notion of murder as 'the greatest pleasure'. Reclus was mad.

And Dupin?

Dupin, if he has become a killer, must be mad, in the same, seemingly rational way as the man he sent to the guillotine, the man who infected him with his terrible, repulsive idea. Already, in the day and night that have passed since the mesmeric *séance* of which I have written, new reports have reached New York of still more killings in France: two sisters, this time, their throats savagely chewed by an unknown creature.

Yet how can I tell the police what I know? More importantly, how can I convince them? A letter is easily dismissed, and if I made the effort of travelling to France to speak to the people in power there, I should probably find myself locked up. I can imagine how Dupin would respond, with a mocking, pitying smile: 'A dead man told you I had killed him? And do you often converse with the dead? This is common in America? My dear friend, I fear you are suffering from a fever of the brain . . .'

Dupin has the ear of the French police, as I do not, but I have something else. I have the ear of the public, in this country and abroad. My readers will not like this story as much as they liked 'The Murders in the Rue Morgue'; I admit, I do not like it so much myself. Yet it must be told. I must beg my readers to supply the necessary ending.

The Third Person

When she got Rachel's text suggesting lunch, Imogen was thrilled into immediate agreement, although the short notice, and her friend's choice of venue, meant a rush, and her colleagues' displeasure that she was taking the full hour for the second time that week.

For once, Rachel wasn't late; eye-catching as ever with her long, red hair and dramatic style, she waved from a booth at the back and announced that she'd already ordered for them both.

'You're going to love the cauliflower cheese soup. And it gives us more time to talk if we don't have to faff around with menus.' She was glowing, radiant, bubbling in a way Imogen had not seen in months. It reminded her of the old days, when they'd shared a flat, before Rachel married Andrew.

Marriage changed everything. Everybody knew how it was: married couples had different priorities, and when they weren't alone together, liked to be with other marrieds. Add to their new status a starter house in a distant suburb and two demanding jobs, and there wasn't much left for their singleton friends. Imogen had thought she might be the exception: after all, the three of them had lived together for nearly a year, so comfortable a threesome that they joked about their Mormon marriage, if too conventional to go farther than flirting with the idea of a sexual *ménage à trois*. Andy's undemanding yet undeniably masculine presence had added a bit of spice to her life, which she missed. She recalled the pleasures of lazy Sunday morning fry-ups over three different newspapers, late-night take-aways and horror movies viewed from the sagging, second-hand couch – even a boring, stupid thing like doing the laundry was almost fun as a threesome. But maybe that was only her. Maybe they would always have been happier without a third person in their life.

She looked at her friend through the steam of soup too hot to touch. 'What's up? I can see you're dying to tell me something.'

Rachel compressed her lips. 'I need you to promise you won't tell anyone.'

She was stung by this distrust. 'Who would I tell?'

'Not anyone. If it ever got back to Andrew . . .'

'Oh my god.'

'Promise?'

Imogen scowled. 'Asking me to promise *now* is a bit stable-doors. You're having an affair?'

Rachel grimaced. She could not deny it, only quibbled over the wording. It was nothing so definite as an 'affair'. Love didn't enter into it. It was just sex.

'But . . . why? Why take the risk?'

'Oh, Immy.' She shook her head and looked chiding. 'I didn't mean to. I didn't go looking for this. It just happened.'

'Yeah? Where, on the bus to work? Oh, I'm sorry, sir, it's so crowded, I seem to have impaled myself upon your manly tool. As we've started, may as well continue.'

Rachel nearly choked on her soup, giggling. 'OK, OK. I am a weak and horny woman who cannot resist temptation. I was feeling frustrated and half dead . . . Andrew, bless him, is just not up for it that often. He's less . . . *driven* by sexual needs than I am. I always knew it might be a problem someday, I just didn't expect it to be so soon. But when Mr. Hotbody came along and woke me up . . .' She gave a fatalistic shrug.

'Who is this Mr. Hotbody?'

'You don't know him,' she said quickly. 'Nobody does.'

'That sounds spooky.'

'Nobody *we* know. There's no reason Andrew would ever hear anything. He's a total stranger I met in a pub.'

Imogen shivered, and took a careful sip of her soup.

'It wasn't a pub I'd ever been in, either. A client had suggested it, and after she left, he came over and offered to buy me a drink. I'd noticed him watching me, and gave him the look . . . it was just like the old days, picking out the sexiest guy in the room, to see if I could pull.'

'So you can still pull. Amazing. Did you tell him you were married?'

'After he put his hand on my leg. He just smiled and said he liked married women the best, because they didn't confuse sex with love, and he sort of walked his hand up my leg, right up to my crotch and started to rub me there, through my pants, looking me in the eye the whole time while he brought me off.'

It was not the heat of the soup that brought Imogen out in a sweat as Rachel continued to describe what followed. 'Sex in the toilet! I don't know what possessed me – I hadn't done anything like that since I was eighteen. And this was much, much dirtier.'

'And that wasn't the end of it?'

She shook her head, eyes glazed over. 'I didn't even know his name. I told Andrew I had to go away overnight, on business, and booked a room in a Travelodge. He met me there. We were at it all night. Never slept. I did things I'd never done before – he made me do things – '

Imogen pushed her bowl to one side, her appetite gone. 'That does not sound good.'

'Are you kidding? It was the best I've ever had.'

'Not good for your marriage.'

'Oh, no, there you're wrong, my friend. Sometimes a bit of danger, the risk of another lover, is just what a couple needs. I went home and bonked the living daylights out of Andrew. He loved it! For a little while, I had my Randy Andy back. Plus, I'm so much nicer when I'm not feeling frustrated. I've stopped being such a bitch at home. What's good for me is good for him.'

'Good for you. You've saved your marriage. End of story.'

'It's not the end.'

'You can't go on sleeping with this guy.'

'I have no intention of sleeping with him, or going out to dinner with him, or knitting little booties, or falling in love. This is just sex. So much spicier than I can get at home. A bit on the side. That's all I want from him.'

'So what do you want from me? A seal of approval?'

'We need a place to go.'

'Oh, no.' Her stomach clenched. 'You can't go to his?'

'He lives with someone. And anyway, I don't want to get involved with his life.'

'So rent a room . . . Travelodge was good enough before.'

'It would be good enough again, if I could afford it . . . or if he could. Please? It won't be very often, I'm sure. Just a few more times, 'til I get him out of my system.'

'Or out of your pubic hair. Where am I supposed to go while this . . . de-lousing . . . is taking place?'

Rachel's face tightened. 'Don't be nasty.'

'You're the one talking about how wonderfully dirty it is.' Before her hurt, angry glare, she caved. 'I'm sorry. I just don't understand why you need to do this thing.'

Her hand was seized and held in a warm, strong grip. 'Of course you don't, my sweetheart, because you're *normal*. This is some kind of madness, but I can't get over it without going through it. And you are the one and only person who can help me, who I can talk to. I don't want to put you out. But you go to the gym and out for a meal with your friends from work every Thursday, am I right? What time do you get home?'

'About nine-thirty,' she said, although ten was closer to the mark.

'I'd want to be on the nine-forty-seven for home anyway,' said Rachel. 'We'd be out by nine-thirty. I promise you, Imogen, you won't know we were there. One evening a week, a time when you wouldn't be there anyway – is that really too much to ask?'

She understood she could not refuse; not unless she was prepared to lose her friendship.

Rachel came by that evening to pick up the spare key, and Imogen was a little stiff with her at first, feeling she had been bullied into abetting a crime, but instead of hurrying away like a guilty thing, Rachel hung around, diffident and awkward, until Imogen thawed and suggested she stay for dinner.

'There's a kebab shop just around the corner; I could run down for something . . .'

Rachel checked the contents of the fridge. 'I'll cook,' she said. 'Spaghetti carbonara sound all right?'

'I don't have any cream.'

'We never did, and I don't recall any complaints in the past, so long as there was plenty of *this*.' With a wicked grin, she produced a bottle of wine from her capacious shoulder bag.

Every remnant of ill-feeling vanished as she whipped up a quick supper. It was like old times again. She phoned her husband to warn him she'd be home late, and put him on speaker so Imogen could hear and join in a joking, friendly, three-way conversation. When they were doing the washing-up, Imogen said wistfully, 'We should do this more often.'

'I don't know about you, sweetheart, but I wash up after *every* meal.'

Imogen laughed. 'Idiot. I've missed you. Missed *us*.'

'Me, too.'

Walking through her front door on Thursday night (9:56 by her phone), although it was dark and still, Imogen felt another presence there.

'Ray?' she called sharply. 'Hello?' Her skin prickled; what if it was *him*?

With the light on, she could see into every corner of the sparsely furnished, open-plan living room and kitchen. There was nowhere to hide, unless—looking one way—behind the half-open door of the bathroom—or, at the other end, in the bedroom. She scarcely breathed until she had checked both rooms thoroughly, even peering inside the built-in wardrobe in the bedroom, and the narrow airing-cupboard in the kitchen. But she remained tense, even knowing she was alone, so she phoned Rachel.

'How'd it go?'

'I'm on the train.'

'I wasn't expecting the porno version.' At the familiar sound of her friend's snorting laugh, she relaxed at last. 'I just wanted to check that everything was, you know, all right.'

'Mmm, good question. Not sure what to say.'

Suddenly suspicious, she demanded, 'Is he with you?'

'What? No, of course not! I said, I'm on my way home. There's the tunnel.'

'Catch up tomorrow?' She was talking to a dead phone.

The abrupt end to that unsatisfactory conversation left her feeling on edge, but she went through her usual routines, tidying the already tidy flat, and put herself to bed before eleven o'clock.

She was tired, and her thoughts soon drifted into the surreal jumble that presaged sleep. Turning on to her left side, she snuggled deeper into her pillow, and caught a faint whiff of Jo Malone's Pomegranate Noir – Rachel's signature scent.

By now her own body heat had warmed the space between the sheets, and with that warmth, other smells were released from the bedding: body odours that were not her own, sweat and musk and ejaculate, the unmistakable smells of sex.

And then she could hear them – laboured breathing, low grunts, the slap of flesh against flesh – and feel them, too, a woman and a man in bed with her, one on either side of her . . .

It wasn't real, of course. It couldn't be. If she'd suddenly found herself in bed with two other naked people she would have been repulsed by it, felt disgust, or fear. But instead, half asleep and knowing she must be dreaming, it was safe to become aroused. These two people, so focused on their own sexual pleasure, stirred desires she kept buried, hidden from her conscious mind. The man behind her was a stranger – it didn't matter who he was. The woman whose soft large breasts pressed against her own was Rachel.

This was Rachel as she'd scarcely dared to imagine her, yet knew she must be, powerfully erotic, sexually voracious. As Imogen allowed herself to be overwhelmed by the power of the fantasy, she heard her friend whispering to her, words she'd actually said once when talking about masturbation:

'You shouldn't feel guilty. That's crazy! It doesn't matter *what* you think about while you're doing it – whatever gets you off is fine, it doesn't matter what crazy, sick thing turns you on, so long as it stays inside your own head. Nobody ever got hurt by a private fantasy. It's the safest sex there is.'

In the morning, though, she was not so relaxed. The first sip of coffee seemed to curdle in her stomach, and she felt sickened by herself, and then angry at Rachel. Why couldn't her friend have followed her own advice, and kept her fantasies locked inside her own head? Why did she have to soil Imogen's bed with them?

She poured the rest of her coffee down the sink and, although there was scarcely time for it, hurried back to the bedroom, intending to strip off the dirty sheets, rather than leave them festering with their alien stains and smells for another day. But as soon as she saw her bed she realized it wasn't necessary. Rachel had changed the bed after using it. The dirty sheets and pillowcases were in the washing machine in the kitchen – a fact she had noticed before going to bed, and then forgotten.

She leaned down and sniffed the pillow. She could just about pick up traces of herself – skin oil, face cream, shampoo – but nothing remotely like Rachel's perfume. When she put her head under the covers she smelled the lavender scent of her fabric conditioner, and nothing else.

Those smells that she thought had triggered an erotic fantasy had been part of the fantasy – part of the dream. It had been a dream, of course, with no conscious desires behind it at all. The knots in her stomach loosened. Dreams were nobody's fault. You couldn't blame yourself for what your unconscious got up to while you slept.

Text messages flew back and forth between Imogen and Rachel over the next few days, but despite reiterated declarations that they must meet, or at least talk, their busy schedules made it impossible before Thursday came around again.

There had been no repeat of that disturbingly erotic dream, and Imogen had almost managed to repress the memory of it until that morning, when she woke up thinking about Rachel and her faceless, nameless lover, who would soon be going at it like knives in this very bed, between her own, used sheets.

She didn't know if knowing his name or what he looked like would have made it better, or worse, but she was tormented by the sense of being unfairly used. Maybe she had no right to judge Rachel for the betrayal of her marriage vows, but wasn't more respect due their friendship? Changing the sheets was the merest gesture; all that frenzied passion must leave traces that could not be easily washed away, a charge in the atmosphere, a kind of miasma in the bedroom that affected her sleep and gave her bad dreams. She wished she had made more of an effort to talk to Rachel; she should have insisted on seeing her. It was too late now, of course, but she decided tonight was the last time. She would ask Rachel to give her back her key.

Mounting the deserted concrete stairs that rose through the large, quiet building at a quarter to ten, Imogen tingled with anxiety, again plagued by the feeling that someone was waiting for her inside. Not even the sight of the clear, empty vista of the main room was enough to calm her nerves, and she was obliged to check out the bathroom and empty bedroom thoroughly before she could relax.

This time, she did not miss the fact of clean sheets on her bed, and deliberately took several deep, calming breaths of the soothing scent of lavender as she settled down to sleep.

But it happened again. As her own body heat raised the temperature within the warm cocoon of the bed, something else was released, as if memories of what had taken place in that space a few hours earlier had left spores ready to blossom into life under the right conditions. All the smells of sex wafted over her and she heard the animal sounds of vigorous fucking, and while a small, civilized part of her was repulsed, and a little frightened, by this activity going on in her own bed, her body was melting, yearning, opening with the longing desire to be a part of it.

They were so close, so close, but at the same time impossibly distant, their desires never meeting hers, so completely focused on each other that they didn't even know she was there. They were all in the same space, but separated by time. And so, although she found herself between them, they were blissfully unaware of any impediment, intent only on satisfying themselves through each other, as if Imogen did not exist, as if she were of less substance than a ghost.

Maybe she was only a fleeting thought passing through

Rachel's mind, a weightless fragment of gratitude and guilt, gone before it could be acknowledged, as the other woman hurtled, with single-minded intensity, towards her own satisfaction.

Imogen could not connect. The other two made love through her, without her, and although she was unbearably close to them, forced to witness their coupling, to smell and hear and *almost* feel their moving bodies on either side of her own, she could not make them feel her. She could only join in, steal a share of their pleasure, by pretending. This was no guilt-free dream, no dream at all. They were in her bed, but she was alone, tensing her muscles, arching her back, opening her mouth wide, nothing to fill it, nothing to assuage her emptiness and bring satisfaction but the quick, impatient movements of her own fingers, angry and dissatisfied with her own, too-familiar flesh, but still practiced enough to know what they must do.

She made herself come again and again until at last her bed was empty and she could fall asleep.

She didn't want to see Rachel again. But they were going to have to meet. Rachel had the key to Imogen's flat. Even more importantly, she thought she had permission to use it. Imogen could not be like the evil landlord who changes the locks without warning. Even if she couldn't tell her the real reason, she was going to ban her from using it and demand the key back. She didn't care if they fell out over it and never spoke again; that would only prove that Rachel had never been such a good friend as she had thought.

They met on Saturday morning, at a Starbucks in a mall, in the middle of a heaving mass of shoppers hunting for a bargain.

'I have to meet Andrew at Ikea in thirty-five minutes, but that should be plenty of time for a coffee,' Rachel said, with a hug and kiss Imogen was not quick enough to avoid. She was as beautiful and bouncy as ever, and Imogen felt like a coward, evading her direct and happy gaze. She ordered a skinny vanilla latte for the look of the thing, but knew by the roiling in her stomach that she would not be able to drink it.

'What's up? Your text was so ...'

No point wasting time. She blurted it out: 'I want my key back.'

'Oh.' Rachel's shoulders slumped. She stared down at her hands. Her wedding band made its own comment. 'Well. Of course. In fact, I'd already decided ... decided to end it. It's crazy – I love Andy, we have a good marriage, I don't want to risk everything for a bit of ... well, *sport*.'

Imogen's tension began to ease as she realized she wouldn't have to argue. 'Good sense wins the day. Did you bring it?'

'Bring what?'

'My key.'

'Oh! God, no, I didn't think – that's not important, is it? I mean, it is a spare, right? And somebody ought to have it, in case you lock yourself out or something happens while you're away – you shouldn't have both keys yourself.'

Imogen recognized the wide-eyed, honest gaze that went with the perfectly logical argument. She'd seen her friend use it on others to get something she wanted. When she was hiding a lie. Her stomach clenched again.

'Ray, this is not about a stupid key. I don't want that man in my flat again.'

'What happened? Did he do something? What did he do? Have you talked to him?'

She felt her ears get hot and prayed she wasn't blushing. 'Talk to him? Of course not! I don't know who he is. You won't even tell me his name.'

'Only because I don't want you involved in this.'

'But I *am* involved. You involved me by using my flat. You've done it in my bed! You can't do that anymore.'

Something flared in her friend's eyes, and for a moment Imogen thought she'd guessed – somehow she knew exactly what she'd experienced –

'Just once more. Please, darling. I'll finish with him this week. I promise.'

'Good. Break up with him in a pub. Or have your final fling in the Travelodge.'

She shook her head. 'It's not that easy. I can't get in touch with him before Thursday. But this Thursday will be the last, I promise. And then, if you really insist I give your key back . . .'

'I do.'

Rachel made a dramatic gesture. 'Next week, same time, same place. I promise I will bring it. And I can provide all the sordid details you like.'

The following Thursday night, at nine-forty-seven precisely, Imogen turned the key and stepped inside. Refusing to let herself be driven again by the now-expected impression that there was someone else in her flat, she did not waste time looking around, but went straight to the bedroom to put away her gym gear.

The light was on in the bedroom, and there was a man there, kneeling on the floor. He had been crouching, apparently examining the carpet, but when she opened the door he straightened, although still on his knees.

Her mouth dried. She looked past him, to the bed, which had been roughly re-made, but Rachel was not there.

He was not someone she would have picked out as the hottest guy in any pub. He had a muscular upper body, but his face was forgettable, and his thinning grey hair straggled down as if length could make up for what was missing on top. He was older than she had expected, a forty-something clinging rather foolishly to the style of his youth. Most surprisingly, he didn't look surprised to see her, but smiled seductively.

'What are you doing?' She spoke sharply, annoyed at Rachel for leaving this strange man alone in her flat.

He looked down at the carpet again. 'She lost her necklace – chain broke. Gold chain. Had to leave . . . couldn't miss her train . . . but so upset, I said I'd find the missing bit.'

She peered down at the thick pile of the carpet, knowing immediately what necklace it must be, a diamond and amethyst pendant on the finest of thin gold chains, a twenty-first birthday present from Rachel's grandmother.

'She could have asked *me* to find it,' she muttered, and then was startled to notice the man, still on his knees, had moved closer.

He pushed up her shirt and rubbed his face against the bare skin of her midriff. The shock of it froze her in place. She caught a

familiar whiff of dried sweat and hair grease at the very moment
that his wet, warm tongue darted into her navel.

She opened her mouth to protest, but the incoherent sound
emerged sounding more like encouragement. Her arms did not
want to push him away. Her muscles seemed to have turned to
jelly, and she might have collapsed entirely without his support.
She seemed to have fallen into a helpless dream as he touched and
rubbed and kissed her from the waist down. When he unhooked
and unzipped and pulled down her trousers, she did nothing
to help or hinder, and they fell to her ankles, followed soon by
her underpants, and hobbled her. He carried on with his more
intimate explorations as she closed her eyes and surrendered to
whatever he would do to her with his hands or his mouth. He
sucked and licked, rubbed and poked and prodded, sometimes
hurting her with a rough touch, but generally skilful, increasing
her arousal to an incredible pitch.

This was no dream. He was doing it all. Doing everything to
her that he had previously done to Rachel, things she could only
imagine before now. Her own hands, unoccupied, hung at her
sides, now loose, now clenched. Her breath sighed and whistled
and caught in her throat. She moaned softly and tried to open
her legs wider, wanting more, but she was trapped by her own
clothes. As she tried to kick free of them, her knees buckled and
she almost fell, but he caught her, and lifted her – so easily; his
arms were even more powerful than she had guessed. He quickly
and efficiently freed her from shoes, underpants and trousers, and
dropped her on to the bed.

Remembering Rachel's description of how he'd looked into her
eyes the whole time he'd caressed her to orgasm that first time in
the pub, Imogen waited for him to look at her, but he was absorbed
by the task of removing his own shoes and socks and jeans, and
when he came back, wearing only his shirt, he stared at only one
part of her, so fixedly that she wondered uneasily if he found her
hairy pubes disgusting. (Rachel was religious about depilating, but
Imogen could not be bothered.) She was disturbed to notice his
penis was flaccid, not even half-erect, but that changed as he pulled
it, still staring, so it was obviously not a turn-off.

With unexpected suddenness, still without a word or even an affectionate look, he plunged inside her and began thrusting away with an odd, jerky rhythm. She was just starting to get comfortable with it when he suddenly withdrew and ejaculated on her shirt.

She gave a startled, disappointed cry.

He stood up and backed away, looking at her now with a smile that was more of a sneer. 'You slut,' he said, without heat. 'You didn't think I'd let you have my baby?'

He began putting his clothes on. She lay where he'd put her, afraid to say or do anything that might provoke him, and wondering what had been going on inside his head while she'd been caught in her own fantasy. She was grateful when he left without another word, and sat up when she heard the definitive closing snick of the lock on the front door.

She felt sick, and desperate for a wash. She wanted to wash away every trace of that awful man. She stood up. About to cross the room, she saw something glinting on the floor, and bent down to find two gold links, snapped from a chain.

Holding them, looking at the minuscule circles lying in the palm of her hand, she had an image of Rachel's necklace, broken as it was brutally yanked from her neck, and shivered as she touched the skin across her own collarbone. Then, closing her hand on the tiny bits of gold, she went through to the main room, where she stopped just short of colliding with Rachel.

She only just managed not to scream. Rachel had been in the flat the whole time. She must have been in the bathroom at first – she should have realized her friend wouldn't have left that man here alone – but when she returned to the bedroom – had she seen them? Looked in, and seen Imogen standing with her trousers around her ankles? And said nothing? Was it a total shock, or something she had suggested or engineered, perhaps pursuing her own fantasy of a threesome . . .

If so, it clearly had not turned out as she'd dreamed. She had not interrupted them or tried to join in, and her continued silence now, and the expression on her face, frightened Imogen. She had never seen Rachel with such a terrible, staring face, and such a murderous look in her eye.

'Hey, Ray, ' Imogen said softly, her heart in her throat. 'We need to talk.'

Rachel's fixed, hideous glare did not soften, and Imogen saw something that froze her heart. Yes, that was murder in her eyes. In one hand, half-hidden by her side, Rachel held the longest, sharpest knife from Imogen's kitchen.

'Don't.' The word jumped out, hot and urgent, forced through the lump of ice in her chest, and then she ran for the safety of the bathroom. She slammed the door and locked it; then, leaning her head against the cool tiled wall, she began to cry.

But she soon regained control. She wouldn't risk opening the door, but she spoke through it, yelling at Rachel that she was sorry, but that jerk wasn't worth it, and couldn't they please at least *try* to have a civilized conversation? Nothing at all in reply from Rachel, so Imogen took her time about having a shower. She knew her friend was no killer. Give her a few minutes to calm down, and then they'd talk.

When she came out of the bathroom, reeking of strawberry shower gel, the flat was empty. She knew it instantly, could tell from the atmosphere that she was alone, but went through the motions of searching, just in case. The long, sharp knife was back in the wooden block where it belonged. Rachel had gone without leaving a note.

She slept that night on the couch. It was not very comfortable, but she preferred a broken night of restless dozing to the company of the ghosts in her bed. When she woke at three, four, five and six, she phoned Rachel, and left humble, apologetic messages begging her to call back, regardless of the time.

At seven-thirty, as she dressed for work, Rachel's phone was still switched off. At eight, she rang the landline number, and Andrew picked up.

'Andy, I need to talk to Rachel.'

There was a silence. 'Imogen? I thought she was with you.'

She swallowed hard. 'She left last night. It was after ten, after her usual train, but there's a later one, isn't there? She didn't say, but I assumed she was going home.'

'What do you mean she didn't say?'

'She – she was upset when she left.'

'What was she upset about?'

Her eyes fell on the tiny gold links she'd brought through from the bathroom. 'You know her gold necklace? From her Nan? It broke.'

'She stormed out because she broke her necklace?'

'There was more to it than that, but it was my fault. I couldn't get her to stay and talk about it.' She touched one of the links with the tip of a finger, staring across the counter to the wooden knife block on the far wall of the kitchen, all four black handles sticking out. 'She was pretty mad – I was sure she'd go home, but maybe she has another friend she stays with sometimes?'

He didn't reply.

'Look, if you see her, I mean, when she comes in, or calls, would you please ask her to call me?'

'I was going to say the same to you.'

She said a rather awkward goodbye, and then, as she broke the connection, felt the hairs rise on the back of her neck, and knew she was no longer alone.

There had been no sound, and the door had not opened, but even before she turned she knew who was there.

Rachel, looking just as she had the night before: same clothes, same ghastly expression, even the knife in her hand, although there had been no time for her to take it from the kitchen. She could only be a ghost.

Then the small, metallic click of a key in the lock, and the door opened. He came in and shut the door behind him, glaring, holding Rachel's black and silver Nokia, which looked ridiculously tiny in his large hand.

'Why'd you keep calling?' he asked. 'You think she'll forgive you for what you did with me last night?'

She realized then that the murderous look in Rachel's eyes, and the knife in her hand, had never been meant for *her*. She could only hope, as she sprinted for the kitchen, that her own attempt at self-defence would be more successful.

The Wound

Once the seasons had been more distinct, but not in living memory. Now, mild winter merged gently into mild summer, and Olin knew it was spring only by the calendar and by his own restlessness.

That morning, Olin's bus took a different route, road repairs forcing a detour through the old city. As he stared out the window at the huge, derelict buildings crumbling into ruin and colonized by weeds, he caught sight of figures through gaps in the walls. No one lived in the old city, but there were always people here. Olin had been one of them once, when he was young, coming here with his lover. He remembered that time as the best of his life.

Recalling the past made him feel sad and prematurely old. His lover had become his wife, and after ten years of marriage they had separated. He had lived alone for the past two years.

Olin reached into his breast pocket for diary and pen, turned to the blank page of that day, and wrote 'phone Dove' in his small, precise hand. About once a month he phoned her, and they would arrange to meet for a meal. Always he went to her in hope, with fond memories and some vague thoughts of reconciliation which would fade over the course of the evening.

As he left the bus two other teachers, senior to Olin, also got off. They did not speak as they crossed the street together and passed through the heavy iron gates onto the school grounds. Olin caught sight of another colleague, a little ahead of them: Seth Tarrant, the new music master. Tarrant was young, handsome, and admired by the students. His cream-coloured coat flared like a cape from his shoulders, and he seemed to be singing as he strode across the bright green lawn. He carried an expensive leather case in one hand, and a bunch of blue and yellow flowers in the other.

Olin felt a brief flare of envy and he touched his breast pocket. He would phone Dove, he thought. She would be glad to hear from him.

During his lunch break Olin went into the telephone alcove by the cafeteria and was startled to see Seth Tarrant there, his long body slumped in an attitude of defeat, his head pressed against one of the telephones. Before Olin, embarrassed, could retreat, the other man looked around.

He straightened up, brushing a strand of fair hair out of his eyes. 'Mr Mercato,' he said.

'Olin,' said Olin, embarrassed still more by the formality. 'Please.'

'Olin. I'm Seth.'

'Yes, I know. Ah, are you all right?'

'I'm fine. Do you like opera?'

'Opera? Yes. Yes, I do, actually. Not that I know anything about it – maths is my subject, really – but I do like to listen. On the radio, and I have a few recordings . . .'

'You don't think it's tedious, pretentious and antiquated?'

Olin wondered who the music master was quoting. He shook his head.

'You might even think it worth your while to attend a live performance?'

'If it weren't so expensive – '

With a conjuror's flourish, Seth produced two cards from his pocket. 'I happen to have two tickets to tonight's performance of *The Insufficient Answer*, and one is going begging. Would you care to be my guest?'

'I'd love to. But are you sure?'

'Do I seem uncertain to you?'

Olin shook his head.

'That's settled, then. We'll meet on the steps of the opera house at seven o'clock, which will give us time for a drink in the bar before it begins.'

'Thank you. It's very kind – '

'Not at all. You are the kind one, agreeing at such short notice. Please don't be late. I hate to be kept waiting.'

The opera house was on the river, in an area of the city far older than the part known as the old city. Olin had been there once before, in the early days of his marriage, to attend a performance of *Madama Butterfly*. Dove had been pregnant then, and she had fallen asleep during the second act. It was probably the quarrel they'd had afterwards, and not the price of tickets, which was the real reason Olin had never been to the opera since.

The steps were crowded with people meeting friends, but Seth's tall, elegant figure was immediately noticeable. When he reached his side, Olin began to apologize for his lateness although it was barely five past the hour. He felt awkward, worried about the evening, certain that Seth had regretted his spur-of-the-moment invitation by now. Seth brushed aside both apologies and thanks with a flick of one long-fingered hand.

'Let's get a drink,' he said.

He seemed distracted and brooding in the bar, but Olin contrived a conversation by asking him questions about opera: after all, music was the man's subject. Olin felt like a student taken on a cultural outing by a master; an odd reversal, since he was at least ten years Seth's senior. It was a relief when the bell rang and they could find their seats and stop talking.

The Insufficient Answer was a love tragedy, a popular story which Olin already knew in outline. He had seen some of the most famous scenes enacted on television, but never with the technical brilliance displayed in this production. By ingenious use of lights and projections, the physical miracle of love appeared to be actually taking place on stage during the opening love-duet. After that breathtaking scene, the familiar tragedy was set in motion as the lovers, Gaijan and Sunshine, discovered they were not cross-fertile. Because there could be no children, marriage was out of the question. Social as well as biological forces drove Gaijan to take other lovers while Sunshine watched, and wept, and waited. For Gaijan still swore that he loved her the best of all, and he returned to her after every coupling. He told her he considered her his true wife and would never marry. His other lovers, led by the young and beautiful Flower, discovered Sunshine's existence and reproached her in the choral, 'We are all his wives.'

When Sunshine protested that she could not live without his love, Flower responded with the thrilling 'Then you must die.' The duet between Sunshine and Flower which followed echoed the earlier duet between Gaijan and Sunshine, only instead of a transformation, it was concluded by a suicide. In the final act, Gaijan threatened to follow Sunshine into death until Flower wooed him away from the cliff edge. As Gaijan and Flower exchanged vows of marriage, Flower promised to be to him all that Sunshine had been, and all that Sunshine could not be. The stage had been growing darker all the while, and Olin expected the curtain to fall on the final throbbing notes of Flower's promise and the lovers' embrace. Instead, Flower turned to face the audience and opened her robe. Olin caught his breath at the sight of an embryo, seen as if through Flower's flesh, growing within her body. It grew, as he watched, and even without opera glasses Olin could see that the unborn baby wore Sunshine's face.

There was a moment of awed silence as the curtain fell and then an explosion of applause. Olin clapped, too, full of emotion he was unable to express in any other way. He glanced at Seth and then hastily looked away again at the sight of tears on the younger man's face.

The murmuring, satisfied crowd bore them away, and there was no need, or chance, to speak. On the steps again, Olin began to say his thanks, but was stopped by a gesture.

'Don't rush off,' said Seth. 'I'd really like to discuss what we've just seen. That's why I don't like going to these things alone – it's never complete for me until I've been able to talk about it. Won't you walk with me by the river? I need to stretch my legs, and somehow I think better when I'm moving.'

Olin felt flattered that Seth had not tired of his company after the strained effort of their earlier conversation in the bar, but he glanced at his watch saying, 'I'm afraid the last bus is –'

'Oh, don't worry about that. I have a car; I can run you home.'

'Your own car? On a teacher's salary?'

Seth smiled faintly. 'No. Not on a teacher's salary. Nor this coat, nor a subscription to the opera. It won't last long at the rate I'm going, but I have a little money. From my wife's family.'

Olin remembered the despairing way Seth had leaned against the telephone, and the flowers that morning, and he was surprised. 'You're married?'

'Separated. It lasted less than a year. A youthful mistake.'

The night was dry and not cold, the river path paved and lighted, but they were alone.

'My wife and I separated two years ago,' Olin offered.

'How long were you married?'

'Ten years.'

'Children?'

'Two. At school now.'

'Not a youthful mistake, then,' said Seth. 'Why didn't you stay together? Why — I'm sorry. Please forgive me. It's none of my business, of course.'

It would have been a rude question even from someone less a stranger than Seth, and Olin knew he should have taken offence. But suddenly he wanted to talk about his marriage with someone, anyone, who was not Dove. He had never had the chance before.

'I suppose we separated because we ran out of reasons for staying together. We'd stopped loving each other long since, the children were at school and didn't need us, and there was no reason for two people who didn't like each other very much to go on sharing the same house. We'd never had much in common except the physical.'

'That's supposed to be enough,' said Seth. 'It is in all the operas, in literature, in ballads. The miracle of love is physical love — a biological affinity. Which would be fine, only it never lasts. And nobody will admit that. Everybody expects it to last, and when it doesn't we think there's something wrong with us. We're failures. Why can't we be taught to see love in perspective, to see it as a physical pleasure which belongs to one part of life but doesn't ever, can't by its very nature, ever last. We outgrow it, and we're *meant* to outgrow it. So why do we ruin our lives, wasting so much time and energy on love, dreaming about it, waiting for it, hoping for it against all odds?'

Although they were walking side by side, not looking at one another, Olin was vividly aware of Seth's anguish.

'You're too young to be talking like that,' Olin said, trying for a cheerful, bracing tone. 'It's all very well for me to resign myself to a solitary life, but you're still young and you should have hope. You can marry again – you *will* marry again. As you say, the first was a youthful mistake. You'll meet someone else.'

'Oh, yes, I'll meet someone else, and start the whole messy process all over again. I won't be able to help myself. But what's the point? To come to this again. Honey's pregnant. Already. I found out today. I suppose I should feel grateful. At least relieved that I didn't ruin her life. It would be so awful for her to find out she couldn't have kids ever, with anyone. It's not so terrible for a man to be infertile, but to be a woman . . .'

'There's no reason to assume you're infertile,' said Olin. 'Lots of people aren't cross-fertile with each other, but that doesn't mean they're infertile. Like in the opera we just saw – it's a question of finding the right partner.'

'So why should it be so complicated? It's just biology. Biological compatibility. Why all this stuff about love? It has nothing to do with physical attraction, or being a nice person, or having common interests, or the meeting of souls. It's not spiritual destiny. It's blind chance. It could have been worked out better, don't you think? So that we couldn't fall in love with someone unless we were cross-fertile.'

'But then it wouldn't be love,' Olin said. 'Then it *would* just be biology – we'd just be animals attracted to each other in the mating season.'

'I think we are, and we just don't know it. In our ignorance we've screwed it up. We try to make it something noble, try to pretend that sex and reproduction are the by-products of love, instead of the other way around. Why should sex get this special treatment? Why can't we see it clearly, as a need like hunger? Why mystify it? Why can't we just admit that we're just animals who need to reproduce, and *do* it?'

Olin was conscious that their argument was operating on two levels. However abstract and intellectual it might become, Seth was speaking out of his own hurt. He was looking for comfort, and Olin responded with the wish to help. But what wisdom could he offer? He was older than Seth, but no wiser. He hadn't found the answer in marriage or out of it. He had told himself that love was for the young, and safely in his own past, but something in him still responded to romance.

After a little silence Olin said, 'We're animals, but not only animals. Yes, we need to reproduce – but we have other needs, too. Emotional, social needs. We have a need for love, however you define it. Maybe it's misguided to connect love with sex, but everyone does, so there must be some sense in it, there must be some hope – ' He stopped talking as they both stopped walking, having come to the end of the paved, lighted river path. The river wound on, out of sight behind the embankment to their left, but ahead of them was a dark, rough wasteland.

Staring into the night Seth said, 'There's a need, but is it natural? Is it something basic in us, or was it constructed? Does it have to be that way, or can we change it? Should we?'

Disturbed, Olin turned away. 'We'd better start back. There's no way through here. It's odd – you'd think the path would go somewhere, wouldn't you? I mean, to pave it, and put up lights – you'd think it would go somewhere. At least to the next bridge, or up to the main road. Just to end like this. Are you coming?'

As they walked back, Olin turned the conversation to architecture, a subject about which he knew little but had many opinions. He soon provoked Seth into disagreement, and by the time they reached the opera house they were arguing as merrily as old friends, all restraint between them gone. Seth's bitter mood had passed, and Olin was glad to agree when he suggested they stop for a snack in a late-night café on the way home. Even knowing he would have to get up in the morning to teach, Olin was not ready for the evening to end. He was enjoying himself with Seth, but he didn't trust their friendship to survive even the shortest separation. In the morning, he thought, they would be strangers again.

But he was wrong. The next day at school, passing each other on the stairs, Seth suggested they meet for a drink after work. He spoke as casually and easily as if they were friends and, suddenly, they were.

Drinks led to dinner and to another walk; to more drinks,

dinners and walks. Despite, or perhaps because of, having a car, Seth loved to walk. It was his only exercise – like Olin, he had developed a hatred of sports at school – and after days cooped up indoors, he longed for the chance to move in the open air. He said that it not only relaxed him, but it helped him to think. Olin, always lazy, enjoyed their walks because the talk that accompanied them allowed him to forget he was exerting himself. Some of their best – and most disturbing – conversations took place while they walked. There were things that could not be said in a restaurant or a bar, looking at each other. But striding along, talking into the open air as if thinking aloud, unable to see each other's expression, anything might be voiced. Anything at all. And one day, Olin thought, Seth would go too far. The thought gave him a strange feeling at the pit of his stomach. It was a pleasurable excitement he remembered from long ago, from the last time he'd had such a close friendship. The feeling was fear, but it was also desire.

Women had friendships among themselves, but women had nothing to lose. Older men sometimes managed it, becoming as if boys again in their age, but for everyone else friendship was a risk. Olin was well aware of this, and thought Seth must be, too. They never spoke of the danger they might be courting, although they came close. For love – or sex, or biology, or marriage – was the topic they continued to be drawn to, again and again, in their night-time, walking conversations. The subject was like a sore Seth could not stop probing, or a cliff edge he had to lean over. It was during those conversations that Olin became aware of what a dangerous edge it was on which they balanced. If one of them fell . . .

But if one of them fell, it would be Seth, he was certain. Seth, with his youth, his passion, his sorrow, his 'mistaken' marriage, would fall in love with his older friend, and not the other way around. Olin could imagine Seth in love with him, and the idea of making love to a transformed, newly receptive Seth aroused him. But Olin did not let himself dwell on such thoughts. He didn't really want it to happen. He liked this not-sexual friendship; he wanted to believe that it could last. He wanted to go on balancing. He didn't want Seth to change.

One morning, about six weeks after the performance of *The Insufficient Answer,* Olin's telephone rang before he left for school.

It was Dove. 'I've been trying to phone you for days, and you're never in,' she said.

He remembered his long-ago, never-kept resolution to phone her, and felt guilty. 'I've been busy – I'm sorry I haven't been in touch.'

'It doesn't matter. But I thought you might have forgotten that it's parents' day this weekend. I thought the 8:45 would be the best train to catch. Could you meet me at the station by 8:30 on Saturday morning? Tristan wants a new football, I know – do you think you could manage to buy one? And some books for both of them – you know the sort of thing they'd like better than I would.'

Olin winced and closed his eyes as his wife's voice poured into his ear. He had forgotten. Worse than that, he didn't want to go. There had been a time when he welcomed the ritual visits to his children at their school. Then, his life had been so dull that any events were treasured as a break from routine. But his life was different now. A day spent with Dove and the boys meant a day without Seth. They had made tentative plans for Saturday already: a drive in the country, a visit to some site of historic interest, some place from the old times. Olin knew what he wanted to do, but he also knew his duty. He told Dove that he would meet her at the station.

They embraced as they always did on meeting – former desire transformed to awkward ritual – and then stood back to examine each other for signs of change.

Her hair was too short, Olin thought, the style too severe. It made her look older than she was, harsher and no longer pretty. But she looked fit, and still dressed well.

'You've put on weight,' Dove said.

He was surprised, and a little indignant, for since spending time with Seth he was not only getting more exercise, but also eating less. He tucked a thumb into the waistband of his trousers to show Dove how loose they were.

In answer, she touched his chest. 'Look how tight. That button's ready to pop.'

He flinched away from her hand. 'Maybe the shirt shrunk.'

'Shirts that old don't shrink. *I* bought you that shirt. You're bigger in the chest, and it isn't muscle. Your face is fuller, too. It doesn't look bad. You look younger, actually. Softer.'

Olin shrugged, annoyed and not wanting to think about why. 'Let's get on the train before it goes without us.' He was dreading the two-hour journey. Usually he told Dove about his life and she listened. But he didn't want to tell her about Seth, and he could think of nothing else that had happened to him in the last two months – nothing that would take more than two or three minutes to tell. He had brought along a book to read, but he was so aware of Dove watching him that he found it difficult to concentrate. The familiar train journey had never seemed longer.

Their children, Tristan and Timon, acted pleased to see them, but they clearly had lives of their own in which parents played no very large role. Olin knew this was normal – he remembered his own schooldays. And it was only fair that they be uninterested in him, considering how seldom he thought of them, but, confronted with them in the flesh, with their inescapable separateness, Olin felt his own estrangement the more. Once they had been at the centre of his life, he thought. When he hugged them, and could feel and smell their familiar bodies, he loved them, but when they moved out of reach he was left with only memories. He loved his babies, but his babies had grown into strangers. He wondered if Dove felt the same way. Perhaps it was worse for her. Or perhaps she had come to terms with it long before. It had to be different for a mother, who had brought forth children from her own body. He had *always* been separate from his children. Suddenly, confusingly, Olin wanted to cry. To cover his feelings, he began to roughhouse with the boys until he realized he was embarrassing them. He wasn't acting like the other fathers. Desperately, Olin watched the other fathers for clues, and tried to act like them. He tried to remember what he had done six months ago, during his last visit to the school. What had he felt then, who had he been? Surely it hadn't always been this difficult, this painful?

Fortunately the day was structured to make life easy for everyone. Olin and Dove were taken around by their children, reintroduced to their children's friends and teachers, observed various competitions, sporting and dramatic events, and then took Tristan and Timon out for the traditional feast. Presents were given out, and then the farewell kisses and goodbyes.

Back on the train, Olin was too exhausted even to pretend to read his book. He didn't think Dove would have let him, anyway. It was obvious she had something to say, even if she was taking her time about saying it.

'So,' she said at last. 'You going to tell me about him?'

'Who?'

'Your friend.'

'What makes you think I have a friend?'

'You always thought I was stupid,' she said. 'But there are some things you don't get to know out of books. You're different than you were the last time I saw you. You're always out, too busy to call me, instead of lonely and bored like you were before. And instead of telling me in detail about your boring life, you got on the train and stuck your nose in a book. Because your life isn't boring anymore. Because there's somebody in your life. Somebody new. Maybe it's early days yet, maybe you're not really sure, and you don't want to jinx it by saying anything too soon in case it doesn't happen, but – I don't think it's that. I think something's happening that you didn't expect.'

'What are you babbling about?'

'The main thing is, the reason I'm so sure, is that you remind me –' Again she stopped short. It was almost like a dare to him to tell her what she already knew.

He gave in. Maybe, after all, he did want to talk about it; maybe he wanted confirmation from someone else. 'What do I remind you of,' he asked gently. 'Do I remind you of how I used to be, when you and I were first in love? Do I remind you of how I was then?'

She shook her head. 'No. You remind me of how *I* was.'

Dove was right, and he was in hell. He had denied it to her, and had tried to deny it to himself, but Sunday morning Olin woke and saw the blood in his bed and could no longer hide the truth from himself. He had fallen in love with Seth.

It wasn't much blood – a dried brownish spot no larger than his thumbnail. He stripped off the sheet and saw that it had soaked through to the mattress. As he scrubbed at the stain with a wet, soapy towel, Olin blinked back tears and struggled to think logically.

He was changing. No doubt about that, but the change was far from complete. Dove had seen the signs, but Dove had been through it herself. It might not be too late to stop what was happening to him. His only hope was to get away get away from Seth before it was too late. Parents did sometimes save their sons from shame by sending them away when they recognized the threat of a developing romance. Olin couldn't actually go away – he couldn't afford to leave his job – but he might be able to contrive something to keep him safely out of Seth's company.

Olin sat back and surveyed his work. There was a large wet spot on the mattress, but that would soon dry. The bloodstain was gone.

The telephone rang, making Olin jump. He stared at the thing, knowing already who it would be. Maybe he should start now, ignore it. But he couldn't resist the summons.

'Took you long enough,' said Seth's voice in his ear. 'I thought you said you lived in one room?'

'I do. I was in bed – I'm not feeling well.'

'Oh, what's wrong?'

'I'm not sure. Probably just tired out from the day with Dove and the boys.'

'Why don't I come over and cheer you up?'

'No!' The leap his heart had given – of pure desire – made him shout.

There was a short silence on the other end. Olin tried not to think about what Seth was thinking, not to worry whether he was hurt or angry.

Seth said, 'What's wrong?'

'I told you. I'm tired. I don't feel well. I'm fed up with people – I just need to be alone.'

'You're the doctor. I'll leave you alone, then. You'd just better be over this by Wednesday.'

'Wednesday?'

'You hadn't forgotten that we've got opera tickets?'

'No, of course not. I'll be better before Wednesday – I have to be well enough to go to school tomorrow. I can't afford to pay a substitute.'

Olin knew Seth's schedule like his own. It was easy enough to avoid him at school, just as, a week earlier, it had been easy to engineer brief 'accidental' encounters. At the end of the day Olin crept out by a side entrance and went to a movie and then had dinner in a café of the sort Seth would never enter. He felt like a hunted animal, following similar routine on Tuesday. But on Wednesday one of the boys brought him a note:

Opera steps, 7 sharp, yes? Don't be late! S.

Olin folded the note and tucked it into his pocket, aware that his students were staring at him and giggling.

'Is that a love note, sir?' asked one of the boys.

Another, in a loud whisper, corrected him: 'Is that a love note, *Miss!*'

The whole class exploded into mocking laughter.

Olin pounded on his desk, painfully aware that he was blushing. He regained control of the class, but he knew how weak was his hold on them. Boys that age were sensitive to hints of sex even where they did not exist, and once they knew the truth about him he would lose their respect forever. He tried to take comfort from the fact that they couldn't really know – and nothing, after all, had happened – and then, with a chill, he wondered if Seth also suspected. If Seth, perhaps, knew.

Against the rules, Olin dismissed his final class ten minutes early. He didn't go to a film or a café. He had decided to do something positive, and he caught the bus which would take him to the north-eastern suburb where Dove lived.

She seemed surprised and, he thought, not pleased when she opened the door to him. Entering at her reluctant invitation, he saw that she already had a visitor, a woman dressed, like Dove, in dark blue overalls. Olin had not seen Dove in her work clothes since the days when they lived together: she always dressed up for him when he came to call. She looked taller and stronger to him now, more of a stranger.

'Is something wrong?' she asked. She did not offer to introduce him to the woman.

'No, no, I just thought I'd like to take you out to dinner.'

'Why didn't you phone?'

He shrugged uneasily. 'It was a spur of the moment thing. I thought you'd be pleased.'

There was a silence, and then the other woman set down her teacup and rose from her chair. 'I'd better be getting along,' she said to Dove. 'I'll see you tomorrow at work.'

'I'll phone you later,' Dove said.

The two women exchanged a look which made Olin feel even more uncomfortable, and then the other woman smiled, becoming almost beautiful. 'Take care, Leo,' she said.

'Leo?' said Olin when Dove had closed the door behind her departing guest. 'Why did she call you that?'

'It's my name.'

'It *was*. Dove –'

'Dove is *your* name for me. I still have my own. I prefer my friends to use it.'

He wondered what she meant by the word friend, and what that woman was to her, and he did not want to know. 'I didn't know you didn't like it. I could have chosen another name if you'd ever said –'

'I didn't say I didn't like it. It's all right *you* calling me Dove. Let's not argue. Come in the kitchen and have a cup of tea. Or would you rather have a beer? I've got some.'

'Tea.' He followed her into the kitchen. 'I'm sorry I didn't phone first. I really didn't think about it until I was on the bus coming out here, and then it seemed too late. If you really want me to leave –'

'No, now you're here, stay.'

'I can wait while you change,' he said as she put the kettle on.

She shook her head. 'I don't want to change; I don't feel like going out.' She turned around to face him, leaned against the counter and crossed her arms over her chest. 'Why don't you just say what you have to say?'

He didn't want to talk to her in such a self-possessed, almost aggressive mood. He had hoped to make her pliable with drink and good food, to lead up to it gently, but she wasn't giving him the chance and he couldn't afford to wait for a better time. He drew a deep breath.

'I want to try again,' he said.

'Try what?'

'Us. I'd like us to try again. I'd like to move back in here with you.'

She simply stared. He couldn't tell what she was thinking. The kettle was boiling. She turned away and poured the water into the teapot.

'He's really got you scared,' she said.

'Who?'

'It won't work,' she said. 'You can't get away from him that easily. You can't just pretend you've got a wife.'

'Why should it be a pretence? We loved each other once – why can't we go back to that?'

'Because we've changed.'

'*I* haven't,' he said furiously. 'I haven't changed! It's started, yes, but *he* doesn't know – we haven't done anything – it's not too late – if I stay away from him – I don't have to be his woman –'

'And I don't have to be yours.'

Olin stared at her. 'But you can't – you can't change back. You can't ever be a man again. Becoming a woman – that change is forever. I changed you.'

She smiled. 'What makes you think I *want* to be a man again? There are other kinds of change. There's such a thing as growing.'

'Have you met someone else? Who is he? Do you want to marry someone else?'

'No.'

But there was something ... Olin felt sick. 'Not her – that woman who was here? Is she your lover? Do women do that?'

He saw her tense, and it occurred to him that she wanted to hit him. But she was very controlled as she said, 'We're friends. We'll probably make love some day. But not in the way *you* mean. It's not that kind of thing. There aren't any men and women among us.'

'I wouldn't try to stop you,' Olin said. 'If that was what you wanted, if you wanted her as well . . . You could do as you liked. Let me move back in here.'

'No.'

'Why won't you help me? Do you hate me that much, for what I did to you?'

She sighed. 'Olin . . . I don't hate you at all. If I can help you, I will. But I'm not going to live a lie for you.'

'Why should it be a lie? We were happy together once, weren't we?'

'We were, but that's over. Olin, you know it is. You spend an evening with me, and by the end of it you can't wait to get away. The Dove you've got in your mind isn't me. You'd know that if you weren't so afraid right now. Why are you so afraid? It's natural; it happens to people all the time. Why can't you just accept what's happening to you?'

'I'm too old,' he said, anguished.

She almost laughed. 'The fact that it's happening means you're not too old. All right, maybe too old for babies, but that can be a blessing. Since you've done your bit for the species already, with Timon and Tristan, you don't even have to feel guilty. Let yourself enjoy it. There *is* pleasure in it, you know. Pain, too, but you might find that the pleasure makes up for it. I remember the pleasure, Olin. You don't have to feel guilty about what you did to me. Oh, I know you feel guilty. Otherwise you wouldn't be so afraid of it happening to you. Don't be. It isn't *so* terrible to be a woman.'

Of course it was terrible to be a woman. Olin had feared it all his life. Everyone feared becoming a woman. Parents feared it for their sons. And friends, in their intimacy, battled grimly not to lose. To lose was to become a woman. Olin had been through that in his youth, and he had won. He thought he could relax, then, he thought he was safe. He had not realized, until it was too late, that the battle to retain manhood never ended. He had not truly understood that one victory was not the end. He had not realized until now that he might yet lose.

After leaving Dove, Olin rode around the city on buses, unable to think what to do next, unable even to decide upon a restaurant. But eventually he became restless and decided that, like Seth, he would be able to think better if he could walk. He left the bus at a stop near the old city, so that was where he went to walk.

Darkness had fallen, and the broken pavement was treacherous underfoot. Here and there among the looming vastness of ancient buildings tiny lights glowed and flickered: candles lit by lovers in the abandoned rooms which were their trysting places. They were all around him – he heard the indistinct murmur of their voices and, occasionally, a cry of pain.

He broke out in a sweat. Once these surroundings would have induced nostalgic memories of his time with Dove. Now they brought only fear. Why had he come here? Why had he chosen these streets, of all there were in the city to walk? He had to get away.

Olin turned around and there, in the darkness, unmistakable, was Seth.

'I knew you'd come here,' said Seth. 'I knew I only had to wait.'

'It was a mistake,' said Olin. 'I'm leaving.'

'You'll come with me first.'

'No.'

As he tried to go past, Seth caught him by the arm. It was the first time he had ever touched Olin, and now Olin knew that it really was too late. They could fight: although Seth was taller, Olin was heavier and better coordinated and under other circumstances he could have taken Seth. But as he stood very still, feeling Seth's fingers like a chain around his arm, feeling the unwanted, unmistakable trickle of wetness between his legs as his wound began to bleed, Olin knew that Seth had already won this fight. He shuddered, as his fear was transformed into desire.

'Where will we go?' he asked.

'I know a room. Come on.' Now Seth, seeming kind, released his bruising hold and laid his arm gently across Olin's shoulders. 'Don't be frightened,' he said, leading Olin away. 'I'll be very gentle; it won't hurt so much.'

It was only the first of his lies.

The Man in the Ditch

There was nothing to look at once they were away from the town, only a long road stretching ahead, bare fields on either side, beneath a lowering grey sky. It was very flat and empty out here on the edge of the fens, and dull winter light leeched all colour from the uninspiring landscape. Occasionally there was a ruined windmill in the distance, a knackered old horse gazing sadly over a fence, a few recumbent cows, a dead man in a ditch –

Linzi screamed when she saw it, an ear-piercing screech that might, had J.D. been a less-practiced driver, caused a nasty accident. If there was nothing else out here, there were still plenty of vehicles travelling fast and close, both front and back.

'What the fuck?'

She saw how red his face had gone, the vein that throbbed in his temple, and felt bad, but she hadn't screamed for nothing. 'Jay, there was a dead body in the ditch back there – a person!'

'Don't be stupid.' His hands tightened on the wheel, and his eyes darted between the mirror and the road, not sparing her a glance.

'I saw it! We have to –'

'What? What do we have to do?'

'I – I don't know. Go back?'

With every passing second the distance grew.

'And why should we do that? Do you see anywhere to turn? And then, even if you could tell me where to stop, there's nowhere to pull over without going right into the ditch. And why? So you can see that what you thought was a dead body was really a load of fly-tipped rubbish?'

She worried at her lip as she tried to recall precise details of what she had seen – a withered, brownish, naked man, lying curled on his side – but she didn't believe it had been an optical illusion. 'It was a man's body. I'm sorry I startled you, but anyone would've yelled, to see a corpse like that.'

J.D. sighed and moved his head around, easing the tension in his neck. 'All right, my lovely. It's over now. A dead body doesn't need our help.'

'But – we ought to tell someone?'

'Tell who?'

'The police?'

He flinched, and she shut her eyes, as if his response to the word had been a slap in the face. She opened them again when she heard him put on the indicator.

'If you really saw it, other people did, too,' he said calmly. Then he turned left, onto a sign-posted road, and then, very soon, took another left onto an unmarked road; a narrow, single-track lane. They were now travelling parallel to the main road, back in the direction from which they had come. With a nervous flutter of anticipation low in her belly, Linzi realized he must be responding to her request, taking her back to the spot where she'd seen the body. From here, the main road was easily visible as a steady stream of traffic; only a short stretch of empty land separated the track they were on from the drainage ditch, even though she couldn't see it. But then she hadn't noticed this road from the other side. She couldn't guess how far they'd gone after her sighting, but she had faith that J.D. knew: he was a professional driver.

Linzi caught hold of her elbows and gave herself a small hug. Wasn't it just *like* him to grumble and pretend he wasn't doing what she wanted? Not that she *wanted* to see the horrible old dead thing again ... and, in fact, as the car slowed and then stopped when the track ran out, she prayed to whatever powers there might be that J.D. was right, and she'd been scared by an abandoned, stolen shop-window mannequin or a crash test dummy.

'Here we are,' he said. 'What do you think?'

She looked at his proud smile and remembered what the dead man had pushed out of her mind.

'Come on,' he said, not waiting for her reply. 'Let me show

you round our new home.' He hopped out and, with the courtliness that had won her heart, opened her door for her.

She fixed a pleased smile on her face, but he must have picked up a hint of her true feelings because he said, sounding defensive, 'Of course it doesn't look like much now, but use your imagination. Think of all the stuff you can plant. Landscape the holy shit out of it. Whatever you like; I'll pay.'

Tentatively, she tried to explain her unease: 'I thought we'd have neighbours . . .'

'Who the fuck wants neighbours? You said you wanted a house in the country.'

'Yes, yes, I did; I *do*. But I didn't think it would be so far away from everything –'

'It's the *country*. And it's *not* far – what, twenty minutes from Norwich? You must have seen the village sign-posted, two miles that way for post office, pub, and primary school.'

At that reminder of the children they'd have someday, she melted against him. 'Oh, honey, I'm not complaining! How could I, when I've got you? I was just surprised. I was imagining a new development.'

'You know I hate those ticky-tacky estates.' He relaxed in her embrace. 'Would Madam like the grand tour?'

They walked over land that was rough but not boggy as the fields had appeared from the car window. She saw the boundary markers – poles sporting fluorescent orange plastic tags – and then came upon a pile of rubble, and a concrete slab.

'What's this?'

'What's left of the house that used to be here. Why'd you think we've got planning permission to build a new one?'

'What happened to the old house?'

'I think it burnt down. I don't know, twenty years ago. Before that there were cottages. People have always lived here. You might not think to look at it, but it's actually on a rise, higher than the marshes out there. And the soil is a different composition, not boggy, so we can plant what we like. And we're never going to have to worry about other houses going up either side, because who'd build on a bog? We won't have noisy neighbours, or nosy ones, popping over every five minutes, complaining that our *leylandii* is blocking their view, wanting to borrow the hedge-trimmer, giving you the eye . . .'

As he worked himself up into a rant she had heard before, staring out at the bleak, blank, featureless plain where the only other life to be seen was in the cars and lorries thundering past, Linzi felt a tremor of doubt. Those things he complained about were leftovers from his past in the suburbs with 'that cheating bitch.' Did their life have to be defined always in reaction to his first marriage?

'Are you cold?' Noticing her sadness, J.D. became tender. He took his coat off and wrapped it around her. 'That wind has teeth. We'll have to plant a line of trees over there, as a wind-break, and a hedge on that side, to screen us from nosy buggers staring out their windows as they drive past. Come on, back to the car now.'

Going back, she couldn't see anything unusual in the ditch. There was nothing in the local news the next day about a body being found, and the next time they drove out east on the A47 she couldn't even identify the spot where she'd thought she'd seen it.

Building soon got started, and a few weeks later, J.D. stopped by the property one evening and took pictures with his phone, sharing them with Linzi when he got home. She made admiring noises until the final picture, when the sound stuck in her throat.

'What – what's that?'

'A side view –'

'I mean down in front, the left-hand corner, that thing.'

He peered at the screen. 'What are you talking about?'

'It looks like – ' But she found she didn't want to say it looked like a dead body, a wizened naked man lying on his side, so she just pointed. 'There.'

'Oh. Not sure. Pile of sticks and some weeds, maybe. The light was going. Waste of space, that one.' With the touch of a button, he deleted it.

A few days later, Linzi accompanied her husband to the building site. She was surprised by how quickly everything had changed, how different the space looked now that there was the frame of a house at the centre of it. She was also a little taken aback by how much clutter there was everywhere. Much of it was equipment and building material, or the discarded packaging for those things, but there were also food wrappings, plastic bottles, beer cans, even the odd item of clothing – a white T-shirt, a single shoe – suggesting the workers considered the space outside the house a dumping ground. It was easy to imagine some accumulation of trash appearing in dim light like a body, and she abandoned her plan to search for the object that had created such a disturbing impression in the picture, and instead clung to her husband's arm and listened to his description of how the work was progressing.

At one time Linzi had made good money dancing in a club – it was where she had met J.D. – but he couldn't stand the thought of other men seeing her naked, so now she worked at Tesco. It wouldn't be too bad as a part-time job when her kids were in school, she thought, but a year into her marriage she still wasn't pregnant, and she was getting impatient. The doctor said there was no obvious reason why she shouldn't conceive in due course, but if she wasn't content to wait and see, the next step would be to check her husband's sperm count. Well able to imagine how J.D. would respond to that suggestion, Linzi decided to explore other options first.

She'd heard there was a woman in Lowestoft who had studied all the old traditional ways to increase fertility. First, she read your cards, then she'd advise on the most propitious times for conception, and would make up a special herbal tea or a list of vitamin and mineral food supplements, based on what the cards revealed. So Linzi made an appointment, and drove down there on her next afternoon off.

The address was in one of the rundown terraced houses across the road from the big parking lot on the seafront. The woman's name was Maeve, and she had a blowsy, sun-tanned, gypsyish look: Celtic motif tattoos, hennaed hair, big silver jewellery. She took twenty quid off Linzi before leading her in to a cramped, over-furnished sitting room that smelt of cats and sandalwood incense, where they sat facing each other across a small table.

'You want a baby,' Maeve announced. 'You have been trying and failing to fall pregnant. Your husband ... no, don't tell me, darling ... is older than you. You are his second ... third ... wife. Don't tell me, I will tell you. You are very keen to start a family, but he, perhaps ... no, he is also keen. But his children ... no, no, of course, he has no children. I see that. But the reason ... Let's see what the cards have to say.'

She opened a wooden box, removed a velvet bag from it, and a deck of cards from that, which she shuffled. She told Linzi to take three cards from the deck and lay them out face up.

These were not the brightly coloured tarot cards Linzi had expected. Instead, each one offered a murky, black and white image like a bad reproduction of a very old photograph, and it was hard to make any sense of them at first glance.

One card showed a dancer, a man who was naked except for a belt tied loosely around his waist and a close-fitting cap on his head, caught mid-pirouette, balancing on one pointed foot, the other leg bent at the knee, arms folded behind his back. His eyes were closed and he was calmly smiling.

The second card had a picture of a woman with a dog's body – or a pregnant bitch with a woman's head. The female face was fixed in a blank, upwards stare, mouth gaping open as if to swallow the object of her gaze, a large, silver egg suspended just above her head.

The third card involved a great number of knives and a bleeding body. Before she could make out anything more, Maeve had scooped up all three and returned them to the deck which she cut and shuffled feverishly, muttering, 'That's bad. Very bad.'

'Shall I try again?' Linzi asked meekly.

The woman shot her a venomous glare. 'He won't give you a baby.'

'You mean J.D.?'

'Don't let him trick you.'

'Are you talking about my husband?'

'You shouldn't have married him if you weren't prepared to be faithful.'

'I *am* faithful!' She stared at the fortune-teller, outraged. 'I haven't slept with anyone but J.D., not since our very first date!'

' "Slept with." So oral sex doesn't count.' The woman sneered at her. 'You can't lie to me. You've been unfaithful to your man once, and the cards show it happening again.'

She felt the blood drain from her head and saw little starry spots in the darkness. The bad thing. How did she know? 'I didn't . . . I wasn't . . . I wasn't *cheating* on him. Do the cards tell you *why?*'

Maeve put the cards away. 'I don't care why. That's *your* problem. But I see what's coming, and it's not good. It would be very bad for you to cheat on your husband, especially with that one.'

'I'm not going to cheat on J.D. – I love him! I came here because I thought you were going to help us have a baby. Can't you make me some tea, prescribe some herbs and vitamins?'

Maeve stood up and began to move towards the door. 'I won't help you with fertility until you sort out this problem with your husband. You'll have to decide what you want: this marriage, or something else.'

Linzi remained stubbornly in her seat, twisting around to face the other woman. 'I want this marriage. And a baby. Are you saying I can't? Not have J.D.'s baby? That he's sterile? Please, you have to tell me. I have a right to know.'

Maeve sighed and stopped in the doorway, playing with one of the heavy silver chains hanging from her neck. 'Your husband won't give you a baby. And the other one can't.'

'What "other one"? There is no man in my life but J.D. I swear.'

The woman responded with a hard, contemptuous stare. 'You have to leave now.'

Linzi's feeling of shock had faded, and now she just felt indignant. Twenty quid for that! Not a proper reading, one little incident, taken out of context, misunderstood . . . it was an insult. Maeve might have some kind of psychic talent, to have picked up something, but she'd got it completely wrong.

The bad thing. She thought about it again as she waited for a gap in the traffic that would allow her to cross the street. They never talked about it, but it had cast a shadow over their relationship, and haunted J.D., a ghost roused every time he had a flash of jealousy over some harmless incident.

But he had no right to feel jealous. Maeve had misunderstood, but J.D. knew perfectly well she hadn't been cheating on him – she'd only sucked that cop's dick so J.D. wouldn't lose his license. She'd felt his desperation; she knew as well as he what it would mean. So, a quick, wordless transaction: I'll do you, and you won't do him.

He could have stopped it with a word, or a look, but he hadn't. And he had been grateful, at least until his gratitude had soured into resentment. She didn't expect thanks – she would have preferred they pretend it never happened – but why couldn't he understand that when you loved someone as she loved him, no sacrifice was too great?

In her dream Linzi plaited narrow strips of leather into a strong, flexible cord, which became a noose around the tanned and weathered neck of a man who wore nothing else except a soft cap made of animal hide, and a flat leather belt loose around his middle. She woke up with the image vivid in her mind, understanding that the 'dancer' she'd seen on the fortune teller's card was the hanged man.

As the house drew closer to completion, Linzi felt more and more unhappy about the prospect of moving into it. Although the house itself was not the problem – that was turning out to be even better than she'd dared to imagine; you'd have to be crazy to prefer any of the flats she'd ever occupied, or the small, end-of-terrace ex-council house that she'd grown up in. She didn't think she was crazy. She hadn't seen anything that looked like a dead body for months, but the creepy black and white picture on the fortune teller's card had merged in her memory with the body she'd seen in the ditch, and became an ominous presence that she sensed lying in wait for her, just out of sight, every time they took the turning off the A47 and headed for what J.D. already called their home.

It was impossible to tell him she didn't want to live there, especially not when he was looking forward to it so much, and had put so much money and effort into it. So they moved in, and she told herself she would soon get used to it.

The first week in the new house was something like a second honeymoon. J.D. took a week off work so they could take their time settling in. They hardly went anywhere, except to the village for supplies, or meals in the pub; the days passed in a pleasurable round of companionable work as they sanded and painted and moved things around, and their nights were filled with sex both vigorous and tender. Linzi had never seen her husband so completely happy. He thought she was only nervy because pregnancy still eluded her, and kept encouraging her to relax.

Mostly, as long as J.D. was around, Linzi did manage to relax. She felt safe enough in their new house, looking inward, happiest when the curtains shut out any sight of the featureless marshes that surrounded them, and she left all the outdoor chores to her husband, having found that no matter what direction she was facing, she was plagued by the uncomfortable sensation that someone was creeping up on her from behind.

And at night, she dreamed about the hanged man.

Sometimes she was plaiting the noose; sometimes she fitted it around his unresisting neck, before or after bestowing a kiss upon his motionless mouth. At other times she was not so immediately involved, but stood huddled at the back of a solemn crowd and watched him die, his legs kicking, feet dancing on air, semen spurting a final blessing on the barren ground below.

After J.D. had gone back to work, Linzi invited her mother over for lunch. It was her first visit to the new house.

'So much light in this room,' said her mother, approvingly. 'In all the rooms, in fact. I love the big windows. What a great view.'

Standing slightly behind her mother, Linzi peeked over her shoulder at the long, flat treeless expanse, stretching away beneath the blue sky. Although more attractive now in summer colours, she still found it a sinister sight. 'You think so?'

'You don't?' Her mother turned to give her a searching look. 'Is something wrong, Linz?'

She shrugged. 'I just think it's sort of bleak. Come outside,' she added quickly. 'Into the garden. Not that it is anything like a garden yet, but . . . I'd like to know what you think.'

Her mother took the request seriously and examined the land from every side. She even got down on her knees and dug into the soil with her hands. Linzi, meanwhile, put her back against a wall of the house and watched her mother closely for any signs that she felt an invasive, invisible presence, but if she did nothing showed.

They went back inside and ate quiche and salad while Linzi's mother made a list of plants her daughter might want to consider, and sketched out two possible plans for landscaping. 'It won't look so bleak once you've planted a few shrubs. Maybe, while you're waiting for things to take hold, you could put out a few pots, and some garden furniture, just things for your eye to rest on.' She put her pencil down. 'Now why don't you tell me what you really wanted to talk to me about.'

'Did you feel anything . . . anything wrong . . . out there?'

'No, I told you, the soil looks very rich and good; not boggy as I'd expect. Whoever lived here in the past must have tended it well.'

'I don't mean that.' Linzi drew a deep breath. 'Do you remember, when I was really little, you were going to leave me and Tilda with a child-minder, and we went to her house – and then walked straight out again? You said there was no way . . . you felt something wrong in the place, and weren't surprised at all when we heard a few months later that her boyfriend was arrested for being a paedo?'

'Of course I remember.'

'You sensed something wrong in her house. Something bad, dangerous, even though there was nothing to see. I want to know if you sense anything *here*.'

Alarm flickered in her eyes. 'Linzi, honey, you can come home with me now, stay as long as you like; if you decide –'

'What? No!' Tears sprang to her eyes and she stared, open-mouthed. 'Why would you think – You want me to leave J.D., don't you? I knew it! You never liked him.'

Her mother threw up her hands. 'I didn't say anything! You're the one who brought up that horrible –'

'I was talking about the way you *sensed* something wrong. That's what you said, that as soon as you walked through the door, you just knew. So I wondered –'

'– if I sensed something here? No. But why should you expect me to, if everything's rosy?'

'I've felt something. Not about J.D. This place is haunted. The land.' It came tumbling out: the dead man in the ditch, the deleted photograph, her feelings, her dreams . . . 'I think – no, I'm sure – a man was killed here a long time ago, hanged and then buried as some kind of sacrifice. I think it's his spirit I sense.'

Her mother sighed, shifted in her chair, shot a glance at the clock on the oven. 'Why ask me about it? I've never seen a ghost in my life.'

'But you're sensitive to atmospheres. You knew Tilda and I wouldn't be safe with that woman – you sensed *evil* – you even said so, later!'

'Yes. I did. She seemed all right on the phone, and she had good references, but the moment I walked into her house –' She stopped. 'There was just something about her. But she was a person; alive. How can a dead man hurt you? Whether he was good or evil in his life, after he's dead, he can't *do* anything.'

'You don't believe in ghosts?'

It was a challenge her mother deflected. 'I'm not saying that. I don't know what you saw. I will say this: I never heard of anyone being killed by a ghost. I'd be more afraid of the living.'

'So you think it's safe to stay here?'

'What does J.D. think?'

She turned to look at the clock. 'He never saw it.'

Her mother stood up, and Linzi rose, too, saying half-heartedly, 'You should stay . . . and say hello to J.D.'

'No, I have to get back. I've got a meeting this evening. Linzi, whatever you're worried about –'

'I just told you.'

'Well, share it with J.D. That's my advice. I know, neither of my marriages worked out, but I do know that what troubles one partner is bound to affect the other. You'll only make things worse if you keep it to yourself.'

Although she ignored her advice to tell J.D., Linzi took heart from her mother's remark that the dead couldn't hurt the living. She didn't want J.D. to feel haunted as she did. His obliviousness was her bulwark. One evening as she passed the kitchen window she caught sight of an unpleasantly familiar shape on the ground, just behind a pile of gravel waiting to be spread, and the shock brought her to a halt, and made her lean towards the glass, peering out intently, just as J.D. came up behind her.

'What are you looking at?'

'Oh! I don't know what it is – there, behind the gravel, can you see it?'

'What sort of something? Big or little?'

She opened her arms. 'Big.'

'I don't see anything.'

And as he spoke, it was gone.

But the sense of a sinister, lurking presence remained, and intensified as the days began to grow shorter. She was aware of it, like an assassin waiting to jump out at her, every time she came home, from the moment she stepped out of her car, until, nerves taut and vibrating with fear, she managed to scurry into the house and shut the door. Only then did she dare to relax, a little.

That her husband was unable to see the dead man, that he was seemingly immune to any sense of its presence, reassured her. She thought his blindness kept her safe when he was home, and the one thing she was dreading was the first time she'd have to spend the night alone.

It would happen very soon. Once a fortnight his scheduled delivery rounds included an overnight stay – mandatory when further driving would push him over the safety limits for hours behind the wheel. Drivers broke those limits all the time, of course, including J.D., but after a recent high-profile fatal accident his company was cracking down.

She was trying to be cool about it, but knew that he'd picked up on her nervousness. The day before he was to leave, as she was coming back from shopping, as she glanced across the emptiness to their house, she saw his van, at least an hour before she'd expected him, and called to let him know she was on her way.

'I've been shopping, too,' he said. 'I bought a surprise – well, it's for the house, but I think it will make you happy.'

She felt happy as she pulled in to park beside his van, until she saw something that gripped her heart with a nameless dread: the front door to the house was wide open.

Leaving her purse, phone, bags, everything in the car, she galloped inside, calling his name, in a panic.

'What's wrong?' He was in the kitchen, a carton, packaging, tools on the counter.

'You left the door open!'

'Jesus, Linz, so what? We can't let a little air in? I heard you slam it hard enough!'

She stood with jaw clenched, hands in fists, and tried to regain control.

He came over and held her. 'What's wrong? You didn't bash into my van?'

'No, no, it's fine. I'm fine. I just – I just saw the door and thought – thought someone might – might be inside.'

'So? You knew I was here; I talked to you a minute ago.'

She could think of no plausible explanation and was determined not to speak her fear aloud, her terror that the dead man she had seen in the ditch and then closer on the ground outside was now inside the house with them. But she knew it was true. She could feel that the tenuous safety of their home had been breached by that old ghost.

'Are you going to tell me what happened?' His voice was gentle; he didn't sound angry at all.

'I don't know,' she said, her voice tiny as she clung to him. 'But when I saw the door hanging open, I got scared.'

'Wow. I definitely made the right choice of what to buy you today.'

She was still trying to summon sufficient interest to ask what it was when he said, 'But I'll show you after we've searched the house and you see we're alone here.'

It was obvious as they walked through the large, light and still sparsely furnished rooms that there were few places a man might hide, but Linzi knew the intruder she feared could hide in plain sight. She didn't know why she'd been cursed with the ability to see him and found herself wishing J.D. *would* see the dead man, just once. Then he'd know what she'd been going through, and they could talk about how they were going to deal with the fact that the ghost of an ancient sacrifice now inhabited their home.

But neither of them saw anything that did not belong, and Linzi had to pretend to be comforted by J.D.'s present to her of a CCTV system. With the cameras mounted outside, she could monitor the property, all approaches to the house, from the TV set in the bedroom. Thus, if she heard spooky noises from outside while he was away, she could check them out without even having to show herself at the window, and find out if it was a fox, or a gust of wind, or even a couple of kids from the village looking for somewhere to take drugs and have sex. She thanked him as ardently as she could, because he had meant well; he couldn't know modern technology was utterly useless against the thing she feared.

But he must have picked up the fact that she was not as reassured as she pretended, because he suggested she invite her mother to stay over while he was away. Considering his prickly relationship with her, the suggestion was staggeringly generous. But she turned it down.

'And then go through this whole rigamarole again in two weeks? No, I have to get used to a night on my own some time. Might as well be tonight,' she told him before she hugged and kissed him goodbye.

The day passed peacefully enough, soundtrack supplied by Radio One, as she painted the upstairs room they'd designated as the nursery. The light, buttery yellow would be a good choice for a child of either sex, although she still thought about wallpaper for one wall, pattern to be chosen when she knew she was expecting.

She talked to J.D. around eight, assured him she was coping. He said he'd try to phone her back later, but if he hadn't, she should phone him at bedtime. She agreed, although she wasn't sure what counted as bedtime when they were apart. She was quite tired by ten, but the thought of going to bed alone made her linger downstairs, drinking the rest of a bottle of wine and watching some rubbish film until she nearly fell asleep on the couch. Then she staggered upstairs, fell into bed and a light, woozy sleep.

A sound, something her sleeping mind recognized without alarm, brought her awake, not frightened, but utterly bewildered. What time was it, and what night? She could feel the still, solid presence of the man sleeping beside her. But if J.D. was home, whose was the key in the door downstairs?

Laying one hand on a sheeted shoulder she whispered, 'J.D.! Honey, wake up!'

From downstairs came the familiar sequence of beeps that meant the alarm system was being disarmed. But who else knew their code? Maybe somebody from the security company, but . . .

'Honey?' Still more confused than frightened, she fumbled for the light switch on the hanging cord, and heard someone mounting the stairs.

'J.D!' She said his name, loud and urgent, as the light came on, and she sat up, shutting her eyes briefly against the flare of light as she tugged at the sheet which he'd pulled up over his head. 'Honey, wake *up*.'

Then she saw what was lying next to her, curled on his side in an almost fœtal position, naked brown skin like ancient leather, face beneath the close-fitting cap serenely smiling in death, and the terrified scream that rose in her throat strangled her, cutting off not only sound but breath. In the instant before she blacked out, she saw her husband standing in the doorway, staring at the bed – but not at her.

Mere seconds later, when she came to, that's when she screamed out loud. Recoiling in horror, she jerked convulsively up and out of the bed before she noticed that it was empty.

She stopped in the doorway, clutching at the doorframe for support, and looked again. Not only was the bed empty, the bedclothes were disturbed only on the side where she had been. There was no depression to indicate that any other head had rested on J.D.'s pillows since she'd plumped them up after making the bed that morning. But J.D. seen him – she had seen the direction of his gaze and, more importantly, the look on his face; a look she knew she would never forget.

'J.D.?' She tried to call, but her voice was little more than a whisper.

Where was he? Her husband had disappeared as utterly as the ghastly corpse. She had to ask herself if the whole experience had been a nightmare from which she had only now awakened.

Stepping into the dark hall, she felt an unexpected draught. Putting on the light, she looked down the stairs and saw the front door was wide open. Descending, she heard the sound of a motor starting, the easily recognizable, throaty note of J.D.'s van, shifting hard into reverse, flinging up gravel, then driving off at speed.

Uselessly, she called her husband's name, ran down the stairs and then back up again for her phone, seeing in her mind's eye the dark, angry flush on his face, the vein throbbing in his temple, tears in his fixed, furious eyes as he pressed harder on the accelerator, as if by going faster he could outpace his own jealous rage.

He thought he'd seen another man in bed with her. Why hadn't he stayed to be sure, stayed to curse her, stayed to fight? She had to reach him, had to tell him the truth, had to make him understand . . .

But his phone went straight to voicemail. She was listening impatiently to the mechanical instructions for leaving a message when she heard the scream of tortured brakes, the slam of metal against metal, the final, shattering sound of a car crash up on the main road. Heart in her throat, she grabbed her keys and ran for her car, barefoot and in her nightgown, unable to think of anything but the necessity of reaching him, imagining there must be something she could do to help him, to save him; clinging to that belief right up to the moment when she reached the site of the accident and saw her husband lying where he'd been thrown through the windscreen when his van went off the road, half curled on his side, neck broken, already dead in the ditch.

The Last Dare

'I'll buy you a Halloween treat,' said the grandmother.

The little girl backed away from the display of walking zombies and howling ghosts, rubber spiders and bloodshot eyeballs, shaking her head: she didn't like scary things.

'Let's keep looking,' the woman coaxed, and, taking her granddaughter by the hand, walked further down the aisle of the store.

They came to a shelf of stuffed toys, featuring ghosts and grinning pumpkins, teddy bear zombies, vampires and witches. The little girl stared, then swooped on a sweet-looking black kitten with green eyes, a conical orange hat rakishly cocked over one ear.

'You like that one?'

Anxiously, the little girl nodded, even as she pulled away.

'Sweetheart, of course you can have it. Or whatever you like. We'll go buy it now. I love Halloween; it's my favourite holiday. How about you, Madison? Do you love Halloween?'

Madison shrugged her skinny shoulders and raised the stuffed cat to her face, rubbing it against her cheek. She whispered, 'Love her.'

'Has she got a name?'

'Holly.'

'Holly? That sounds more like Christmas to me.'

'Holly – for Hallo*ween*.'

They had reached the line for check-out, and at the grandmother's characteristic short, sharp bark of a laugh, another woman turned, looking startled.

The grandmother apologized. 'I was just laughing at myself for being silly.'

The other woman, a well-maintained platinum blonde of indeterminate age, widened her eyes. 'I know you. Elaine Alverson? Is that you?'

'Yes, but how – Bobbi? Bobbi Marshall?'

With exclamations of surprise and delight, the two women embraced.

'Gamma, who is it?'

The girl who spoke was dressed like a tiny Goth in a black T-shirt and ripped leggings, her hair teased and gelled into spikes.

'Ruby, my youngest granddaughter,' said Bobbi. 'She doesn't *always* look like this.'

'Just for Halloween,' said Ruby. 'Tonight, I get to wear eyeliner and black lipstick, too. I never met you before, did I?'

'No, you didn't,' said Bobbi. 'This is Laney ... Elaine ... Ms Alverson?'

'Call me Lane.'

'Lane and I were best friends when we were little, since second grade.'

'I'm in second grade,' said Ruby.

'Me, too.' Lane was startled by Madison's voice, no longer a whisper, but piping and clear, the way it had been before she left New York. Her daughter had told her that Madison was finding it hard to settle at her new school, having arrived late in a class where friendships and pecking order were already firmly established. Someone had made fun of her accent, and the child's response had been to clam up. Lane was even more surprised to hear Madison address the other little girl: 'Your hair looks so cool. How do you get it like that?'

'Actually, my mom did it. With a ton of hair gel. She's going to do my make-up, too. Black,' she added, with relish.

'Mine won't let me wear make-up.'

'Not even for Halloween?'

Madison cocked her head. 'Well – maybe. I'll ask.'

As the girls chatted, Lane's attention was claimed by her old friend. 'This is so amazing! When did you move back?'

'I didn't.' She barely repressed a shudder. 'I would never move back to Texas. But Kate – my daughter – came here for her husband's new job. They wanted me for Thanksgiving, but I'd made other plans.'

'You must miss them. Your only grandchild?'

Lane nodded, glancing at the girls who had progressed to exchanging secrets, hunched close together, whispering and giggling.

The two women traded personal details as Bobbi's purchases were scanned, and with the impulsive warmth Lane remembered so well, her old friend invited them to lunch. 'We have so much to talk about – and I do believe our babies feel the same – look at them! Best friends already. You don't really have to rush off.'

'I was just going to look for somewhere nice for lunch.'

'My house! I've got a heap of fresh shrimp.'

'Where do you live? Is it far? I don't know my way around any-more, the city has grown so much.'

Bobbi grinned, a familiar, mischievous gleam in her dark brown eyes. 'Oh, you'll find my house all right. It's on Cranberry Street.'

Cranberry was one street over from Blueberry, where Lane had spent the first twelve years of her life. She remembered well enough how to get there, but since the girls wanted to stay together, Ruby came along to direct: 'When you get to Cran-berry Street, she'll show you Grandma's house.'

The entrance to the old neighbourhood was a wide, quiet boulevard that wound like a slow, concrete river through the heart of the residential area, divided by a central esplanade.

Lane had not thought the children were paying attention – she never did, at their age – but when she put on her turn signal, Ruby cried out: 'No, not this street! Cranberry is the next one.'

'I know, Ruby, but this is Blueberry – where I lived when I was your age. Wouldn't you like to see my old house?'

'I would,' said Madison.

The pink brick house on the corner was as she remembered, but Lane stared in bafflement at the house next door. Her old home had disappeared. A chain-link fence enclosed the property, which boasted a mini-mansion so new it was still under construction. The tree she used to climb, the bushes she played under, the flowerbeds and lawn were all gone, churned up in mud in front of a house that was patently too big for the lot, dominated by a huge garage.

'Which one?' Madison asked. 'Did you live in that pink house, Nanny?'

'No. That was the house next door. My house is gone.' She felt hollowed out, and did not understand why.

'How can your house be gone?'

'Somebody bought it, and tore it down to build a new house.'

'Why?'

'Well, probably the people that bought it wanted to live in this neighbourhood, but they needed a bigger house.' Glancing along the street, she saw this was not the only new, much bigger house to replace a modest, single-storey home from the 1950s.

'Why?'

Putting the car back into drive, she moved on. 'Can you think of reasons somebody might want a bigger house?'

'If they have lots of children.'

'Or lots of pets.'

'So they could have a home movie theatre, and a gym, and a game room.'

While the girls competed to come up with reasons for a bigger house, Lane drove to the end of the street, then took a left and went on six blocks to cross the boulevard. Ruby noticed as the car turned right into Azalea Court.

'Hey, where are we?'

'Haven't you been here before?'

'Don't think so.'

Blueberry, Cranberry, Blackberry, Bayberry, Gooseberry – and she could not remember how many other -berries – had been part of a brand-new subdivision in 1950, streets filled with affordable starter homes built to an identical plan. On the other side of the esplanade the streets were named after flowering plants, and the houses were larger and more expensive. It had been unknown territory to her when she was seven, like the girls in the backseat, but once she was a little older, she went exploring.

'Spiders,' gasped Madison. They all stared at the oak tree, draped in white gossamer strands. A spider the size of a large dog clung to its trunk; two others, puppy-sized, dangled from the branches.

Ruby laughed gleefully. 'Cool! And look next door – zombies! A zombie invasion!'

Lane checked her mirror, tilting it to see her granddaughter's face. The little girl was pale, but her eyes were wide, absorbing the sights that delighted her new friend. She was reminded of her own long-ago relationship with bold Bobbi who never worried, the way Lane did, about dangers or getting into trouble.

The residents of Azalea Court had really gone to town with their seasonal decorations, she thought, turning her attention back to the street. Ghosts, witches, a multitude of jack-o-lanterns, flapping bats, black cats, and gravestones decorated the well-tended lawns. One red-brick walkway hosted a parade of brightly painted skeletons – more *Día de los Muertos* than Halloween.

There were no construction sites, no tear-downs here: the handsome old houses, designed by architects to appeal to their well-heeled clients, had retained their value into the twenty-first century.

She stopped the car in front of one she named after its most striking feature, a rounded, tower-like end construction topped by a roof peaked like a witch's hat. She stared up at it, trying to remember why it made her feel uneasy, but the memory would not be caught.

Ruby breathed heavily on the back of her neck. 'What are you looking at, Mrs Madison's Nanny?'

Madison chimed in: 'What do you see? I just see a house.'

'The tower house. Sit back, please.' She drove on.

'What's the tower house?'

'That's what I called it. It used to fascinate me. That tower appealed to my imagination, I guess. It didn't seem to belong to the world I live in; it was more like something from an old book, a fairy tale or a fantasy. I wondered what might be inside, and what sort of people lived there.'

'Did you go there for trick-or-treat?'

Her stomach gave a queasy lurch. 'Of course not.'

'Why not?'

'*I* would,' said Ruby.

'It was across the boulevard, and we weren't allowed to walk that far. We didn't know the people who lived over here,' she explained, as she reached the intersection.

'I'll ask Gamma to take me there tonight. She will. I'll find out who lives there – maybe a witch!' Gasping with excitement, Ruby clutched at Madison. 'You too! Madison's Nanny, can she *please* come trick-or-treating with us?'

'Please, Nanny!'

Lane had not yet crossed the boulevard, although there was no reason to wait, with no other vehicle in sight. 'Sweetheart, you're going to a party – '

'I don't want to. I want to go trick-or-treating with Ruby.'

'You'll have to ask your mom. And Ruby will have to ask her grandmother.'

'She'll say yes, I know she will! You can meet my brother and my cousins,' Ruby said.

Lane spotted Bobbi's silver Lexus and pulled into the driveway behind it. Bobbi was waiting at the door. 'What took y'all so long?'

Ruby clutched at her grandmother. 'She showed us the tower house. Can we go there tonight? Can Madison come trick-or-treating with us?'

Startled, Bobbi met Lane's eyes. 'The tower house? You told them that story?'

'Gamma, *can* she? What story? Can we go trick-or-treating at the tower house?'

'No story,' said Lane quickly. 'I just wanted to see if it was still there.'

'Of course it's still there.'

'My old house isn't.'

Bobbi winced. 'I should have warned you.'

'Gamma, Gamma, please? Please can she come?'

Bobbi looked at Lane, who shrugged. 'I told Madison she'll have to ask her mother.'

'Phone,' said Madison, with an imperious thrust of her hand towards her grandmother.

Lane handed over her cell. 'Do you know your number?'

She frowned. 'Don't you have us in your contacts?'

'Of course – your mom's cell is under 'Kate' but your land-line –'

She'd already found what she wanted. 'Mommy? It's me. Can I – *may* I please go trick-or-treating with Ruby tonight? Her granny says it's okay. *Ruby*. What? Yes, she's here. But can I? Okay, okay.' She handed the phone to Lane.

'Where are you? What on earth is going on? Who's Ruby?'

Slowly, carefully, but as succinctly as she could, Lane explained.

'She's *talking*?' Kate's voice was hushed, reverential.

Lane couldn't help smiling, as smug as if it was her own doing. 'She and Ruby hit it off right away – like best pals already.' She watched Madison put her arm around Ruby's waist, saw the other girl reciprocate with a friendly squeeze. 'Wait till you see.'

'I didn't know you still knew anybody here. Where do they live?'

'Not far. Actually, it's the same neighbourhood I lived in when I was Madison's age.'

There were a few more questions, Kate needing to be reas-sured, but the outcome was never in doubt. Madison did not want to go to the school Halloween party, and this alternative, the appearance of a new friend, was a godsend.

Lane stowed her phone away and followed the others inside. It was a strange experience, to be inside a house with the very same design and floorplan as her childhood home; it struck her like a weird sort of *déjà vu*. Even the furniture was familiar – maybe Bobbi had inherited it from her parents. In the kitchen, there was a lunchtime feast of cold, succulent Gulf shrimp to be eaten with either red sauce or Thousand Island dressing, a mound of fresh salad, saltine crackers, grapes and apples.

'Tell us the story about the tower house,' Ruby commanded once the ice tea had been poured and they were sitting around the table.

'What story? I don't know any stories.'

'Oh, you liar,' Bobbi drawled, and cackled before addressing the children: 'This lady used to tell stories all the time – scared me half to death, some of them. The one about the tower house was really weird. And she swore it was true. Most of the time I didn't believe it, when she said that, but that story, I believed. I kind of had to.'

The girls stared at Lane, open-mouthed, eyes gleaming. 'Tell us!'

Not since her own daughter had grown out of make-believe had Lane known such an eager audience. She shook her head. 'Sorry. I don't remember.'

'I do.' Bobbi's look was a challenge. 'Go on – you can tell it much better than me.'

Lane mimed helplessness.

'Well, okay then.' Bobbi cleared her throat and began. 'As I recall, an old, old lady lived in that house, all by herself. One summer, all her grandkids came to stay. There were seven of them. She was too old to keep up with them, so she told the older ones to watch the little ones. The house was big, and she said they could play anywhere, outside or inside, with one exception. They were not allowed to go into the tower room, and never, ever go near the big wooden chest in that room.'

Smiling slyly, Bobbi glanced at the girls. 'Well, you know what kids are like, don't you? Do they ever do what they're told?'

'I do,' murmured Madison, but Ruby grinned proudly, shaking her head. '*I* don't.'

'That's what these children were like. Too curious for their own good. At first, the older ones kept the younger ones in line, but one day, one of the little boys was bored and he decided to go into that tower and see what was there. The only thing in a big empty room was this big old carved wooden chest.'

'Carved how?'

'With designs and things. Pictures of animals and people. The little boy traced these pretty carvings with his finger and made up stories about them until he got bored again and decided to see if there was anything to play with in the chest. So he lifted up the lid and looked in, but it was too dark and the chest was too big, and finally he just had to get inside and feel around and then, while he was sitting there, the lid came down, slowly and quietly. And nobody ever saw that little boy again.'

'Did he yell? Did he scream? Couldn't he push it up again and get out?'

Bobbi shook her head.

'Why didn't they look for him?'

'Oh, they did. They did at first. And his favourite sister went on looking even when the others had given up. And one day she went into the tower room – for about the tenth time – all by herself, and she lifted up the lid of the chest that none of them were supposed to touch, and she could see that it was empty, but just to make sure, she climbed inside, to check that there wasn't a secret compartment, or another way to get out, and slowly and quietly, the lid closed down.'

'No!'

'She had been such a quiet girl that they hardly noticed she was gone, and, after a while, they forgot about her.'

'No!'

'And one day, they were all playing hide and seek, and one little kid went to hide in the chest in the tower room, thinking that nobody would ever find her there – and she was right. And another time, two of them went into it together, thinking, you know, they would protect each other, but again the same thing happened. Finally there was just one girl left, and she meant to be good and mind her grandmother, but one night she was dreaming about her missing cousins, and she got out of bed and went walking in her sleep to the tower, and opened the chest and climbed inside.'

She stopped speaking. The girls stared at her. 'But the parents? Why didn't the grandmother call the police? What happened?'

Bobbi speared a large shrimp, dunked it in the red sauce and ate it. 'Lane made it up. Ask her.'

'I didn't make it up,' said Lane. It had come back to her while she listened. 'I used to tell you stories I'd read – I never made them up myself. That one was written by Walter de la Mare. Back then

I thought it was a ghost story, but now I realize ... He called it "The Riddle", which gives you a clue – really, it was more of an allegory. About memory and the passage of time. The old lady's thoughts were drifting, she remembered the child she had been, her friends, maybe her own children, even grandchildren, now all grown up and lost, the way time takes everyone.'

They all stared at her blankly.

'Ruby, don't play with your food; eat that shrimp, or leave the table.'

'Can we go trick-or-treating at the tower house?' asked Ruby.

Bobbi shook her head. 'Forget it.'

'Why?'

'It's too far, for one thing – '

'It's *not*.'

'And I don't know who lives there.'

'*Please.*'

'It's nicer to go to the neighbours who know you – or know me, anyway.'

'Please, Gamma, please, pretty please can we go to the tower house?'

'No. I said no, and I mean it. Now stop nagging and finish your lunch.'

Lane thought that was the end of it, but after the children had left the room Bobbi suddenly asked, 'So what did happen in the tower house?'

'What?'

'Were you just pretending, to scare me? After you came out. Why wouldn't you talk about it?'

A sense of unreality swept over her, the opposite of *déjà vu*. 'I never went inside that house.'

Bobbi laughed scornfully. 'This is me you're talking to, remember. I saw you with my own eyes.' Reading the bafflement on Lane's face, she slowly shook her head. 'Really? How could you forget?'

'Why would I go into a stranger's house?'

'Because I dared you.'

Suddenly it made sense. They'd played the 'dare' game for a

year or more, and some of Bobbi's challenges would make any parent quail. 'Honestly, I don't remember anything about it.'

'I could never forget,' Bobbi said emphatically. 'I can practically see the look on your face now. And the way you told the story–'

'How?'

'You went into the house, and you met a girl – older than us – who told it to you. All her brothers and sisters and cousins had disappeared into the tower room, and she was afraid to go in to look for them by herself, so you agreed to help. She led you up a winding staircase into the tower room, which was empty except for this big old chest, and while you watched, she opened it and climbed inside, and the lid came down.

'You rushed right over and opened it *immediately* but she was gone! You were leaning in, looking, trying to figure it out but afraid to lean in too far in case you fell inside yourself. It looked completely empty. Then you heard a soft voice speaking behind you, a high old lady voice saying, 'Go in, go in' and you looked around and saw this little old lady – she was only little and frail-looking, but you were sure she meant to try to push you in, so you ran out past her, down the stairs and outside.

'Laney, you were scared. You were as white as a sheet. It was obvious *something* had happened to you. You really don't remember?'

'When is this supposed to have happened?'

'I don't remember the exact date. We were eleven. It was the last time we ever played dares. You told me that was the last dare, and you'd won, and I couldn't argue. You'd never talked to me like that before. And afterwards, you were ... different.' She turned her head sharply. 'What was that?'

'Sounded like a door slam.'

'Ah, that will be Ruby giving Madison the grand tour of the backyard. Coffee?'

'Sure.'

Lane wanted to ask her more about that long-ago dare, but was wary of showing too much interest in something that might be a hoax. If she had gone into a stranger's house and seen something that frightened her, surely she would remember it? She didn't quite trust Bobbi and thought her story might be a Halloween trick to pay her back for all the times Lane had scared her with ghost stories when they were children. And yet, there must be some reason for the hold the tower house had on her imagination. Maybe it would come back to her.

They talked about their children and jobs as the coffee brewed, and then Bobbi remembered she had made chocolate chip cookies. 'I'll call the girls.'

There was no response from the house, or the backyard.

The front yard was a small, bare, open patch of grass and flower beds, with nowhere to hide. Before the echoes of her own voice calling could die away, Bobbi was walking briskly down the street. Fearful and sick at heart, Lane hurried after.

There was no need for discussion; they had the same idea of where the girls had gone. The only question was what route they had taken, and how far ahead they were.

'Maybe we should take the car?'

But turning back, the search for keys, seemed a promise of more delay. Bobbi was power-walking; Lane had to break into a run to catch up to her.

At every corner they paused just long enough to peer down each street, hoping to spot two small figures, but they saw no one except a boy doing lonely wheelies on his bicycle, who shrugged when asked about two little girls, and a man raking leaves, until at last they reached the boulevard.

At the corner of Azalea, Bobbi gasped, 'Ruby!' and Lane squinted against the sun and made out the solitary, diminutive figure dressed in black.

'Where's Madison?' Despite her pounding heart, Lane sprinted forward, intent on grabbing the little girl and shaking the answer out of her, but Bobbi was in her way.

'Don't you ever, ever go off like that without telling me! You are in trouble, young lady, big trouble – no treats for you tonight.'

'Where's Madison?'

Looking scared, the little Goth pointed at the tower house.

'She went inside? When? How long – ' Then she saw Madison stumbling down the walk, a wobble in her course suggesting she'd been forcibly ejected from the house. Lane rushed and caught hold of the child. She was shivering. Freckles stood out boldly on cheeks otherwise drained of colour, her eyes were wide and staring.

'Sweetheart, I'm here, it's all right, you're safe now – oh, what happened? What happened, what did you think you were doing, you silly girl?' She jabbered, a mixture of fear and relief driving her questions and not allowing her to pause and wait for answers. 'Come on, let's go, you can tell us all about it later.' It seemed imperative to get away from this house as far and as fast as possible. Bobbi must have felt the same, for she was already nearly at the end of the street, hustling Ruby along.

Madison moved slowly, leaning on her grandmother and dragging her feet as if the force of gravity were too much. Lane felt wildly impatient, but the child was too big to lift and carry. Then, just as they made it across the boulevard, Madison swooned, and Lane only just managed to catch her dead weight before she hit the ground.

'No! Oh, Madison, wake up,' she groaned, but it was no good, she had fainted.

They sat, the woman supporting the child, like a living pietà on a stranger's front lawn for perhaps as long as a minute before Madison stirred and sat up.

'Sweetie, what happened? Are you all right? What happened? Can you remember?'

Too many questions, but Lane couldn't help herself. 'Honey, tell me, please.'

The little girl opened and closed her mouth a few times before she whispered, 'Save her.'

'What?' She bent closer to catch the faint, breathy little voice.

'She's in the box. Save her.'

'Who?'

But Madison only struggled to her feet and together they walked back to the house on Cranberry Street, where they found Bobbi waiting anxiously, half in, half out of the front door. 'Is she okay?'

'I don't know. She fainted.'

'Come in; what shall we do? Water? Juice?'

'She's cold; could you get a blanket?' Ensconced on the couch, cocooned in a fluffy blue blanket, Madison shut her eyes and relaxed. She fell asleep at once, her breathing shallow but steady.

'Probably best we let her rest,' said Bobbi, looking down with a worried frown before trailing Lane back to the kitchen. Lane picked up her purse. 'You're not going?'

'If I can leave her with you; she needs rest. I won't be long.'

'You're going back there?'

'I need to know what happened. I'll talk to whoever lives there, get their story.'

Bobbi stopped her at the door. 'Wayne will be back at five, he'll go with you.'

'I can't wait.'

'Call the police.'

'And say what, my granddaughter entered a stranger's house and when she came out said . . .' Lane shut her mouth and turned away. 'No. I need to find out if there is a *reason* to call the police, or if it's just . . . kids fooling around.'

'What did she say?'

'A girl in a box.' Lane shook her head, scowling. 'That *story*.'

'Call me,' said Bobbi, following her out the door. 'Call me when you get there.'

Lane got into her car without answering.

'Call me,' Bobbi repeated. 'I mean it. Leave your phone on.'

Too late, as she watched the car leaving, Bobbi remembered they did not have each others' phone numbers.

It had been half an hour. Madison woke as Bobbi was carrying her out to the car.

'What's wrong?'

'Nothing. Go back to sleep.' As she started the car, she heard the girls whispering to each other in the backseat. She glanced in the rearview mirror and saw Madison sitting up. Her colour was better and she looked more alert.

'Oh, no,' said Ruby as they turned onto Azalea, and when Bobbi stopped the car in front of a driveway, 'Gamma, no!'

There was no sign of Lane's car. Bobbi opened her door.

'Don't go in there!'

'Ruby, settle down. I am just going to knock on the door. You kids wait right here.'

Ruby moaned as her grandmother got out of the car, and Madison whispered, 'It's okay, it's okay now, she's not there.'

No one answered the knock on the door, and the bell made no sound. Tentatively, she tried turning the knob, but the door was locked. A scattering of dusty advertising flyers littered the doormat. The longer she stood there, the more Bobbi felt that no one was home, and the more frightened she became.

The police broke down the door. The house was empty and appeared to have been unoccupied for many months. There were a few pieces of furniture, but nothing in the tower room, and nothing anywhere remotely like the carved wooden chest Bobbi insisted they had to find.

The police were polite, and as patient as they could be, but they must have thought she was a crazy old bat. Ms. Alverson was a competent adult. There was no reason to believe any harm had come to her, and certainly no reason to put out an alert, especially as her own daughter was of the opinion that her mother, who had been a reluctant and difficult guest, had probably made a spur-of-the-moment decision to go home early.

Bobbi never saw or heard from Lane Alverson again. Only in her dreams, she sometimes heard her old friend calling, but when she went to look, the room was empty, except for the presence, inexplicably sinister, of a carved wooden chest.

No matter how many times she had the dream (and it would haunt her the rest of her life), Bobbi never dared to open it.

A Home in the Sky

Cara longed for her own home as once she had wished for a lover.

It annoyed her, how much time and energy she had wasted in her twenties and early thirties, as dreamy and thoughtless as if she had all the time in the world. She had spent too much on clothes and holidays, money she should have saved and invested. Even if she found the love of her life and they married, he might not be rich. Fate was not her fairy godmother.

She had been happy sharing flats with friends, but over the years those friends had peeled away into marriage, motherhood, a house in the country or jobs abroad. Cara's job was in London, and it was the only place she had ever wanted to live, but renting was a zero-sum game. There was no security except for the owner-occupier as rents continued to rise. Even if she gave up every little luxury, after she had paid all the bills, there was nothing left to save for a deposit on any sort of London property.

Moving back in with her parents had not been an easy decision, but it enabled her to save. After two years, she was sure to have enough money for a deposit on her first home: small, in one of the outer suburbs, not ideal, but it would be a beginning, the vital first rung on the property ladder. She had only to sit tight and wait it out. It could be worse.

People often said about things remembered from childhood: 'It seems so much smaller.' Cara felt that about her old room. It no longer fit.

Her parents had been kind enough to clear their spare room and let her furnish it entirely, and now it was filled with the stuff she had acquired over the years, things she would want in her new home, packed into boxes. Piled high, they left just enough room for her bed and chest of drawers, with a narrow pathway clear to the door. When she retreated, craving solitude, exhausted by her parents' well-meaning attempts to include her in their lives, all she could do was huddle on her bed with her laptop and headphones.

Her parents had not shrunk in scale with their home. Instead, she had the awful feeling that they had expanded. They certainly took up far more space than she remembered, and in the narrow, low-ceilinged rooms she was forever getting in their way or colliding with some piece of furniture. Even her room offered small escape; she was always aware of them living their lives on the other side of the thin walls, watching rubbish TV and shouting at each other – not in anger, but because they'd grown deaf. It was like being in hospital, she thought, where existence was concentrated in the span of a single bed, screened off by curtains beyond which other dramas played out on and around the other beds, unseen but not unheard.

She stayed away as much as she could; went out early and came home late from work, wishing she could afford more of a social life and making do with long walks.

One evening, walking slowly back from the random overground station at which she had alighted, Cara saw something strange: a house in the sky.

It was not floating there, but fixed – apparently atop some distant hill – but where was there such a hill in this densely populated sector of South London?

She felt dizzy for a moment, stopped and stared at this vision through the trees, trying to make sense of it, telling herself it must be an optical illusion. There was undoubtedly some perfectly ordinary explanation – she simply had not walked down this street before, so of course she had not noticed ... whatever it was.

Lately she had taken to getting off at different stations south of the river, taking pleasure in the exercise in the mild summer evenings, not minding the risk of getting lost when she was in no hurry to get back to her parents' house. Unplanned detours could result in interesting discoveries – like this.

The street on which she found herself was generically familiar: rows of detached villas and the occasional bungalow with tiny front gardens or parking areas. Mature trees lined both sides of the street. She took another quick, shifty glance at the sky, and was almost surprised to see the house had not disappeared. It looked like a new build, a plain modern box, white painted walls beneath a sloping black roof, a shiny black front door with a window on either side – as simple as a child's drawing.

There must be a hill or high point she had not previously noticed. Houses didn't spring up overnight like mushrooms, but maybe a pre-fab kit-house could be assembled in a week or two. Or it might be visible only from this street, from a particular angle.

Determined to solve the mystery, Cara continued walking ahead, keeping her eyes fixed on the view above the rooftops, through the leafy summer branches of the trees, until she turned a corner, and there it was.

What she had taken for a normal-sized house on a hill in the distance was in reality a very small house set up on a scaffold.

Below the model house she saw a fenced-off area of rough ground, a building site in waiting. A hoarding affixed to the fence promised six new homes to be priced between £250,000-£295,000, and there was an artist's impression, a row of neat, cheerful white houses with bushes and flower beds in front. The picture reminded her of an illustration from an old Ladybird book – old-fashioned even in her childhood. The image was simple, stereotyped, yet somehow embodied a promise of comfort and stability and stirred a nostalgic yearning.

She wondered at the little house – presumably it was meant to attract potential buyers, but a one-dimensional theatre flat would have been just as effective an advertisement, and surely easier to make. What she was looking at was not the doll's-house-sized scale model you might find in an architect's office, but a three-dimensional structure at least as big as a garden shed.

Cara walked around the base of the scaffold and examined it from all sides, taking its measure. The front door had a shiny brass-coloured doorknob. There was no back door, but there were windows on three sides – not just painted on, but real – fitted with clear panes, through which she could see curtains.

Frowning, she stopped and stared harder, and noticed a wire running from the rooftop to an overhead power line. Yet she couldn't see spotlights, or any other obvious need for electricity. What was it for?

Her heart beat faster as she recognized how easy it would be to climb up one side of the scaffold – not quite as simple as mounting a ladder, the struts weren't set close enough together, but she could do it.

Turning sharply, she looked around. Fences and the blank brick sides of houses stared blindly back. No one was watching; there was no one to see what she did.

She checked the straps of her rucksack to make sure it was well-settled, then stepped forward and hauled herself up to the first rung, steadied herself, and began her ascent.

In a matter of moments, she was standing on a narrow wooden platform, facing the house. The smooth metal doorknob turned easily in her hand. The door opened.

She had to duck her head to enter, but once inside she found she could stand erect. She was surprised by how large it was, how comfortable the space felt around her. The air smelled good, of new wood and paint, the odour of new beginnings. She couldn't see much; it was darker inside, and the windows let in only a faint, ambient glow.

Reaching almost unconsciously to the left, her hand found a light switch on the wall and pressed it. Recessed lighting came on, and Cara saw the whole room for the first time. It was a bit like a bedsit she'd once considered renting, but nicer. A pleasant, surprisingly spacious atmosphere had been created by careful design and the use of neutral colours. There was a plump-cushioned two-seater couch, a side table with drawers, a table that could double as a desk, two matching wooden chairs, and a neat little *armoire*. One corner was a kitchenette, and in the opposite corner was a door that must lead into the bathroom.

Must? She laughed at herself, but was sure she was right; all the evidence revealed that this little house, despite its unusual location, had been designed as a place to live.

The sound of a toilet flushing startled her, but before she could decide what to do, the door opened and a man came out.

He was young, very thin, and wore a cheap-looking, shiny grey suit. His eyes widened in surprise, and Cara jumped in first: 'What are you doing here?'

'Ah.' Nervously, he glanced around, then stooped and grabbed a briefcase off the floor. She had not noticed it, half-hidden where it leaned against the couch.

'Working,' he said, brandishing the briefcase as proof. 'A little bit late, I know, but I was about to leave, when – ' He stopped and looked at her more intently. 'You're not from the company.'

'Yes I am,' she said quickly.

He shook his head. 'I don't know you.'

'I don't know you either, but I know you shouldn't be here.'

But she had lost her brief advantage as he gained in confidence. 'Of course I should. This is my *job*. But it is late. I wasn't expecting any more visitors today.'

She blinked at him, confused. 'What do you mean? What job? What *is* this place?'

He looked surprised by the question, but sure of himself. 'A model home, of course. A scaled-down version of what will be down below. Mr Lancaster thought it would be a good gimmick to attract attention – in a crowded market you always need something to make your product stand out. Would you care for a cup of tea? While I show you the prospectus?'

He set his case down on the table and snapped it open to reveal stacks of printed papers.

'No, thank you.'

'At least take one away with you. And if you wouldn't mind filling this out?'

She took the full colour, three-fold brochure, but looked askance at the A4 sheet with rows of questions and boxes for her answers that he flapped at her.

'It's okay,' he said quickly. 'Really. Don't bother with all of it, just your name and email or phone number is enough.'

'Why?'

'Contact details, so the company can send you more information. You *are* interested in buying a home?'

She looked down at the brochure, to avoid the view of his bad skin, red-rimmed eyes, and hungry expression. 'Yes, yes I am looking to buy.'

'Great! You have come to the right place.'

Beautiful, modern detached homes starting at £250,000.

Cara sighed with frustrated longing. 'Too expensive.'

She tried to give him back the brochure, but he backed away, shaking his head. 'Are you kidding? In this area? It's a fantastic opportunity, and a great investment. Get in now, while you can, before they're built – prices will only go up. You need to think long-term, stretch yourself a little –'

'Thank you for the advice,' she said coldly, and stuffed the brochure into a side pocket of her rucksack. 'I'll get in touch if I win the lottery.'

'Wait – at least give me your name and details, so I can show I tried.'

He sounded plaintive and she almost relented, but really it was too absurd. What sort of employer would invent such a scheme? How could he be expected to gather data, or interest potential buyers, perched up above the ground like this? How many people, besides herself, would climb up on a whim?

Eager to escape, she made no reply but moved quickly towards the door. She was aware that he followed, even when she stepped outside, but she did not look back until she heard him scream.

'What?' She whirled to find him staring open-mouthed, eyes bulging. 'What's wrong?'

'Bastards! Bastards!'

'Who?'

'Fucking cunts took the stairs!'

His explanation tumbled out, and she understood that he had expected to find a movable staircase – she imagined something like the steps wheeled up to airplanes for embarking and disembarking passengers. According to him, it was part of his job to wheel it away and store it safely overnight behind the fence around the building site. And now, someone had stolen his exit.

It must have been a professional operation, thieves coming pre-pared with bolt cutters and a vehicle large enough to transport it, and doing their thievery so quickly and silently that he had heard nothing.

The young man was clearly distressed, taking it personally, on the verge of tears, and Cara naturally pitied him, and offered to help. But he struggled to compose himself, and said roughly that he was perfectly able to report the theft to the police and to his employers. 'I'll wait until they get here, but you – ' Again, he looked helpless. 'But how can *you* get down?'

'Same way I got up. Watch me.'

Cara put the whole strange experience out of her mind. The weather turned wet, so she travelled by bus rather than walk, and took more direct routes. Summer was nearly over before she came upon the brochure lying wet and crumpled in her rucksack, and noted the name of the development company: Perger, Gallane & Lancaster.

Having nothing better to do, she searched for details online and discovered that the website had been taken down. She was redirected to a static page with contact details for Perger & Gallane in Brussels, and Lancaster Estates in London. She rang the London number.

The perky voice that answered the phone gave the name of a well-known estate agency, and fell silent when she asked about Lancaster Estates. She heard the faint sound of keyboard click-ing. 'Lancaster Estates has ceased trading. I really don't know any more than that.'

'But this was the number given for enquiries.'

'Of course. Well, we did handle the sale of a few properties, but that's finished. What was your enquiry?'

'I was just curious about one thing. There was a building site with planning permission for six homes ...'

'That will have been sold. However, if you are interested in an opportunity for development, we do have a number of properties on our books ...'

Although the speaker's cultured voice and smooth manner

were nothing like that of the young man she had met in the house above the building site a few weeks earlier, it was his thin, tired, acne-scarred face she saw in her mind's eye.

'No, I'm not looking for anything like that at the moment, thank you. I'm sorry to have troubled you,' she said, quickly ending the conversation.

Her curiosity had not been satisfied, but rather stimulated, and the very next day after work she decided, since it was warm and dry, to retrace the steps of her previous journey. She could find out for herself if the little house was still there.

After a few false turns she found the right street and was able again to see the surreal vision of a distant house floating in the sky, glimpsed through the tops of the trees. Excitement quickened her footsteps, but then she slowed, wondering what had become of the thin young man in his cheap suit and briefcase full of glossy brochures. Surely he could have been paid no more than a pittance for handing out brochures and collecting details of potential buyers, but it might have been worth more than that to him, if he had made his office his home. His employer might have turned a blind eye to it – if they even guessed. When he lost his job, probably without any notice –

Cara was convinced by her own chain of logic. The man she had met had been squatting – and probably still was. No one would abandon a rent-free home in London – especially one as nice as that – unless he was forced out.

She arrived at the building site in a jittery, unpleasant mood, feeling envious and angry. Who was he to have such a sweet little home in the sky – for nothing – when she had worked hard all her life and could only camp out in her parents' house while struggling to save up enough money to qualify for a mortgage on a maisonette or a mid-terrace, something that would not have half the charm of what was hardly more than an architectural folly, a treehouse without a tree, where the occupant could look down on the dull earth-dwellers and laugh.

A light rain started to fall. What was she doing here? The building site looked the same as before, pointlessly fenced off from the street, still with the sign advertising an artist's impression of homes worth over £250,000 each. When she looked up at the house that had brought her here, that still called to her imagination, she felt puzzled by the sight, and frowned as she tried to figure out what was different about it.

She squinted up through the raindrops and the gathering darkness. It looked smaller than she remembered. Or was the scaffold higher?

The only way to find out was to climb up. The rain was getting heavier, but she knew that if she left now she might never return, so, after checking that the nearest strut felt secure and strong enough to take her weight, she pulled herself up and began to climb.

It did not take long, no longer than the first time, and when she stood in front of it she could see quite clearly how much smaller it was than the house in her memory. The peak of the pitched roof came only to her chin. She would have to walk through the door in a crouch. Other details had changed as well. The windows were only painted on; the shiny doorknob was glued to the door. When she could not turn it, she tugged, and then, getting no response, she pushed, leaning into the door, and used the whole weight of her body to push until it suddenly gave way.

Surprised, she stumbled as she fell inside. Her head bashed painfully against the lintel, and the sharp, unfinished edges of the narrow frame sliced into her arms, tearing her sleeves and cutting her skin.

Head spinning with pain and confusion, Cara struggled to rise. Her head bumped the ceiling and she was forced to hunch over, nearly to crouch. How could that be? She remembered clearly how easily she had stood erect when she was here before, and even the young man, who must have been six inches taller than she was, had been in no danger of hitting his head. There had been space and light and air and the fresh smell of wood and paint, not this terrible stench. It smelled like something had died in here.

This could not be the same place.

It was too dark to see much, with the only light coming from the half-open door behind her, but there was something that might have been a couch or a table shoved up against the back wall. She pulled out her phone and pressed it, to use the light from the screen to see what was there.

In its brief flare she saw the thin, ravaged face of the young man she had met last month. His eyes were open but unseeing. His flesh had started to decompose.

She screamed and lurched backwards, bashed her head, fell to the floor, sobbed with pain and fear and scrabbled desperately for the door. Where was it? She could not find the opening. Had she knocked it shut when she was flailing about? At least she had managed to keep hold of her phone; it had gone into screensaver mode, and she jabbed it, desperate for light.

But even with its aid she could not see a door. It seemed to have shut itself so firmly as to merge with the walls. When the phone went dark she did not press it again but waited, letting her eyes adjust, and tried to pick out the exit by the thin lines of light that should have come through naturally around the edges. Even if night had fallen, there were streetlamps, the eternal ambient glow of the city.

There was no light, and no way out. It was as if there had never been a door, as if there had never been any way in or out of the box in which she was trapped.

It was only a box. She ought to be able to break through. She remembered the cheap, insubstantial look of the painted plywood from outside, and began to beat her fists against the wall, harder and harder. She tried to force an opening with her shoulders and the weight of her body, but the walls were more solid than they had appeared. Her arms were sore and her hands were bleeding when she fell back and used her feet, which had the protection of shoes.

It was no good. At last, exhausted, she lay back on the rough wooden floor. She felt she was hyperventilating and tried to slow her breathing. But she could not properly fill her lungs. It must be panic, a wooden box with a door could not possibly be air-tight, she told herself, and tried to relax. She was light-headed, not thinking clearly — perhaps she'd suffered concussion when she hit her head.

She was trapped, yes, but not forever. She could call for help.

Not her parents, of course – they would not know what to do. Too bad her best friends lived so far away now. She tried to think of someone in the area, someone cool-headed and practical whose number was in her phone and who would come right away without wasting time on too many questions. Then she knew that her increasing dizziness and difficulty in drawing breath meant there was no time to waste, and she had better call 999 while she was still capable of giving directions.

At that moment, her phone gave the final, despairing bleep that meant the battery had died.

The darkness that surrounded her was absolute.

Voices in the Night

Katya had come to the city of necessity, to work.

By birth, upbringing and inclination she was a country-woman, but after the loss of the family farm, there was nothing left for her, and although she felt too old for such a radical new beginning, as always she did what was required.

Without friends or family to help, lacking in experience as she was, she did not feel hopeful; but, after all, there were plenty of jobs in the city. She found work almost immediately in an old people's home.

Finding a new home for herself was more difficult. Rents were high in the city and her wages low. For the time being she stayed in a hotel that offered discounted rates for long-term residents – the sort of place that relied on low-paid workers to fill its rooms. It was old and shabby but clean, located on a quiet street in a slightly run-down commercial district, an area devoted to offices, small factories and the occasional shop, with nothing to attract noisy customers at any hour. Katya thought she would be able to get a good night's sleep there.

She was wrong. Although the bed was more comfortable than the sagging old mattress she'd been used to, the small room felt hot and airless with the window closed, and with it open the bare two inches it had been fixed to allow, all the noises of the city assaulted her ears. Every eruption of car horn, squeal of brakes or distant siren jolted her awake, and even when it was quiet, it was never *really* quiet, not as she thought of it: the city grunted, snored and muttered even when it seemed to sleep. She tried ear-plugs, but they caused a muffled effect that made her anxious. She didn't like to think she might miss something that she ought to have heard: a shouted warning or cry for help.

Eventually, through experience, her sleeping mind learned to filter out the things she did not need to hear, and within a few weeks she slept through the night, the normal ambience of the city beyond her window no more upsetting than the country sounds she had known all her life.

Two and a half months into her new life Katya woke suddenly, heart pounding, to the sound of voices – many voices. For one confused moment she did not understand what was happening, but imagined someone had called her name.

She fumbled for her phone and saw the time: 2:43. Outside the voices went on – not screaming, but conversational, amplified as they echoed off the street and walls around about. It sounded as if a great many people had gathered in the street just below her window. She could think of only one likely reason, but how had she slept through a fire alarm? Perhaps not in the hotel itself, but in a neighbouring building . . . yet what alarm? Apart from the voices, everything was as still and silent as you'd expect at this hour.

Rolling off the bed, she took two steps to the window and pulled aside the curtain to look out. Beneath the yellow glow of the lights, the street was deserted. She stared, bewildered, as the voices continued to boom.

Across the street from the hotel, occupying the entire block, was a disused factory. She had never seen anyone go in or out and the building appeared derelict, but maybe it was not as empty as she thought. Maybe squatters had moved in, and they were holding a party to celebrate, or it had been commandeered for one of those late-night events – did young people still call them 'raves'?

But she could hear no music, only voices, and the voices were too blurred and distorted for her to have any idea of what they might be saying. Hard as she tried, she could not make out a single intelligible word. It was just noise – human noise – amplified not intentionally by technology but, she presumed, by acoustical effects caused by the specific shape and structure of wherever they were gathered, hidden from her view.

Gradually, the voices died away. Within an hour, they were

gone. But they continued to haunt Katya, a puzzle that would not let her relax.

The next night it happened again. This time, she did not get up. She tried to will herself to ignore them and fall back to sleep, but the noise was too intrusive. She could not tune out the voices, and she could not understand what they were about.

The ebb and flow sounded conversational, if not exactly relaxed, but occasionally she heard a cry – once, a long, wailing sound abruptly cut off – and then it was all she could do not to go to the window and call, 'Are you all right? What's wrong?' She told herself that laughter could sound like crying, but was not convinced. Whatever was going on out there, it was *wrong*.

The next day she spoke to the hotel manager about it.

He gave her a fishy stare. 'Voices – outside? What about it? *How* late?' He sniffed, disbelieving. 'People passing by? No one else has complained. You can hardly expect absolute silence at any time. But *that* street – I cannot imagine what you think you heard. Better speak to your neighbours. One of them was probably watching TV.'

That was the end of the discussion. Katya would have to solve this mystery herself. That evening after work, tired as she was, she went out to investigate.

It was summer, so the evening was long and light. A faded painted sign on the side of the disused building across the street revealed that it had formerly been a corset factory. Now the windows were shuttered, and the big, arched entrance was barred and locked. She guessed at a yard or loading area behind the heavy wooden double doors. The opening would be wide enough to accommodate a lorry, or even a double-decker bus. But there were no gaps or knotholes to peek through – not even a keyhole. A steel bar was secured with a heavy metal lock. Without the key, no one could gain entry this way. She walked around to the next street, where the back of the building pre-sented nothing but a long, windowless expanse of high wall, blank except for a weathered sign advertising COMMERCIAL PREMISES AVAILABLE FOR LEASE. Evidently there was no other way in.

She took a picture of the sign, to have a note of the phone number. Although it was not a conversation she was eager to initiate, at least now she had a way to get in touch with whoever owned the property. They should be informed if someone was using it illegally; if they already knew about it, she would complain to them about the noise.

But that night, she heard nothing.

Not until several nights later, when she had got out of the habit of expecting them, did the familiar booming echoes of distant voices wake her again.

Rising, she went to the window. The street outside was as empty as it ought to be at three a.m. From her position she could not see if the factory gates were still locked shut. In the morning, she told herself, she would call the owner. She could not imagine any other source of that noise, and yet, until she was certain . . . the thought of a faceless stranger on the phone being as disbelieving and dismissive as the hotel manager had been made her clench her teeth.

Grimly determined to know the truth, Katya got dressed and left her room.

Never had she known the place so quiet. Not a footstep, no hum of machinery, not even a gurgle of water in the pipes. Slipping silently down two flights of stairs, she wondered if anyone else in the whole building was awake.

Outside, in the empty, lamplit street it was nearly as quiet. Where were the voices? They had sounded so loud in her room, but she could hear nothing now. Surely there had not been time enough for a crowd of people to disperse.

She hurried across the street. As she drew near the entrance she saw that the bar was down, unlocked, and one side of the double door hung ajar. And she could hear voices.

They did not sound as loud booming echoes, but as more normally pitched voices. Most were little more than low murmurs. Someone was crying. The painful sound tore at her heart, reminding her of her mother near the end of her life.

She slipped inside. There she found the space she had imagined: a large paved yard surrounded by concrete walls but open to the sky; a well in which every small sound was echoed and magnified as it was broadcast to the air above.

It was full of people, a crowd of forty or fifty, she guessed. As her eyes adapted still more to the dark she saw there were both men and women, mostly middle-aged or older, with a sprinkling of younger men. She was struck by *separate* they all were. This was surely a crowd of strangers, no coherent group. Like travellers in an airport, or commuters waiting for a bus, they ignored everyone else in their focus on their own concerns.

What she had overheard was not any number of conversations, but individuals talking to themselves. Now she could see that none of them spoke to or even looked at anyone else. They conducted private monologues, rehearsed grievances, or worried aloud. At least, that was Katya's interpretation, for she still understood nothing of what she heard. She didn't think they spoke foreign languages, but she could not know, unable to distinguish any single words or phrases; the sounds remained incomprehensible as voices cut across each other and bounced and echoed in the enclosed space, a babble that made her head hurt.

She began to regret her rash decision. But as she turned to leave, she saw an old woman against the wall, near the entrance. She wore a long white dress – surely a nightgown – and her face was screwed up in obvious distress. A high despairing wail came from her gaping mouth and sent a shiver coursing through Katya's very bones.

She forgot she had meant to leave and responded as she would to one of her old ladies in the home.

'There, there, it's all right, dear. I'm here now. Let me help you. Here, take my arm.'

The old woman, cut off in mid-wail, fixed her watery blue gaze on Katya's gentle smile. Her fearful expression relaxed, and she moved to rest a cold little hand on Katya's proffered arm. Her lips moved, she smiled, but her gaze remained utterly vacant.

Katya's heart sank. What now? This was not the care home, and she had no idea what to do with this poor old soul.

Surely she had not come here on her own. Yet, as her gaze once more swept the crowd, Katya could see no one less self-absorbed than the others, no one who appeared to be looking for a missing relative. But she did notice another figure nearby, crouching in the shadow of the wall, and although it was only a faint hope, she steered the old woman in that direction.

'Hello? Excuse me?' The words were scarcely out of her mouth before she realized the figure was not crouching but standing. It was a child; the first she had seen in this strange gathering. Well, children might look after their grandparents as well as the other way round, and while at first, from his size, she was expecting a four-year-old, when she saw his face she revised that impression. Stunted and undernourished he might be, but surely old enough to cope with one weak old lady.

'Look, who's this?' She pressed her companion, but the old lady remained unresponsive. The boy likewise gave no sign of recognition or welcome, and she was forced to press him: 'Is this your Nan? Nana? Granny? Hello? Answer me, please!' Her tone sharpened and she raised her voice, trying to get a response.

The dark eyes set deep in the thin, drawn little face shifted towards her and the narrow lips parted. A torrent of meaningless sounds poured out.

That was no language, but the sound of madness.

Her skin crawled. Reflexively she stepped back, causing the old lady to stumble.

'Oh!' Catching her roughly around the waist, Katya managed to arrest her fall. 'There, there, you're all right. I've got you.'

She looked frightened, trembling, and opened her mouth. But instead of a wail, to Katya's relief, the pale lips emitted a dry little chuckle.

A second, louder chuckle came from the boy. There was no expression on the shrivelled young-old face, nothing to indicate if the sound was anything more than a mindless echo.

These two . . . Katya shuddered. She felt they *were* a pair, they belonged together, although clearly incapable of looking after themselves. She wondered who was in charge here. There must be someone she could pass this unwanted burden on to, she thought, looking around. To her shock, the crowd had grown smaller. In the few moments in which she had been distracted by the boy, the yard had nearly emptied. A booming clatter of voices still filled the air, but she saw only a dozen individuals.

As if they'd been given orders, they were all moving slowly in the same direction, towards the far end of the yard. Supporting the old lady with one arm around her, Katya hurried her along after them.

There was a recess in the wall, with stone steps leading down. That was where the others had gone. Katya stared at the retreating backs and addressed the nearest person: 'Excuse me ... will you wait? Stop a minute please.'

He paid her no attention, nor did the next one, although she continued, her voice rising with her increasing desperation. 'Please! Help us! This old lady needs your help. At least tell me where you are going?'

They might have been blind as well as deaf for all the notice they took. Each was locked into his or her own little world, obsessed with their own concerns, muttering away to themselves in their own language with no attention to spare. Even when Katya was driven to grab one woman's arm it made no difference; she did not look at her or pause, just continued relentlessly on until Katya was forced to let go, or be pulled after her down the stairs.

She next tried to release her unwanted companion – reasoning that having got this far on her own, the old lady might be left to find her own place among the crowd – but as she loosened her grasp on her waist, the old lady wrapped her own arms around Katya.

She clung like a limpet. Her legs went slack. She felt much heavier now that she was not supporting herself, and Katya realized that if she was not careful they would likely both fall down the steps, and quickly gave up the undignified struggle.

She saw that she had two choices, equally unappealing. She could take the old lady to the authorities – at this time of night, it must be the police – and let them deal with the problem of a nameless, homeless, demented, unknown person, or she could take her down the steps, allowing (or forcing) her to go wherever she was meant to go with the others.

Katya could not imagine how she would explain herself to the police. And it is always easier, especially in a queue, to continue moving forward.

The steps were wide, solid and dry, and there weren't too many. When they ended, there was a short tunnel, and then she found herself with everyone else outside, standing on the built-up bank of the river.

Katya knew the city was built on a river, and she had seen it often enough from the windows of a bus, but she had not thought it ran so near her hotel, and was surprised to find it here, hidden away below street level. She looked up and across to the other side, but she did not recognize the backs of buildings she had never seen from this angle, or at night when everything always looked different.

The voices were stilled as everyone waited in silence for whatever they expected to happen next. Katya found herself standing near a woman with a lined and kindly face; something about her reminded her of a teacher from her schooldays, and she seemed like someone she could trust to look after the old woman, if she could just get her attention. Unable to catch her eye, Katya opened her mouth, but closed it again. It seemed wrong to break the silence, as awful to speak as it would be to shout during silent prayer in church. The other woman's attention, like that of everyone else, was fixed upon the river ahead – and now she saw the reason.

A strange, old-fashioned kind of boat – something like a gondola, or a punt – was gliding closer, propelled by a pole operated by a mysteriously robed and hooded figure standing in the stern.

It drew up to the shore, and the waiting crowd surged forward. They boarded the boat, one by one, without hesitation, argument or conflict. Somehow, each seemed to know when to wait and when to take his or her turn, although they achieved the same end in different ways. Some lowered themselves slowly and gently from a sitting position and others hopped down. Katya was surprised by the courtesy this formerly selfish crowd demonstrated, with the more able-bodied assisting the weaker ones; it gave her fresh hope that her old lady would get the help she needed, even though she worried how she would know when it was her turn. She was still clinging like a limpet, showing no inclination to move.

As the crowd cleared, Katya hauled her reluctant companion closer to the river, looking around for someone who might help. But the boarding process was going too quickly; finally there was only one man left standing on the bank, and as she opened her mouth to call out to him, he broke into a run and took a flying leap off the bank.

Already heavily laden, it rocked and wallowed, then veered away from the shore.

The pilot pushed down hard on his pole and the boat steadied; then, as he pushed down again, the boat moved – not back in place as Katya hoped and expected, but further away. As she stared, open-mouthed, disbelieving, it glided steadily on down the river until it looked like nothing more than a shadow, merging with the surrounding darkness.

'I don't believe it,' she muttered. Then she sighed. 'It'll be the police, after all. And how am I supposed to get up and go to work in a few hours, after dealing with you? You might at least be a bit more helpful.'

The old lady made no reply, but neither did she resist; although she still clung fixedly to Katya, at least she was walking again, no longer a dead weight to be pushed and carried.

The little boy stood in front of them.

How could she have forgotten? He was now her responsibility, as well. She sighed to herself, and opened her mouth to say something. Mirroring her, he opened his mouth, and made a low hissing sound.

The hostile sound pulled her up short. She stared into the deep, impossibly deep, darkness inside his mouth. It wasn't *all* dark – as in the clear night skies over her lost home there glittered a myriad of tiny, brilliant points of light. But how could the sky be inside his mouth? She felt awed and terrified. She wanted to close her eyes against the sight, but was afraid of making herself more vulnerable, so instead she turned her face away, which saved her from having to witness that impossible vision, while still allowing her to see if the boy made a move against her.

A soft splashing sound called her back to the river, where an empty boat, identical to the first, was approaching. It drew up by the bank and waited.

The old woman had started snoring, asleep on her feet as she leaned unconcerned against her protector. The boy stood where he was, blocking the way to the tunnel and steps.

Katya gently woke the old woman and managed to get her to stand unaided, then propelled her towards the river, pointing and miming in an attempt to make the old woman understand what she must do. The boatman was no help – he stood stock-still and wouldn't even look in their direction – and she had been too frightened by the boy to consider approaching him again. At last she decided there was nothing else for it: she must get into the boat herself, and help the old woman down after her.

She sat down on the bank and gently lowered herself feet-first. Despite her caution, the boat rocked as wildly as if an elephant had jumped in. 'Didn't think I was *that* heavy,' she muttered, and then told herself it was probably just because the boat was nearly empty. It stabilized quickly enough.

When she felt certain it was stable, Katya looked up at the old woman on the shore and reached out her arms, giving an encouraging smile and nodding her head.

The old woman frowned and then hugged herself and began to back away.

'Silly old thing – come here! I'm trying to help – give me your hands –'

The blank expression gave way to a look of horror, and suddenly the woman was propelled forward by a powerful shove and almost flew off the bank. Then she fell, plummeting into the boat, knocking Katya flat.

For a moment she could not move with the old woman lying shivering and crying on top of her. Then, pricked by terror, she struggled to get up.

'What the – let me up – get off me, I have to –'

In the endless seconds it took to free herself, Katya felt the boat veering away from the bank and out into the swift flow of the river.

'No! Not me – Take me back! You must take me back!' – That, or something like it, was what she meant to say, but the words flew out all broken and wrong. She abandoned words for a long, keening wail, and then she clutched at the boatman, determined to make him do what she wished. There was no one – no living being – beneath the long, hooded coat, only some sort of mechanism, roughly man-shaped, attached to the pole that drove the boat.

Katya tried to turn the boat around, but the pole would not respond to her hand, no matter what she did.

The old woman sat in the bottom of the boat, staring fixedly into the darkness ahead. Katya saw no lights, no sign of the city that should have been there. A feeling of revulsion made her turn away. She looked back at the shore and wondered what had happened to the boy. Had he run away after pushing the old woman?

'It should be *him* on the boat, not me. *Him*,' she muttered angrily. 'It's all his fault I'm here with her.'

He had escaped. She could not see him on the river bank.

But something was there – some sort of animal, skulking in the darkness and now loping along beside the river. From its size and shape it could only be a dog – or even a wolf – but there was something not right, something wrong with it that made her crane her neck and frown and squint to see it. Were there *three* dogs? But, no: she counted four legs, one tail, one – no, *three* heads.

A dog with three heads was running after the boat. A moment later it disappeared along with everything else, and she saw nothing but darkness.

The Hungry Hotel

I never told anyone I knew him, and in fact I hardly knew him at all.

It happened more than twenty years ago, when I was twenty-two and engaged to Marshall, who was away all summer, doing an internship out of state. Our impending separation had pushed him to propose. We loved each other and all that, three months wasn't going to make any difference to our feelings, but the formality of an engagement was better, it left no room for doubt.

I never even thought about being unfaithful, and didn't imagine I could be tempted. So I can't explain why, when this cute but short and dark and scruffy character (he couldn't have been more different from Marshall) looked at me, and our eyes met for a moment, I responded as if I'd gone into that bar desperate to hook up with some guy. In fact, I was only there because I was supposed to be meeting a girlfriend – she was the one who wanted to hear the band – but she bailed at the last minute.

When he came over, I let him buy me my low-alcohol beer, and we talked as best we could in that noisy place – I could hardly hear a word he said, but it didn't matter because our bodies were having their own conversation. When he indicated the crumpled pack of cigarettes in his shirt pocket, although I didn't smoke, I went outside with him. We sat in my car and made out for about an hour. We didn't do more than kiss, but that was a lot.

He had to go – his band was doing the second set – and asked if I would wait for him. Could we get together after the show?

Breathless, dizzy, drunk on his kisses, I agreed.

But I did not follow him inside. I got behind the wheel and drove away. There was no light on in our apartment, and as I drew in, I remembered: Lauren was spending the night with her boyfriend. So I kept on driving. I don't know how long I drove, past familiar landmarks and around the campus where I used to be a student, before entering neighbourhoods unknown to me, where dark, winding roads doubled back on themselves or turned into dead-ends.

I drove without aim or destination until I finally ended up back in the parking lot behind the bar and he was standing there, smoking. His face lit up when he saw me.

'I thought you must have changed your mind,' he said, getting into the car. 'I told myself, I'll give it one more cigarette.'

I said, 'I must be crazy. I have a boyfriend; I mean, my fiancé.'

'But he's not here, and I am.' He put his hand on my leg. 'We don't have to *do* anything. I'd like to get to know you, and spend some time with you. Just – whatever you want. I'm going away in a couple of days. I sure don't want to mess up your life.'

I asked him if he had a hotel room. No. The band had been put up in a borrowed house, sharing bedrooms. It might be empty now, but the others would turn up sooner or later; there would be no privacy. But if I didn't mind, if I only wanted to hang out . . .

I told him again that I was engaged. I said I couldn't risk it; I couldn't stand it if somehow word got back to Marshall that I'd been hanging out with some strange guys. Would I have been so worried about how it would look if it was an innocent friendship? Of course not. But I already knew – we both did – that it wasn't innocent. Those kisses.

So I took him to my place. This would be a very different story if my roomie had been home that night. But I knew she wouldn't be, just like I knew we would do more than talk.

It's funny, though, because while you might think sex was the main thing – it was what our encounter was all about, this unexpected, inconvenient, undeniable physical desire that had drawn us together, and it was certainly the aspect of our time together that Marshall might have considered unforgivable – it isn't what I remember.

Of course I don't mean I've forgotten the things we did that night in my bed; I remember his lips and his hands and his skin, how smooth it was, and how good it felt against mine, in places

I hadn't thought of before as erogenous zones – and yes the erotic details would come back to me for a long time afterwards. That's not the point. He wasn't a better lover than Marshall, just different.

What I remember most about that night is how much we talked, and that we never slept. We were each too excited and disturbed by the presence of the other to finally let go and fall asleep. So you could say that we made love or had sex, but we never slept together.

When I was little, before I knew what were called then 'the facts of life,' I was told that to make a baby, two people must love each other very much, and be married. But then it became clear that the teenager next door had a baby in her tummy, and she wasn't married; there was no loving father anywhere in sight. Someone said she had *slept with* a boy . . . and from that I came to believe that lovers created a baby in their dreams. If the baby was meant to be (already at the age of five I knew, from observing the miserable girl next door, that what the potential parents *wanted* was irrelevant), then by sleeping together in one bed, at the same time, they would each dream the same thing, and that dream would somehow get into the tummy of the mother-to-be, and grow into a baby.

'So people are dreams made flesh,' he said. 'I love it!'

Our talk was not like a normal conversation, at least, not like one I'd ever had before. We weren't on a date or planning a life together. We didn't have to impress each other, or assess each other for suitability, or lay down the beginnings of a lasting relationship. We were strangers, free to say anything. I didn't tell any lies about myself – I don't know if he lied to me – he fantasized and made up stories, but I knew that was what he was doing: he wrote songs. He made up one just for me: it was kind of silly, forcing unlikely words to rhyme with my name, but I was charmed. I wish I could remember it now. I'd sing it to cheer myself up.

No one had ever been impressed by my creativity, and I thought of myself as practical and unimaginative, down-to-earth. He didn't know that; he had no particular expectations, and it didn't matter if I disappointed him. The situation set me free.

When I heard Lauren coming in the next morning, I made him leave by the window. It was easy to do, perfectly safe, and I gave him directions to a nearby café where I said I'd meet him for breakfast in half an hour, but seeing him clamber out of my bedroom window added an element of old-fashioned farce, as if it was happening in a black-and-white movie, or an old cartoon, certainly not part of my real life.

I regretted having suggested breakfast as soon as he'd gone. What if someone I knew saw us together? I stopped by the café to order coffee and bagels to go, and greeted him like a casual acquaintance – 'Hey, good set last night!'

We exchanged a secret, conspiratorial grin. He looked wrecked, but happy, telling me he was about to go crawl into bed to sleep for the rest of the day. I said Thank God it's Saturday so I could do the same. He told me he'd leave a comp ticket, if I wanted to come to the show that night, and I said I would.

When I got to the venue, I was immediately hailed by some friends of Marshall's, so there was no chance for us to talk. When the band began to play, I was surprised to learn that he was the drummer. When we'd first stood together talking in the noisy, crowded bar the previous night, when I had let him buy me a beer, he had told me a couple of drummer jokes, so I knew that the Drummer was to the musician what the Blonde or the Aggie was in a similar context, but I hadn't realized he was making fun of *himself*.

Getting away from Marshall's friends was not easy. Eventually I left, drove off, feeling sick at the thought that I might never see him again. But the unspoken bond between us held; when I drove back some time later, he was waiting for me in the parking lot, like before. He crushed out his cigarette under his heel and got into the car.

Lauren was at home, so I couldn't take him there. Feeling like a teenager again, I drove west, towards the lake, until I found a sufficiently secluded spot to park. We got into the back seat and started making out, but it was cramped and uncomfortable and soon unbearably hot. There wasn't a breath of wind, and the open windows invited flies and mosquitoes, and added to my fear that someone unseen in the darkness could be spying on us.

For the first time I asked myself what I thought I was doing.

I didn't want to linger. As soon as I could, I scrambled back into the driver's seat, hastily adjusting my clothes.

'What's wrong?'

'Nothing.'

He didn't ask again. We drove back into town, and the only voices in the car came from the radio, the songs either wildly inappropriate, or offering ironic counterpoint to our sordid little affair.

I dropped him off at an intersection he said was near the house where he was staying. For years afterward, whenever I chanced to stop at the lights there, I remembered that moment, watching him walk away from me, not looking back, thinking that was the end.

It should have been, but when I finally went out the next morning, an envelope that had been wedged between the door and frame fell at my feet.

Inside the plain white letter envelope was a sheet of paper folded in thirds. The handwriting was unfamiliar, but I knew who it had to be from.

It was his last day in town, the band was driving down to Houston – late tonight, to miss the worst of the traffic and the heat – and he hoped he could see me before they left. Could he take me out to lunch and/or dinner? Would I take him sightseeing? He hoped he hadn't missed me already. He was just going off to have a late breakfast in the café I had suggested to him before. If he got to the bottom of his bottomless cup of coffee before I showed up, he would probably smoke a couple of cigarettes before he wandered off and tried to find something else to do. He would be sorry not to see me to say goodbye.

I had woken up that morning with the sad, empty feeling of having done something irrevocable. His letter offered what I thought I wanted: the chance to part as friends.

But it was already past noon, getting close on to one o'clock. I had no idea what time he'd stopped by with the note. Would he still be drinking his coffee, or smoking his cigarettes, or had he given up on me?

I was wearing my usual outfit for a weekend laundry run – ragged cut-offs, a promotional T-shirt, and flip-flops. I thought of going inside to change, at least to put on eye makeup. But what if that five-minute delay meant I missed him? Did it matter what I looked like, even if this would be his last memory of me? After all, I wasn't out to seduce him – quite the opposite.

Deciding that speed was of the essence, I hurried out to my car just as I was, threw my bag of dirty clothes into the trunk, and headed for the café.

Being a Sunday, the place was packed. I recognized a couple of cars belonging to people I knew before I saw him, grinding a cigarette out under his heel and giving me a shy, crooked grin.

'You got my letter. What's the plan?' he said, opening the door on the passenger side.

I drove off as soon as he was buckled in, thinking that it would be just like Fate to have one of Marshall's friends – or maybe the ex-girlfriend who carried a grudge – see me giving a lift to a guy from out of town, a musician I shouldn't even *know*.

My plan was to get out of town. 'You said something about sightseeing. I thought we'd head for the hills. There's a state park, and some cute little towns, markets, a German bakery, good barbecue ... I'm just going to stop off at home first to change my shoes.'

'A lot of walking?'

'Could be.' Mostly I wanted my make-up.

Those cute little towns, and the state park, attracted a lot of visitors, especially on the weekends, but it was a very different crowd from the people Marshall and I knew. The last time I'd taken this route I had been with my parents, when they came to visit me during my first year of college.

Going there with him felt strange, it made me feel different, like I was playing a part. I *was* playing a part, and like an actor who can't get to grips with it, I kept wondering, 'What's my motivation?'

Why had I agreed to meet him? Why were we here? Before, at night, it had been like a shared dream. In daylight, part of the crowds strolling around the quaint town square, walking into the pottery, or investigating the dim recesses of a room stuffed with old junk optimistically described as 'Collectibles and Antiques', our being together was all wrong. I tried to think up an explanation, in case I was asked. He could be my cousin from out of state . . . but not if it got back to Marshall, who knew the names and ages of all my cousins . . . The safest thing would be to connect it to work. If my boss had asked me to entertain a visitor for her . . . it was unlikely, but as Marshall knew, she *had* once asked me to take her mother to a doctor's appointment.

Soon I was treating him as if we'd met for the first time that day. I 'made conversation', asking him about the band, their touring schedule, and he obliged with answers and anecdotes. He tried to take my hand, and I flinched away.

We had a late, heavy lunch in an ostentatiously German restaurant, and talked about food, our favourite dishes, that fact that neither of us knew how to cook. Then we talked about recent movies we had seen.

Driving back to the city, the sun going down behind us, we were silent, exhausted by the effort of working through every possible subject for conversation. I noticed, as we drove through the practically deserted back road leading into town, that there was a new development on this western outskirt. In addition to the houses, town homes and a shopping mall still under construction there was a brand new hotel, towering over the landscape from its hilltop perch, its multitude of windows glittering like faceted gems in the last rays of the sun.

'Turn here,' he said suddenly and I did, off the highway, onto an empty access road which wound around and around and brought us into the parking lot in front of the hotel. Although the building looked finished, and there had been a sign advertising it, I wondered if it was actually open yet, as there were only four cars in the vast concrete expanse of parking lot around it, and no one to be seen. I stopped the car and gave him a quizzical look. 'Why here?'

'From the top floor, we can look down and see the whole world spread out before us.'

I was slow; not getting it, I craned back my head and looked up. 'You think there's a restaurant up there?'

'Let's spend the night together.'

My heart lurched. 'You're going to Houston.'

'*They* are. I don't have to. I could get on a bus tomorrow ... unless you want me to stay. We could have one more night – or forever. What do you say?'

It had taken Marshall three years to decide he wanted to marry me, and this guy, who hadn't even set eyes on me three days ago was talking about 'forever'.

I didn't say anything. I took my foot off the brake and steered the car around to drive back onto the highway.

He sighed deeply. 'I mean it. I want to spend my life with you. But if that's too much – I know you've got a man, you love him and he loves you, and you'd probably have a better life with him than *I* could ever give you – he's –'

'Don't you talk about him,' I growled, feeling my face flame.

'I'm sorry. I didn't mean ... Of course. It's nothing to do with him.'

'That's right.'

'I was just going to say – if you don't want me for *all* the time, I'm happy to be your wayfarin' stranger, see you when I'm passing through. If you're lonely –'

'I won't be. And it would be wrong, when I'm married.'

'OK.'

We went for a little way in silence before he said, 'Can we be friends?'

I wanted to say yes, and I wanted it to be true, but I didn't see how that would work.

'If I came back ...'

'Then I'd have to make up some story about how we met. I'd have to lie ... I'm not good at that.'

'Leave it to me. I'm good at making up stories. Stories and songs,' he said cheerfully. 'You know, it's just as well we didn't go into that hotel. It had a hungry look about it. I have a feeling that if we went in, we might never have come out again.'

I was happy to let him change the subject, and to listen to

something that was not about *us*. The fanciful story he began to tell turned into a song. I wondered if he was making it up as he went along, like he did with his song for me, although it seemed so much more polished and clever, it must have been something he'd already written. But I think I was the first, and maybe the only, person to hear it.

I wish I could remember the words now, or even the tune.

All I can recall is the title – 'The Hungry Hotel' – and that it was somehow both whimsical and sinister, scary and sweet at the same time. But how did it end?

It cheered me up, it wiped out the whole estranging experience of the afternoon and the unhappiness we both felt at what was a necessary, unavoidable final parting, and it also filled most of what remained of our journey, down into the city, and back to the parking lot of the bar where we had first met. There was nothing going on, and only a couple of cars parked out back at that hour on a Sunday evening.

'You sure this is where you want me to leave you?'

'I don't want you to leave me.'

'Stop it.' I was only annoyed with myself for that unfortunate turn of phrase.

He sighed. 'I know you don't want to hear it, but I have to say it –'

We spoke at the same time, our voices overlapping: 'No you don't.' 'I love you.'

Tears started in my eyes. I had to bite my lip not to say it back to him.

One last time we kissed, and then we parted.

A year later he was touring Europe with his new band and I was honeymooning with Marshall in Mexico.

A few years after that, when I was a wife and mother, juggling work and family life, too busy and too happy to have any regrets or even think about the past, I would have forgotten all about him if he hadn't suddenly gotten famous.

Fame is relative, of course; he was already well known in certain circles, as a performer and a songwriter, and he'd written a couple of hits that had made him rich. I'd sung along to one of them in the car never knowing, or even wondering, who had written it. It was only when he married a *real* celebrity – the mega-talented, sexy young singer who'd made hits of two of his songs – that his face as well as his name began to appear all over the place.

I saw him on TV very late one night, as I was trying to feed the baby, my dull eyes fixed on the screen where a music video flashed hypnotically. At first I thought I'd fallen asleep and only dreamed it was him I saw playing the keyboards, dancing (badly) with the singer, dressed like Charlie Chaplin, doing the funny, cane-twirling walk as the music swelled and the singer laughed, and finally in a clinch with the beautiful, sexy singer, the camera zooming in on their lips as they kissed.

And after that – he was with his wife on the red carpet at some event; snapped by the paparazzi; bounding onto the stage with a big grin to accept an award; speaking earnestly to a popular talk show host; his picture in magazines like *Heat* and *People*; on the internet, popping up, usually with her, whether I wanted to know or not.

I wanted to say that I had known him – that it was *me* he had picked before he met *her*. But if I could not tell Marshall (and I couldn't; more than ever, now, I did not dare) I could not tell anyone. It had to stay my secret.

That was probably just as well. Even if I had confessed all to Marshall before we were married, and if he had admitted in turn to some small infidelity of his own, and we had agreed to forgive and forget, and truly had – even if I could now, in good conscience, talk to others about this famous person I'd bedded – well, how *could* I? What price reflected glory? I was no groupie, to brag about the notches on my bedpost.

Anyway, his stardom was fleeting. The marriage ended; he moved to Berlin to be with his new girlfriend, a designer of bizarre and expensive footwear, and although he continued to write songs and published a book of whimsical short stories, his fame now encompassed a smaller, or at least a different, sphere, and made no impact on the world I lived in.

The club where we had first met was demolished to make way

for a towering bank building, and after we moved to Montana I no longer drove past it, or the intersection where I'd watched him walk away. Before long, there was nothing to remind me of that particular weekend so long ago.

The kids grew up so fast. It had seemed like a lifetime before they started school, but after that, the years went by like months. And then Jesse went away to college. Sarah was still at home, but it would not be long before she moved out, and then Marshall and I would be left alone, to finally have that long-delayed conversation about our marriage. I knew things were going to change, one way or another.

One day I got a letter.

A letter! Who wrote letters anymore? Sometimes charities would try to fool you with an envelope that looked hand-addressed, but this one really was. My name and address were written in blue ink, in a looping casual hand that was naggingly familiar.

Inside, though, there was no note, no explanation, nothing but a grey plastic card with a magnetic strip on one side and an arrow on the other. A hotel room key, offering no clue as to what room in which hotel it belonged.

I looked again at my name on the front of the envelope, and suddenly remembered the letter left in my apartment door twenty-two years ago, and — and I thought of the hotel on the western edge of the city where he had wanted me to stay with him.

But how had he found me now? We had no friends in common; I didn't think he even knew my married name.

But it should be easy enough to find *him*. I had not heard anything of him for years, but when I entered his name in a search engine, right below his Wikipedia entry (which read to me as if it had been hacked by a malicious joker) was his own website. It had not been updated in over a year. He did not blog or tweet. The most recent 'news' I could find was a three-year-old interview: he had moved to Brooklyn following his divorce and was writing a novel. I could find no clue to why he should have gone to the trouble to find me.

I returned my attention the envelope, stretching it open and peering inside, as if somehow I could have missed an enclosure. But the only thing I had missed was the number pencilled in a bottom corner; a number, it now occurred to me, that might be a room number.

In what hotel? Surely not the one we'd stopped outside twenty-two years ago, the one that had inspired a song I might think of as his gift to me, if I could actually remember it. But that was in another state, and besides . . . he knew where I lived.

The postmark on the envelope was local.

He had sent me his room key.

I was sure of it. I still didn't know *why,* but the idea that he still thought of me after so long was balm to my soul. And I knew where to find him.

There weren't that many hotels near where I lived. In fact, until recently, I would have said there were none within thirty miles. The area had been still pretty wild and unspoiled when we bought the land to build our house, but since then, the surrounding acres had gradually filled up with houses, and with the expanded population had come restaurants and banks, a big store, a new school, a church, offices and boutiques, and most recently the ground had been broken for an upscale shopping mall. And near the mall-to-be — I had noticed the sign for it just the other day — a hotel.

He was waiting for me there.

How unlikely; but I so wanted it to be true!

Like the impulsive, thoughtless kid I'd been two decades before, when I had imagined the whole universe conspired to bring us together, I responded to his desire. I left without so much as a note to tell my family where I had gone.

I parked near the entrance and went in boldly, hoping to look like a registered guest, clutching my key in case anyone asked, but the woman behind the desk didn't even look up as I marched past to the elevators.

It was only when I stepped out on the top floor that I had second thoughts. I should have called him from the lobby. We'd have lunch. What did I care if the woman at reception, who looked almost young enough to be my daughter, saw us together?

I turned around, but it was too late, the elevator had gone. I pressed the button to recall it. I would start this story over. Maybe I'd meet him in the lobby as he came in from smoking a cigarette – hotel rooms were all no-smoking now. Maybe he'd given up smoking, like everyone else I knew, but even if he didn't want a smoke, he wasn't going to sit alone in a hotel room all day, waiting for someone who might never arrive. I'd ask the receptionist to call his room. If he was in, he would come down. If he was out, I'd leave a note. And if he wasn't here at all, and I had been completely wrong about what the card had meant – I'd go home and forget about it. No one else would ever know.

My stomach growled. Where was that elevator? I strained to hear any sound of it, and stabbed the button several times with no result. I was hungry and impatient. Since I was here, I might as well try the room.

Immediately outside the elevator niche a sign on the wall showed the numbering system and indicated which way to turn. The number I was looking for was on the right, about halfway along the long, curving hallway. I stopped outside the door and listened. The silence was undisturbed. I held my breath and knocked: timidly at first, then more assertively.

Nothing happened.

Then I looked at the brass-coloured door handle, set into a brass square with a slot at the top. He had sent me the key so I could let myself in – but suddenly I didn't want to.

What kind of game was this? Sending an anonymous plastic key card did not constitute getting in touch. What made him think that after twenty-two years without a word, he only had to whistle? No, not even whistle; make me guess and seek for him. But what made *me* think this was *his* game?

The back of my neck prickled. Was somebody watching me, silently, through the fish-eye lens of the spy-hole?

I hurried away, back to the elevators, and slapped the button, my breath coming fast and anxious. I imagined Marshall waiting behind that closed door, waiting to humiliate me. But even if, somehow, he knew – that was not his style. I imagined a psychotic, murdering stranger, or him, horribly changed.

'Come on, come on!'

But the elevator would not be summoned. How long had I been waiting? I shouldn't even be here. I was wasting time. I charged away down the other curving arm of the corridor, the branch I had not taken. But I saw no sign for Emergency Exit or Stairs, although I went to the very end and then walked slowly back, checking each door as I passed.

There *must* be a staircase, if only for use in case of fire. It was surely illegal to erect a multi-story building without fire escapes. Most big hotels had more than one. Yet I found no doors that could be opened without a key, and I couldn't remember seeing any kind of exit sign on the other side, either.

Returning to the elevator niche, looking down the other half of the long, curving corridor, I remembered his song about the hungry hotel, 'built in the shape of a smile'.

I knew then that the elevator was never going to come, no matter how long I waited. I wasn't really surprised to find I couldn't get a signal on my phone. I can take pictures with it, and record this message, but how is that going to help?

Eventually I will have to use the key, because that's the only thing left to try.

Maybe I'm dreaming, and when I use the key, I will wake up. Maybe it will open an ordinary room, with a window looking down onto the parking lot, and a telephone that works. But I don't think this is that kind of dream.

I've been thinking about my childish belief that babies got made by people dreaming together, and I've been thinking about that song he made up for me, and now I seem to be inside it. (I wish I could remember how it ended!)

Maybe we dreamed this hotel together, and maybe the key will open the door to a room where he's waiting for me, and it will be like the one night we spent together, only it will last forever.

Or maybe it will just be the end.

The Dragon's Bride

The black notebook

I was early marked for sacrifice.

Two months of my life are gone from my memory. How? Was it done to me, or did my mind retreat in self-protection? Whatever happened, it was something terrible and traumatic. Those memories, I am certain, hold the key to my fate. I must remember before it is too late.

It happened the summer that I was twelve, when I was sent away to stay with a relative in England, but although the memory is gone, it left a mark on my soul; a mark only I can see.

What I *do* remember is the day that I came home.

My mother picked me up at the airport. She was alone. She didn't mention my father, and I felt afraid to ask about him. At home, everything was different, even the smell of the house and the way the light came through the windows, yet there was nothing I could positively point to as having changed. The same furniture occupied the same places, but although it all looked the same, I knew it was not. My father was gone, and I no longer belonged in this house where I had grown up. Yet I had to go on living there until I was old enough to leave, and in all that time neither my mother nor I ever said a word to acknowledge the distance that now lay between us.

I woke in the middle of the night. The house was dark and silent. It would be hours before I could watch TV or go outside. But I was wide awake. In England, it was time to get up. So I got up, deciding I might as well unpack my suitcase.

My clothes were all in a jumble. I had not learned how to pack. To make up for my careless haste, I tried to be especially neat and careful as I put everything away. I was shaking the creases out of a red dress when something small and hard flew out of its folds, hit the floor, and rolled under the bed.

I went after it, scrabbling at the carpet until my fingers closed on something. It was round and flat, about the size of a quarter, and made of some light, pale metal. It looked like a coin or medallion made in the shape of a sleeping dragon, intricately detailed, the working so fine that I could see each individual scale picked out, and the tiny slits of closed eyes. It slept curled around itself, nose to arrow-pointed tail. It was oddly beautiful, but I could not recall having ever seen it before. I moved it closer to my eyes.

As I breathed on it, it came to life. The little eyes opened, flashing like points of fire, and the beast uncoiled. It flowed like quicksilver through my hands, and wrapped itself around my ring finger, caught its tail in its mouth, and froze. It was once again cold, hard and solid, as if it had never known another form, as if it had always been a ring on my finger, fashioned in the likeness of a snake-like dragon swallowing its own tail.

I must have stared at it for a full minute, trying to make sense of what had happened. I felt drowsy and confused. Was this a dream? No, I was awake, and beginning to be frightened. The weird ring did not disappear. Finally, determined to be rid of it, I seized hold of it with the thumb and forefinger of my right hand and tried to pull it off.

It would not budge. I couldn't even twist it. It seemed to have grown into my flesh and become a part of my hand.

Soon I was hysterical, rubbing my hand along the carpet and then smashing it against the wall, screaming. My mother found me like that, my left hand torn and bloody. Before the doctor arrived to sedate me, I'd broken two of my fingers. It might have been worse. If my mother hadn't been strong enough to stop me. I think I'd have torn or even bitten the finger completely off.

I don't know why it scared me so much. Waking from sedated sleep, I accepted the thing on my left hand as if it had been a new mole or freckle. No one else ever remarked on it, and I wouldn't be thinking about it now, if it weren't for the letter from my aunt, calling me back to England. My time has come. Suddenly it is urgent that I remember, that I understand what's going on, before it is too late.

I need more time.

*

The Golden Bough was the book that gave him his excuse, but Fitz didn't pretend even to himself that books had anything to do with it. One sight of the girl's tall, slim figure, glossy auburn hair, and the endearingly awkward way she wrapped one long leg around the other, perching stork-like as she read, and Fitz was hooked. It would have been the same even if the fat paperback in her hand had been a bestseller by Judith Krantz.

Moving in close, he said softly, 'There's an illustrated edition on the remainder table.'

She looked up, startled, and stumbled slightly as she came down on both legs. She had slanting grey eyes, a small nose, pale skin: a pretty but unremarkable face. He guessed her age at twenty-two, five years younger than he was.

Smiling, Fitz gestured at the book in her hands. 'It doesn't cost much more than that one, and it's worth it for the illustrations. It's also a hardcover, with bigger print. I think it might be slightly more abridged, but it's more readable. If you're planning on reading the whole thing, that is. I don't think anybody does read it these days; it's become a part of the collective unconscious. You keep it on your shelf long enough and you absorb it by osmosis, you know? I must have had my copy for ten years – bought it when I was reading *The Waste Land* in high school, probably even listed it in the bibliography for my term paper, but I never actually read more than a couple of pages here and there. I'd open it at random, read a few lines and feel like I'd learnt something.'

She was nodding. 'Me too. When I get curious about some subject, I go to a library or a bookstore and just kind of . . . browse around. It doesn't always work, but usually it does. Sometimes it's the only way to find the exact thing you most needed to know.'

He relished the intensity of her gaze and adored her faint

southern drawl. He especially liked the way she talked to him, as if they'd never been strangers.

'Serendipity,' he said happily. 'What's the object of today's search?'

'Dragons. The truth about dragons. Most of what I've found so far is useless.'

'What kind of dragons? Chinese?'

'European, I guess. The real ones they used to have in England and Wales and I guess in other places too. The ones in folk tales and legends and all. You know?'

Inwardly, he groaned. Dragons – at least she hadn't mentioned fairies! He hoped she wasn't a total flake. 'You mean as in St George and the?'

'I guess so. Did he rescue a maiden?'

'Didn't they always? Not much of a story without the princess bride for the noble hero. Although, if the guy was such a saint –'

'But why? Why this connection between virgins and dragons? In here,' she waved the book, 'it connects dragons with water-spirits, and says maidens were sacrificed to ward off floods. Did it only work with virgins? Would the dragon refuse the sacrifice if they weren't virgins?'

'Well, sexist attitudes in a patriarchal society,' Fitz said with a shrug. 'Virgins were the prize. It was about purity, or men wanting to own their children. That means controlling female sexuality. It's a wise child who knows his own father ... unless you make sure that only one man has access to the woman he expects to provide him with offspring. The other part – I've never really understood the logic behind sacrifice. Probably comes of not being religious.' He laughed, while watching for any signs that his heathenism was offensive to her. He didn't pick up any, and her obvious interest encouraged him to go on.

'So, I don't know, but could there be a connection between sacrificial offerings and sacred marriages? I mean, it might be a stretch, unless the dragon was some kind of god, but why not? If the women were given to the dragons as brides, then of course they'd have to be virgins. The people who believed in that stuff would expect the dragon to be mightily pissed off if he got damaged goods, so to speak. Hey, don't blame me, I didn't make up their stupid rules!'

'I didn't say anything –'

'You didn't have to – I saw that look!'

'But it wasn't about you,' she said earnestly. 'Please, go on, this is really interesting.'

'You do realize I'm not an actual expert on mythology, religion or ancient cultures?' He winked and saw her flush and drop her gaze. 'However, I am always more than happy to share what I've gleaned from years of unsupervised study.' He cleared his throat. 'Not to mention my opinions, one of which is that it is an awfully sexist assumption, don't you agree, that the dragons would not only be male, but would be wanting to marry a human female. If I remember right, Jung described the dragon as an archetypal female image. It represented the devouring aspect of the mother, and the maiden it held captive was an aspect of the hero. By killing the dragon, he was actually setting himself free . . . but maybe that's just another kind of sexism, blaming the mother for anything that could go wrong in a man's life?'

Her grey eyes were wide. 'The dragon is the mother?'

He shrugged. 'It's one interpretation. Hell, you can make these things mean whatever you want.'

He felt the atmosphere chill. 'Symbols are not a game. Things have meanings. You can't just stick labels on – it's not a joke. You don't get to change the meaning just because you like it better than the truth.'

What had he said? He scrambled to repair the damage. 'I only meant – well, different cultures invest different meanings in the same symbols, the way that they use different words for the same thing. Jung had this theory about universal archetypes, but, well, I'm not an expert on Jung, or dragons – or anything, to be honest.'

'Young, you said? Who was he? Why did he think the dragon was female?'

'Carl Gustav Jung.' He spelled the last name. 'His books will be in the psychology section. But I don't know where I read that thing about the dragon; I haven't read much by Jung, so it was probably in an article, and it might have been about almost any-thing, but probably not about Jung *or* about dragons.'

Her gaze was warmer now. 'What else do you know about dragons?'

He laughed. 'Hardly anything. I thought I already warned you. I read widely but not deeply. As someone once told me, my mind is a vast warehouse of trivial information. I'd never make an expert. My mind could never settle on one subject for long enough. But tell me, what's your particular interest in dragons?'

She turned to replace *The Golden Bough* on the shelf, and his eyes travelled down her backside. 'It's complicated.'

'Most interesting things are. Hey, have you had dinner? There's a Greek place right around the corner. We could talk more there ... I could rummage through the vast warehouse of trivial information I laughingly call my brain for anything else dragon-related.'

She smiled. He admired what it did to her face and felt encour-aged despite the shake of her head. 'Come on. My treat. Why not?'

'I don't even know your name.'

'Officially, Lawrence Fitzgerald. To my friends, Fitz.'

'Isobel,' she said, and thrust out her right hand.

He took it in his and gently raised it to his lips. Looking up, he saw her blush. 'Shall we?'

'No one's ever tried to pick me up before.'

'You must not get out much.' He smiled into her eyes. 'Well, I've never rescued a maiden from a dragon.'

He'd been angling for another smile, but her expression turned grave, the pinkness fading from her cheeks. 'Would you if you had the chance?'

'If you are the maiden, I'll do everything in my power.'

They left the bookstore together. Fitz had always had luck with women, despite being neither handsome nor rich. He was short, his hair was thin and almost colourless, and his nose, as his sister had been the first to point out, looked rather like a potato. But, as his sister also admitted, he had beautiful, puppy-dog eyes, great intelligence, a sense of humour, a sweet nature, and one other, less-celebrated, attraction: 'You look harmless,' she said. 'They think they're safe with you, and then, before they know it, they're in deep. And then you meet someone else, and, sweet as you are, you break their hearts.'

Fitz didn't like having the term 'harmless' attached to him, but certainly he meant no harm to anyone. He thought women liked him because he liked them. Hearts got broken only because being in love with one woman had never stopped him from falling in love with another.

'Do you like Greek food?' he thought to ask as they approached his favourite restaurant.

'I don't know. I've never tried it.'

'Never? How long have you been in New York?'

'I only got here today.'

'Where from?'

'Tennessee.'

Entering, they were greeted by Milo, the owner's son. Milo glanced at Isobel, gave Fitz a knowing look, and conducted them to a table near the back. There was much discussion over the menu, as Fitz explained things and made suggestions for what Isobel might like. Milo brought over a bottle of retsina without being asked and took their order, and then they were alone together.

Fitz looked across the table at Isobel and sighed happily. He loved beginnings. In the romantically dim light Isobel looked even prettier than the stranger he'd noticed in the bookstore. He had been too taken by her body then to really examine her face. He raised his glass to hers. 'To happy endings.'

'What do you think dragons are, really?'

He managed not to sigh. 'Tell you the truth, Isobel, I've never given the subject much thought. In the Bible, the dragon is the devil, the old serpent. In China, the dragon symbolized leadership, and only the emperor could use the dragon sign. In fantasy stories, they can be faithful friends or deadly enemies. There's a science fiction writer called Anne McCaffrey who's written – ' he stopped, seeing she was about to interrupt. 'Right, you said "really". OK, I did read something once that suggested all the old stories about dragons terrorizing populations and being slain might have had some basis in fact. That there might have been some sort of large land reptile, imagine something like a cross between a crocodile and a gila monster, that survived into the Middle Ages in Europe. Maybe a leftover dinosaur.' He grinned. 'That idea has an appeal to me. I've always liked dinosaurs. It seemed so unfair that all of them were wiped out before human beings came along.'

Her hands on the tabletop tugged and worried at each other. 'But could something like that could have survived into our time?'

'Like in the depths of the Amazon? Or in a deep canyon on a remote volcanic island, never explored until . . .'

She shook her head fiercely. 'Not like *The Lost World*. It would have to be in England. Maybe just one incredibly old animal that was still in a cave. Or maybe it wasn't real, but some people thought it was? Oh, I don't know. Have you ever read about anything like that?'

'In England? No. It seems unlikely, but, hey, what do I know? There's the Loch Ness Monster up in Scotland. I don't know much about England. But people do find strange creatures all over the place. There are still plenty of mysteries in the world. There've been sightings of Bigfoot and the Yeti, and just because I haven't read about dragon sightings doesn't mean there aren't any. There are some big reptiles in the world; imagine what you'd think if you saw one of those big tortoises without its shell, or if it turned out there were crocodiles or even monitor lizards living in Central Park? But why are you so interested in dragons, real or imaginary?'

'It might not be a real dragon,' she said slowly. 'In fact, since dragons are generally agreed to be fantastical, it probably isn't. It could be a symbol. Probably is a symbol. I'm just trying – I don't know if there's even any point to this, but I am trying to find some kind of answer, a key, connected to the idea of a dragon.'

He was none the wiser. Did it matter? Time to leave the subject.

'Hey, you haven't even tasted your wine,' he said. 'I want to know what you think of it.'

Obediently she sipped and looked startled. 'Oh!'

'Like it?'

She took another taste and nodded slowly. 'I think so. It tastes like pine trees.'

'Yes! The resin. Some like it, but it's not for everyone.'

'It's nice.'

A waiter arrived and set down a dish of olives, a basket of flat-breads, and small bowls of tzatziki and taramasalata. Fitz nodded thanks and picked up an olive.

'It is perfect with Greek food, ideally on a Greek island, dining on the beach after dark – or so I've been told. I have yet to get there. You ever been to Greece?' He popped the olive into his mouth.

'I've never been anywhere outside America except once, to England.' She looked at the table, gulped some wine, looked unhappy and put down the glass.

'Easy – if you're not used to it – have a bite to eat first.'

'England,' she said. 'That's where it happened. It was after I came back from England that I started wondering about dragons.' She clutched her hands close to her chest, then let them fall to her lap, below the table. They were out of sight, but from the tension and faint tremors in her upper arms he knew something was going on: she was clenching or tugging at her hands.

'Something you saw in England?'

She began to nod, then shook her head, frowning. 'I don't know. I can't remember! That's the thing. I spent two whole months there, and I've got, like, total amnesia about it. I remember the day I got back, my Mom picking me up, but the whole time I was away is a blank.'

'Except for something about a dragon.'

She looked down at her lap. 'Yeah, well, it was just a little thing. I don't know what it means. I need to find out.'

He waited, but she was no more forthcoming. Fitz ate another olive and tore off a piece of pita bread and dipped it into the tara-masalata and handed it across the table. She stared at it but made no move to take it. 'What's that?'

'Try it and see.'

Slowly, her right hand came up to accept it. She bit and chewed, then nodded, looking pleasantly surprised.

'Have some more.'

She took her knife and smeared more of the pink stuff on the bread. 'What is it?'

'Does it matter, if you like it?'

Moving it away from her mouth, she gave him a look. 'Tell me.'

'Taramasalata.' He hesitated. 'Olive oil, garlic ... and, don't freak out, but the main ingredient is cod's roe.'

'Why would I freak out? Cod is a fish, and roe ... I thought roe was caviar?'

'It is – but from a different type of fish, and they don't treat it the same way, obviously.' He pointed to the other small dish. 'That's tzatziki, which is mostly yoghurt and cucumbers. It also has garlic and olive oil, same as the pink stuff.'

'You know a lot.'

'I can sometimes give that appearance.' He grinned. 'But remember, all I have upstairs is a vast warehouse of useless trivia.'

'Not always useless,' she said, taking another piece of the bread. 'The stuff about dragons ... you probably think I'm crazy.'

'No, why should I?'

'I don't really believe in dragons. I'm just trying to make sense out of something that happened to me when I was twelve. I think something terrible must have happened, really traumatic, and that's why I can't remember anything about those two months.'

That put a different spin on things; he had been thinking the trip to England was more recent. 'Your parents can't help?'

'They weren't there. I went to stay with my aunt, and when I got back, I had this – ' she moved her hand down, then seemed to recall she was still holding the bread and arrested the movement. Her left hand was in her lap. 'I had the idea that whatever it was that I couldn't remember had something to do with a dragon. That's why I've been trying to find out what a dragon *means*.' She sighed and dropped the end of the pita bread onto her plate. 'I can't explain it any better than that. I'm sorry.'

'Don't apologize. Have you talked to anyone else about it?'

'No. I wanted to forget about it. And I almost did until –' She swallowed hard. 'Until Aunt Margaret sent for me. She wants me to visit her again. And I don't want to go. I don't want to go back there.'

'Then don't.'

'You don't understand.' She looked at him imploringly; he saw tears welling in her beautiful eyes. 'I have to go.'

'No you don't.' He caught her hand and gave it a gentle squeeze. 'Isobel, you're not a little girl. You don't have to go just because your aunt wants you to.'

'It's not just her, it's my mother. I don't know why, because I thought they fell out, years ago. They haven't seen each other in years, maybe not since I was born, and I didn't even think they'd kept in touch, but now my mother insisted I had to go. Poor Margaret is all alone. She doesn't have any children; I'll be her heir, she'll leave me everything, but I don't care, even if she's a million-aire, she can leave it all to charity. If Mom is so concerned, why doesn't *she* go, I said. *She* can be her sister's heir, and pass it down to me – or not, her decision, her sister, their choice to make up or not, but don't make me their go-between . . . I made my mother cry,' she ended in a wondering tone. Her own eyes were dry.

'That's good, you stood up to her.'

She made a wry mouth. 'Until I caved. She wore me down. It would be a fun vacation for me. Aunt Margaret had already bought my ticket. Mom just rode over all my objections. She even called the agency where I'd been temping and said there was a family emergency, and I wouldn't be available for the rest of the month. She packed my suitcase and drove me to the airport and waited to see me onto the plane. I told myself I didn't have to stay with her the whole time; I had enough money to travel around, staying in youth hostels, if I was careful. Maybe I wouldn't stay with her at all – but she was going to pick me up from the London airport and drive us down to Devon. I started to get scared. Once I was there, what if she didn't want to let me go? I was supposed to change planes in New York. When I got here, I knew it was my only chance, so I just walked out of the airport. My big bag was checked through – I guess it's on its way to Gatwick right now.'

Their moussaka arrived, making for a natural break in the conversation. It turned out that Isobel was not a complete novice when it came to Greek cuisine: she'd had moussaka once or twice before at a covered-dish supper.

They traded more information about their lives, minus the fraught subject of relatives. Isobel had majored in art at college but hadn't used her degree since she graduated the previous year. She'd been scraping by doing clerical and secretarial work, just as she had done during her summer breaks, and didn't know what sort of career she might have. She didn't have the talent to be a fine artist, or the skills to be a successful illustrator, she told him earnestly, but thought she'd like a job in design, maybe working at an advertising agency, or on a magazine? She thought it would be cool to work in a gallery, but there never seemed to be any jobs going. She'd thought about moving to New York, where there were more art galleries, ad agencies and magazines in a few square miles than in the whole of the state of Tennessee, but it had been too intimidating to go on her own to a place where she didn't know anyone.

'Well, you're here now – and you know me.'

'What do you do? Your turn now.'

He told her he'd grown up in New Jersey, unable to decide if he'd rather be an astronaut, a baseball player, or Ernest Hemingway. In college he'd wavered between journalism and anthropology and American studies before dropping out to spend more time writing his great American novel. A temporary job delivering telephone books in Manhattan put him in the right place to hear about the job he still had, writing copy for an in-house publication.

'So you are a writer?'

'In a manner of speaking. It's not literature, but I get a kick out of turning management-ese into plain English and spicing up dull stories with strange and interesting factoids.'

'From the vast warehouse of trivial information?'

He pointed his fork at her. 'You got it, sister.'

'What about the great American novel?'

'Someone else will have to write it. The job pays the bills and keeps me busy – enough writing, already, I think when I have time off.' He signalled Milo for more wine.

'Oh, no,' said Isobel when it arrived.

'I thought you liked it.'

'I did, but I've had enough.' She pressed her hands against flushed cheeks. 'I'm not used to drinking.'

'I will not be the cause of your ruin,' he said solemnly and then, to Milo, 'Never mind. We'll have two Greek coffees instead.'

He turned his sweetest gaze on Isobel. 'I promise, I am a gentleman. You can trust me to put you in a cab and send you safely back to your hotel whenever you say the word, no matter how much or how little you've imbibed.'

'I don't have a hotel.'

'Okay. You want me to suggest one?'

'I'd rather go home with you.'

He nodded slowly. 'Sure. Delighted. But I ought to warn you it's a one-room apartment where the couch also happens to be the only bed.'

'I want to sleep with you.'

Her words were a jolt of electricity. Fitz wanted to keep his cool, but knew he was grinning, on the verge of slobbering like a dirty old man. He reached across the table and took her hand. With a gasp, she jerked it away.

'Sorry,' she said breathlessly.

'No, I'm the one who should apologize. Only, if you share my bed, I am not sure I can be a perfect gentleman about it.'

'You don't have to be. I don't want you to. When I said sleep – I didn't mean "just sleep".' She took a deep breath. 'I just – I'm funny about my left hand, that's all. It's a silly thing, but sometimes, when I'm not expecting it . . .' Abruptly, she thrust that same hand towards him like someone daring fire.

Cautiously, he put out his hand and touched hers, letting it rest in his palm. He ran his thumb across the backs of her fingers. For no reason, he suddenly shivered. It was a soft, lovely hand, just like the one he had held earlier. There was nothing wrong with it at all, but he was glad when the arrival of the coffee gave him an excuse to let it go.

★

The black notebook

I can't even remember what she looked like. The only picture I've ever seen of her is one with my mother, when they both still lived in England, and that was taken before I was born, and it's not good because she moved her head just as the picture was snapped, so her face is blurred, half turned away. My father took that picture not long after he had met the two sisters, one of whom he would marry. Was he already in love with my mother then? Or did he love Margaret first?

I might not remember how my aunt looked ten years ago, but I know how she looked when she was young. All I have to do to see her again is sit and stare into the mirror until her face starts coming through. I hate it when that happens; it scares me, even though I know it's only a trick I am playing on myself. I know what Aunt Margaret looks like because she's my mother's twin.

Identical twins, in love with the same man, but only one could have him.

I used to think he was the reason for the rift between the sisters. I imagined a love triangle. I thought Margaret was angry at him for choosing her sister, or mad at my mother for stealing him from her. Maybe that was true, once upon a time. But it's such a simplistic, old-fashioned view. Life goes on. Things change. They each made a choice. Even if they'd both fallen for the same man, it didn't have to be forever. It wasn't forever for Mom, as it turned out, and surely Margaret could have found another man if she'd wanted. She could have moved away, had other lovers, had children. She didn't. The fact that my mother is the one who went to America, got married and had a child, while Margaret stayed behind, unmarried and childless, in the house where she'd been born, doesn't imply she was the loser – or does it? My mother would never talk about it. I've had to put together my own explanation. And I think it was just that simple: one who won and got away; one who lost and had to stay.

Two girls were born. Only one was needed to be the dragon's bride.

The sacrifice.

What does my aunt want with me? I think I know. And I also think I know how to resist that fate. A man saved my husband, so why shouldn't a man save me? Sexist and old-fashioned – but so is the idea of sacrificing a maiden to a dragon. It ought to work. I'd be damaged goods, after. And a woman can't have two husbands.

★

Fitz's apartment was in its usual state, stinking of cats, dirty clothes, and mouldering cartons of Chinese takeout. Newspapers and magazines were strewn about, and the unmade bed had not been folded back into a sofa. He had not expected, when he went out for an evening browse in a bookstore, to be bringing anyone back with him.

He apologized for the mess. 'I could say it's not usually this bad, but I won't insult your intelligence. Let me feed the cats and put a few things away ... can I get you anything? Coffee? Tea? Beer?'

'No thanks.'

'I won't be long. Make yourself at home, if you can stand the thought.'

He felt suddenly, weirdly nervous. He had not been so nervous around a woman since his virginal teens, but now he thought the problem was not with him, but her. There was something wrong, but what was it?

As he fed the cats and dealt with their litter box, Fitz tried to work it out. Isobel was a strange one, but he'd known other ladies who were stranger: shy, skittish, neurotic or fey. Sometimes their emotional or psychological issues had precluded anything more than a brief encounter, but not always. The real problem was that as attracted as he was to her, he'd sensed no more than a flicker of interest on her part. She wasn't repelled by him, but she had shown no actual desire. Physically, she was remote, in some other dimension. Something other than lust was driving her. He'd bought her dinner, and she'd told him she had nowhere else to stay – maybe she thought sex was the expected price for a bed for the night?

When he came out of the small kitchen, he found her standing just as he had left her, beside the untidy mess of his bed, doing nothing at all but waiting for him.

'Sorry about the mess, but it won't take long to clear it away. Sure you won't have a drink?'

Staring, she reached out and let her hand rest on his arm. 'Kiss me.'

It would have been rude, even cruel, to refuse, he thought, but as soon as he embraced her, all his unease melted away. He expected her to melt, too, but she was like a living statue in his arms, passively accepting his kiss without returning it.

'What's wrong?'

'Nothing.'

'You don't seem comfortable . . . want to sit down?' He was used to kissing taller women, but maybe the disparity in their height bothered her.

She let him guide her to the edge of the bed and perched there while he tossed aside a stray newspaper. Then he began kissing her again. He held himself back, kissing without intensity or pressure, nuzzling her face and neck in a friendly sort of way. Gradually, she relaxed and kissed him back. His hand slipped to her breast, and she tensed up. Mentally cursing himself, Fitz removed the offending hand: oops, sorry, no harm meant.

'Should I get undressed?'

He drew back to look at her. 'Somehow I don't feel like we're in the same movie.'

'What do you mean?'

He sighed and dropped his hands, moved until there was space between their bodies. 'Forget what I said before – you can share the bed with me and the cats, at no cost. We can talk, cuddle a bit if you like, but not if you don't. You have a safe place to spend the night. Say the word, and I'll leave you alone. The cats might not.'

Her mouth sagged open and her eyes widened in hurt. 'Don't you want to make love to me?'

'Of course I do. You're adorable. I think you're swell. What man could resist? But this isn't just about what I want.'

'I want it, too.'

'Sure you do.'

She bit her lip. 'Why don't you believe me?'

'Because, to twist an old saying, though your lips are saying yes, yes, yes, your body is saying no way, Jose.'

'I don't know what you mean.'

'I mean that I'm getting the distinct vibe that says you'll put up with whatever I want to do to you, but you aren't enjoying it.'

She shuddered. 'But I want to! I just don't know how!'

Suddenly he understood, and almost laughed at his own stupidity. 'You mean you're never done this before?'

She nodded.

'You're a virgin.' He repressed a smile and said gently, 'Sweetheart, that's no crime. You should have told me. Well, I guess you did, in a way, only I was too dumb to take it in. I guess I couldn't believe that a girl as lovely as you could have remained virgo intacto past the age of twenty unless she was kept locked up. They didn't keep you locked up, did they?'

She smiled, looking more relaxed. 'Never. Well, hardly ever.'

'And you've never had a boyfriend?'

'Not really. I went out with a boy in college, and people thought he was my boyfriend, but we never did anything more than hug and hold hands. He came out as gay in our junior year. I don't know if he knew he was before . . .'

'And that was it?'

'Sometimes guys asked me out, but I never . . . well, I guess I just never liked them enough to, you know.'

He put his hand on his heart. 'I am deeply, deeply flattered that you like me well enough to choose me as your first lover.'

'So we're going to do it?'

'Yes, *we* are – together. Making love is not something one person does to another – it takes two. Don't think of this as something I know how to do and you don't. This is not an endurance test. I want your first time to be as good for you as it possibly can be. That means you've got to tell me what you like and what you don't, and if I need to take it slower, or if it hurts –'

'I thought the first time always hurts.'

'I don't know about that. I don't think it has to. Anyway, that's penetration; I'll be as gentle as I can. Most of what we're going to do should just feel good – unbelievably good, but you do need to relax.'

He couldn't tell if she believed him. It was clear to him now that his perception of what she was like had been skewed by her nervousness – maybe fear was not too strong a word. He wondered about her upbringing. She hadn't said anything to imply a particularly strict or religious upbringing, but maybe there was something like that in the background. And then, to fall for somebody who was never going to find her sexually attractive must have been a blow to her self-confidence. It was pretty amazing that she'd had the nerve to fling herself at the first halfway decent stranger who happened along . . .

There was something off-kilter about the whole thing. Fitz started feeling nervous again. Maybe he should ply her with the cooking sherry and hope she'd fall asleep before anything had to happen. Despite his assurances to Isobel, he'd had no actual experience with virgins. His own first lover had been an experienced older woman, and he had learned more from even his youngest girlfriend (Amy, eighteen to his twenty-one) than he'd ever been able to teach them. He'd never been anyone's first time before, and that was a heavy responsibility. What if something went horribly wrong? He was struck by an unwelcome memory, vivid as a flashback, of an episode from Sylvia Plath's *The Bell Jar,* in which the heroine had nearly bled to death after her hymen was torn. It seemed too grotesque to be possible, but the scene was based on something that had happened to Plath herself under similar circumstances. It might be more common than he thought. Maybe they should stick to oral sex.

'Fitz?'

'I was just thinking – I don't suppose you're on the Pill?'

She looked anguished. 'I'm sorry.'

'We wouldn't want you getting pregnant, would we?'

Tears glistened in her eyes, and the sight undid him. 'Don't worry, it'll be fine. I've got something – pack of rubbers in the bathroom. Just wait. I'll be right back.'

He did not hurry. Maybe she'd reconsider and decide to leave. But when he came back, she was naked, lying curled on her side on top of the sheets. The sight of her slim, pale body, so defence-less, and her tense, expectant expression caused a rush of tender-ness. She was counting on him, and he would not let her down. By the time he had undressed and joined her on the bed, Fitz felt as if they were both virgins embarking on this journey for the first time.

'Aren't you cold? Let's get under the covers,' he said. In fact, the room was warm and stuffy, and he was trembling with nerves. When he took her in his arms the feel of her naked flesh and her faint, warm scent aroused him almost unbearably. His erection was like those he remembered from adolescence, so hard it was painful. He felt on the verge of exploding.

Isobel in his arms was no longer the girl he'd seen in the book-store, the girl he'd had dinner with and found attractive, like so many others. She had become a stranger when she took off her clothes and lay down in his bed. She was a dream, a fantasy, unat-tainable and forbidden. Her breasts were soft and strange against his chest. So this was what women were like under their clothes. His sister raised her dress, to show him. He was afraid to look, sure the sight would make him go blind, but he was dying to know more. He was afraid his father would come in. He had no right to be here; he would be punished.

She moved her thighs against his and murmured, 'Kiss me.'

Fitz groaned as, helplessly, out of control, he came.

In agony and pleasure he pressed himself against her and then, abruptly, it was over.

Repulsion seized him, a disgust with himself. He pushed himself away from her, turned his back, found the tissues. Every muscle was trembling in the aftermath of intensity, but what shook him more profoundly was the loathing he felt. It was like nothing he'd ever experienced, and while he knew it made no sense, the feeling was directed mostly at her, the strange woman in his bed. Beyond all sense he blamed her for what had happened, for the images that had flooded his mind, the forbidden desire, and the brief, dirty pleasure. It was as if she had taken control of him, demonstrated her power over him, and then, contemptu-ously, let him go.

Gradually, after a few seconds (it could have been no longer) he calmed down. Those feelings were like a bad dream. It had been some sort of mental glitch, he decided; nothing to do with what he really felt, and certainly nothing at all to do with Isobel, an innocent young woman who could not be blamed for some unwanted, ugly thoughts stirred up from the depths of his subconscious.

Fitz rolled over and put an arm around her. He kissed her on the mouth. 'Sorry about that.'

She looked wary and confused. 'What for?'

'I got a little too excited. It's never happened to me before. I don't –' he stopped himself. She didn't want an explanation, only reassurance, and words would not provide that.

He began to make love to her, without passion, but with tender skill. Having no desire himself, he concentrated on creating it in her, relying on past experience and alert to her every slight response. As he kissed and touched and stroked her he became aware of her reactions almost before she was herself. He found the tiny sparks of her desire and fanned them to flame. Her body changed, reshaped by his hands. What had been a hundred separate nerves leaping beneath her skin combined in one strong, steady pulse, and her urgency transmitted itself to him. He forgot about her inexperience and stopped being so gentle. He didn't know, or care, if the sounds she made were of pleasure or pain: it was all the same. She was no longer a virgin, if she ever had been. She twisted and flexed beneath him and wrapped her legs around his waist as if she'd known this dance for years. Her excitement drove him on; now, she excited him, and he'd forgotten his aim of giving her pleasure, too lost in his own. He imagined he was being watched; he was at the centre of a crowd of other people who were willing him on, encouraging him to prevail. His eyes closed, and he was in darkness, not just in his own familiar room, but inside a cave, deep beneath the earth. She was there, too, squirming beneath him and he was stabbing her with his sword. He had to kill the dragon, to save her and to prove his love. She was watching him kill the dragon. She approved. She was the princess, and she was his reward. She raised her dress to show him where to come. The cave was hot and moist around them, she was hot and moist as she enveloped him, but the dragon was still alive. He felt the dragon moving, although it was impaled by his sword, as he impaled the princess, hearing her groans of pleasure, and although he knew he must pull out and kill the dragon before it was too late, it was too late.

He shouted as he came. The orgasm seemed to empty him of everything: pain, pleasure, memory, desire, understanding. The years rushed away. He lay, stunned, on top of her, unable to move, and tried to count the closely woven blue threads of the pillowcase as he waited for his personality to come back from wherever it had gone.

★

The black notebook

There wasn't any blood. There wasn't any pain. I liked how it felt. But it didn't hurt at all. And there was no blood.

It can only mean I was not a virgin.

I feel sick.

I was sure I'd never had sex with anyone. Never been with a man. Never had a lover. That's not something I would forget. But if Fitz wasn't the first, it must have happened in England, during those two months I can't remember, when I was twelve years old. Still a little girl. Just a kid. How could she? If something like that happened to me, though, it makes sense of my amnesia.

But I think I do remember something. Something to do with blood, and terror. The blood was my own, between my legs, smeared on my naked thighs. I've had flashbacks about it before, but always thought it was a memory of getting my first period. They hadn't started before I went to England, but after I got home, there was a big blue box of sanitary napkins in the bathroom cupboard, ready and waiting. So, although I don't remember anything else, nothing about discussions with my aunt or how she might have calmed me down and explained this natural process, I thought I could account for those nightmarish memories of blood and terror if it happened away from home.

But now I have to wonder if what I remember was caused by something else. If the blood and the fear I recall were the result of rape; my loss of memory the result of being sexually abused. Only that could explain why I was not a virgin like I thought. Ignorant and innocent, yes, but not really a virgin.

My aunt gave me to her master. That was the betrothal; a promise of the greater sacrifice to come.

Aunt Margaret was a witch. I've always known that, putting together various snatches of overheard conversations between my parents. Only, when I was ten, eleven, twelve, being a witch seemed cool. *Bewitched* was my favourite show. I wanted to grow up to be Samantha – but I would never marry a stupid spoilsport husband like hers. I imagined Aunt Margaret as more like Sam's mother, Endora, with an attractive splash of wickedness that meant she might turn some unpleasant man into a toad, and Sam would then exert all her best efforts to restore him without letting mere mortals learn she was a witch. I didn't realize then that Samantha and Endora were cuddly fantasy figures, and that REAL witches worshipped the devil and did terrible things to other people.

Fitz said the devil was the dragon, the old serpent. My aunt gave me to him, and he marked me for his own. Now she's called me back for the consummation. To make me his bride.

In bed with Fitz, when he was making love to me, I kept seeing dragons and snakes, huge serpents coiling and writhing in the air. It didn't make any difference if my eyes were open or closed. I more than saw them; I felt their flickering tongues lash me, like ice sometimes and sometimes like fire. But I thought they couldn't hurt me, not with Fitz there to protect me.

I thought that giving myself to a man would change everything and make me safe. But Fitz is no dragon slayer. He might want to protect me, but is he strong enough? Is any man?

The ring is still on my finger. The dragon is waiting for my return.

★

Fitz had more than half expected Isobel to vanish like a dream.

He hated to leave her, but he had to go to work. Once in the office, he could not concentrate; twice he tried to call her. There was no answer, but was his phone ringing in an empty apartment, or was she too nervous to pick up? He fell to daydreaming, imagining going in search of her, first throughout the city, and then, perhaps, flying to Tennessee or even to England to track her down. Colleagues noticed his abstraction and teased: 'In love again, Fitz? Who's the lucky lady this time?' He left work an hour early, claiming he had to pick his cat up from the vet.

Isobel was waiting for him, curled, like one of his cats, on the sofa. Unlike the cats, she was reading, but put the book down at his approach, smiling shyly.

He sank down beside her, took her in his arms, and kissed her. The whole day had been leading to this moment. Neither spoke, but their bodies spoke, and there was no mistaking her response. Soon they were undressed, hungrily making love.

Afterwards, Fitz was disorientated when he turned to kiss her again and saw the flushed, young, pretty face of a stranger. Who was this woman? He felt remote from her and yet joined, as if they were strangers who had experienced some great disaster, a flood or fire or earthquake, and clung to one another from fear, united only by their shared humanity.

'Are you all right?' he asked, suddenly anxious.

She smiled dreamily. 'I didn't know it would be like that. That . . . powerful. That . . . strange. Does sex change you?'

'Uh, sure. I guess. Everything that happens has that potential, don't you think?'

He had the sense she was not really listening. She went on, 'I mean, maybe it's not about virginity. Not in the physical sense. Maybe virginity is a symbol, and what's important is not who does what to who, but what it *means*. It can't be one-sided. It can't just be one person making the decision for somebody else. So if it's rape it doesn't count. It wouldn't be fair. Especially not for a child! I still don't understand how she . . . but she can't control me. I won't let her make me.'

He pushed up on his elbow and looked down at her, blinking. 'Who? What are you talking about?'

'My aunt. Just because he didn't marry her ... that's not my fault. If she's mad at my mom, that doesn't give her the right to take it out on me.'

He was reminded again of how little he knew this young woman. 'That's right.'

She met his eyes. 'She can't make me do anything I don't want to do.'

'Of course not.'

The telephone rang. After a little while, Isobel said, 'Aren't you going to answer?'

He smiled at her. 'What for? The only person I want to talk to is right here.'

She tried to smile back, but it was not a success.

'Hey, don't worry about it. It's probably somebody trying to sell me insurance.'

'It's not that. It just made me think –' The phone stopped ringing. She went on. 'Nobody knows where I am. My mother must be worried. I should call her. Would you mind if I used your phone?'

He tried to ignore the sudden dive his spirits took, a premonition of loss, and quickly told her to use the phone whenever she liked.

'It's long distance – I'll pay you back – or should I reverse charges?'

'Don't be silly. You should let your mother know you're all right. And maybe your aunt, too.'

She frowned. 'I'm not calling England.' She sighed. 'I guess I should write her a letter. I do need her to send my things back. But ...'

'Ask your mother to do that. Tell her to send your stuff here.'

Her eyes widened. 'You mean I can stay?'

He wrapped her in his arms and kissed her vigorously. 'For as long as you can put up with the cats and the mess – and me, of course. I'll help you find a job. I'll buy you some new clothes to tide you over.'

This time, her smile lit up her eyes. Then she made a rueful face. 'My mom won't like it. I might have to pretend you're a girl – Lauren Fitzgerald?'

'Ugh!' He rolled his eyes. 'Come on, you're not a little girl anymore. At least, I hope you're legal – I should have carded you! Please tell me you are legally an adult.'

She made a face at him. 'I'm twenty-two.' She sat up, pushing him off when he tried to pull her back. 'And I am absolutely starving. I haven't had anything except a couple of pop-tarts all day.'

He frowned. 'You didn't have lunch?'

'I finished the pop-tarts.'

'But I left you the extra key – I thought you'd go out and get something.'

She shrugged and looked down. 'I don't know, it just seemed safer – better – to wait for you to come back.'

He realized how foolish his earlier fears had been. She wasn't going to leave. She wanted to stay. Here was cause for celebration. He kissed her again, then rolled off the bed. 'Get dressed. We're going out for dinner.'

She looked at the phone.

He was about to suggest waiting until later, but it was probably best to get it over with. 'Tell you what. I'll go out for Chinese – you like Chinese food? Great – and you can talk to your mom in private, tell her whatever you think she needs to hear.'

On his return, the cheery greeting froze on his lips when caught of Isobel huddled on the floor, weeping. Her face was red and tear-streaked, her eyes swollen and nose running: clearly she had been crying for some time.

He put the bags of take-away and the bottle of wine down and went to her. 'Izzy? It's all right, love. Whatever she said –'

'She's dead.'

His heart lurched. He dropped to the floor and cradled her in his arms. 'Your mother?'

'No!' She drew a long, shuddering breath, wiped her eyes on the back of her hand, and wriggled away from him. 'Kleenex, please.'

Baffled but obedient, he went to fetch the box beside the bed.

'I don't know why I'm crying. Not because my aunt is dead.' She blew her nose. 'Why should I care? But my mother ... she was so angry . . .' Her voice quavered and broke. 'She was mad at me! Almost like she blamed me.'

'For your aunt's death? That's crazy.'

'I know. How could that be my fault? Even if I'd gone like I was supposed to . . .' She stared at nothing and took a long, shaky breath. 'She's really mad about something else. It goes back a long way, to that summer when I went to England. I knew there was something, when I got back. I could feel it. But she wouldn't talk about it. I guess she thought, since I was there, that I was in on it, and so she did kind of blame me. But really I didn't know anything about it. In fact, I completely forgot until she reminded me just now. I didn't go to Aunt Margaret's by myself. My dad went with me – and he didn't come back. He stayed in England, with her. I guess she was the one he really loved all along.' Isobel shook her head slowly.

'Look, whatever happened, there's no way it was your fault.'

'I know. But I was there. I was involved.'

'You were just a kid. Don't let her guilt-trip you. Mothers can do that, I know.' He was getting uncomfortable, squatting there on the floor. 'I think you need something to eat.'

'Oh, gosh, yes, I'm starving. Let me just go wash my hands and face.'

He cleared his typewriter and books off the folding table and laid out the feast. He had generously over-ordered, eager to expand Isobel's appreciation of Chinese food, but also thinking that any leftovers would be nice for breakfast.

She ate with appreciative appetite, and they'd killed nearly half a bottle of wine between them before she said, quite calmly, 'I guess I'm going to have to go to England.'

He felt a hollow ache inside. 'No, you're not.'

'Yes, I am.' She smiled sadly.

'You've let her guilt-trip you. Is she going to pay your expenses?'

'She is, actually. But it's not about that.' She took a breath. 'It's my dad. He's still there. He's bound to be at the funeral. I'll have a chance to talk to him. I want to do that. I need to. I told you that I don't remember what happened. Now that Margaret's dead, he's the only one who can tell me anything.'

'I get it.' He reached for her hand, careful it was the right one. 'You have to go.'

She clasped his fingers in her own. 'I know. But I'm still scared. I'd feel better if you came with me.'

'Really?'

'I know it's a lot to ask, but if you could . . .'

'Are you kidding? In a hot second, sweetheart. There's nothing I'd rather do than run away with you. When do we leave?'

★

The black notebook

Is it a trap? Maybe she's not dead.

But no, why would she pretend? And then for my mother to be in on it? She wasn't acting, I'm sure. She was so mad at me for not going over there when I was supposed to.

Anyway, now I know my father stayed behind and sent me home alone, I have my own reason for going. I'm not a go-between for my mother. I need to find out the truth for myself.

★

Fitz had already used his week of paid vacation time; asking for another two, even unpaid, earned him an incredulous laugh from the boss. 'Sorry, maybe at the end of the year, but not before.'

'I need it now – or at least this month.'

'No way.'

Without stopping to consider, he announced he was quitting. 'Sorry for the short notice. I can stay till the end of next week if you like, but I'd rather just finish what I've got to do today.'

Arnold was not exactly a friend, but had always been friendly, and now he looked concerned. 'Is there a problem, Fitz? Family emergency?'

Tempting as it was to take the offered excuse, Fitz didn't want to lie. 'Not my family, but . . . it's something I just have to do.'

He told no one but his sister Sally that he was going. He usually tried to keep his girlfriends away from his sister, who could be unpleasantly perceptive and very sarcastic about their foibles and failings, but somebody had to look after the cats, so the meeting was inevitable.

Isobel was in one of her down moods. Feverish excitement about going to England and, as she kept saying, *finding the truth,* had given way to the dull fear that she was making a terrible mistake. Sally tried to strike up a conversation, but Isobel scarcely responded to her overtures, huddled on the sofa, looking miserable. Fitz had managed to sedate the cats and get them settled in their baskets before Sally arrived, so he was able to hustle her out in record time. 'Best to get these guys over to yours before they wake up. And you don't want to get a ticket.'

She gave him the side-eye, but said goodbye to Isobel, and did not speak again until they were on the street. He braced himself for one of her cruel parodies, but she only said, 'Is she always like that?'

'Her aunt just died.'

'So you said.' Sally sighed, and, when the cats in their carriers had been loaded into the back seat of her car, she surprised him with a hug. 'She's lucky to have you looking after her. But.'

'What?'

'It's awfully sudden, that's all.' She drew back and gave him a searching look. 'I've never seen you like this before. Is she really the one?'

'I've never felt like this before. Yes.' The question burst out of him almost against his will: 'What did you think of her?'

'I think I don't know her like you do. I hope she cheers up soon and the two of you have a wonderful time. And I think that if I find out she's hurt my little brother, I will track her down and wring that long white neck of hers.'

Little more than a week after their first meeting, Fitz and Isobel were driving through a fairy-tale landscape of gentle green hills and valleys, thatched cottages and picturesque villages. The sky was grey, the air misty, the weather more like March than late

June, but Fitz was enchanted despite his concern for Isobel, who was tense, on edge, switching between manic determination and silent fear.

She'd already reserved a car and insisted on driving directly from Heathrow down to Devon, although there was no obvious reason for hurry since her aunt's funeral (or 'supposed funeral', as she had said once) was over. She also insisted on doing the driving, and Fitz, who had seldom been behind the wheel of a car in the three and a half years that he'd been living in the city, did not protest.

'Just remember to stay on the right side of the road,' he said.

'The *left* side.'

'That's right, the left side is the right side – Who's on first?'

She either did not get or did not appreciate his jokes. He shut up and let her drive.

It was nearly four when they arrived in Taviton, a little grey-stone town of narrow, cobbled streets nestled on the edge of Dartmoor. The solicitor (Fitz loved the word and corrected Isobel when she called him a lawyer) who was handling her aunt's estate had his office there. Isobel spotted a parking place in the central square and neatly inserted the car, then let her shoulders slump as she gave a great sigh of relief.

Fitz rubbed her back. 'You did good. We're here. You can relax now. Maybe we could get a room in that hotel over there – it looks nice and Olde English.'

'We need to find the lawyer.'

'The solicitor can wait. I could do with something to drink and I bet you could too.'

'I want to find him before he closes.' She opened her door and got out.

Fitz got out, stretched, and gazed around with hungry curiosity. He'd seen nothing of England except through the car windows, and he longed for the chance to go exploring. The air still felt chilly, but the sun had broken through the clouds and burnt off the last of the mist long since. The small town appeared a lively enough place, the streets around the square full of people, some obviously local, like the women with their little shopping carts, the groups of school children and people walking their dogs, others, like the backpackers who had stopped to consult a map, presumably tourists.

'Okay, the office should be just up that street off the square on the right.' Isobel came up beside him and gave him a little push. He wondered if he had fallen asleep on his feet. Somehow, while he had been gazing dreamily at his surroundings, she had evidently found someone who was able to give her directions.

Fitz had imagined an ancient, Dickensian office stuffed with quires and rolls of parchment, but the reality was disappointingly modern and ordinary: airy white rooms on the ground floor of a grey house halfway up a street of similar houses. The solicitor, Felix Barnes, was a bland-featured young man in a sharp three-piece suit, and no wig. He was laid back to an extreme that came across as boredom. At first he took Fitz for Isobel's husband; when he learned that this was not the case, he addressed himself entirely to Isobel. As if, thought Fitz, I was the lady's butler. He wasn't bothered; he found it funny. And, of course, it was Isobel's business. If she wanted his help she would ask.

The entire estate had been left to Isobel. In addition to the house and furnishings, there was sixty thousand pounds in a savings account. It was all quite straightforward, and although it would take some time – months, probably – for the probate, in the meantime he saw no reason why Isobel should not visit the house or even stay there for as long as she liked. Indeed, her aunt had specifically mentioned this in her will. In due course, after probate, said Mr Barnes, he would be happy to handle the sale of it under Isobel's instructions.

'Thanks. There's no hurry. I'm sorry I couldn't get here in time for the funeral. Was it well attended?'

'I couldn't say. The person to ask would be Mrs Teggs, or her daughter, at Trescott Farm. They were your aunt's nearest neighbours and saw her every day. It was the daughter who found the body.'

Fitz jerked his head up, startled by the phrase. So the old lady hadn't died in a hospital bed?

Isobel did not query it; she had something else on her mind. 'Has anyone asked for me? Or left a message or . . . ?'

'I'm sorry?'

'I'm trying to find my father. Bill Mannering. William Mannering. I thought he would be living there?'

'We haven't had any enquiries. It was my understanding that Miss Ward lived alone and had done since the death of her mother. I couldn't say as to visitors – again, your best source might be the Teggs. My only instructions were those left in the will, which makes no mention of anyone else. Would you like me to make enquiries?'

'Oh, no, no thank you. I will ask Mrs Teggs.'

The solicitor gave Isobel a copy of the will, a map of the area, and directions to the house which was now (or nearly) hers.

Outside in the street, Isobel shivered. Fitz put his arms around her. 'Come on, let's go get something to eat, go inside and get warm, and I can warm you up another way.' He stroked her back, then slipped his hand beneath her shirt to feel her silken-smooth skin. It had been so long since they'd been flesh-to-flesh; the longest stretch of abstinence since their first night together. He tried to kiss her, but she slipped away. 'Not here.'

'We'll get a room.'

'Why spend money on a room when I've got a whole house?'

He frowned, imagining the house of a dying woman, the smells of illness, soiled sheets, dirty dishes piled up in a filthy sink . . . 'But there won't be anything to eat. We'd have to drive back here, and then – you may not realize, but we are both jet-lagged, and after a good meal and a glass of wine, neither one of us would be in any fit state to drive back into the dark countryside, so we might as well be sensible and get a room now.'

From the way her shoulders relaxed he thought she'd given in, but then she said, 'We should get something to eat before we go.'

Taviton was not New York City. There were only a few restaurants, and none of them would be serving before six-thirty or seven. There were no fast-food franchises, and the fish and chip shop (take-away only) also closed between the mandated lunch and dinner hours. They managed to find one café open, but it was closing in half an hour, and could offer only cakes, rolls or sandwiches with a hot drink. Fitz knew when fate was against him and agreed to that. As they waited for their inevitably disappointing repast, Fitz examined the map. It was an enlarged photocopy of part of an Ordnance Survey map to a scale walkers would find useful, with every building, ruin and geographical feature marked. The solicitor had put a red dot to mark the tiny square that represented the house that Isobel had inherited, and a yellow one for 'Trescott Fm'. They were about six miles from the town.

'Why did your aunt live there?'

'It's where she was born. She stayed on after Grandmother died. My mother was the one who got away.'

'But what did she do?'

'Besides her witchy stuff?'

'Is that how she made her living?'

'I don't know. Maybe.'

Isobel had referred to her aunt as a witch a few times before, but he didn't know how to take it. 'You're serious?'

Their coffees arrived then. She waited until the woman had gone back to the kitchen before replying.

'I always thought so. My grandmother knew all about it, only my mother didn't want to have anything to do with that stuff.'

'Wait – you're saying your grandmother was an actual, practising witch?'

Isobel took a sip of coffee, made a face, and reached for the sugar pot. 'I never met her, and my mom never really talked about her. I looked her up when I was at college. They had a couple of her books in the library, all about folklore, witchcraft, old religions and stuff. She was an anthropologist, I guess. At Oxford, but she rented a cottage on Dartmoor so she could study the folk beliefs and history of the area. Later, she bought the cottage and lived there full time. There were rumours that she'd 'gone native' and started up a witch cult, or coven.' Isobel shut up when the door to the kitchen swung open and the same woman trudged across the floor bearing two plates of rather sad-looking sandwiches.

Fitz waited to ask: 'And was that true?'

'Who knows?' Isobel picked up her sandwich and put it down again. 'She was an unmarried mother. That wasn't something they let you get away with in those days. That could be why she left Oxford. My mother never knew her dad, but we can guess he was married, most likely one of her colleagues. Maybe he sent them money, or maybe he never even knew about the girls. He wasn't part of their lives. They had their mother's name.'

Fitz had already finished his sandwich. He gestured at hers. 'You should eat.'

'I'm really not hungry.'

'You should have something besides this horrible coffee.'

She smiled slightly, shook her head, and pushed the plate towards him. 'You have it.'

'You sure?' He was too hungry to refuse. 'So, about these books your grandmother wrote . . .'

'I only read one. *Survivals of Pagan Religion in Modern Britain.*'

'Agatha Ward? Your grandmother was Agatha Ward!'

'You've heard of her?'

'Author of *Pig Cults in Pre-Christian Britain.*' He gave a startled laugh and turned to look out the window at the narrow street outside. 'And here we are! The site of the Taviton Pig Fair. I knew there was something familiar about the name.' In response to Isobel's blank stare, he explained: 'It's an annual event – and ancient, supposedly one of those relics of pagan times that brought her to Devon in the first place.' He laughed again. 'I wish I'd known; I'd have brought it along to read on the plane.'

'You actually have that book?'

'How could I resist a title like that, and priced at just a quarter? And here I am with the author's granddaughter. Talk about serendipity.'

'Excuse me, but I'm going to have to close in a few minutes.' The proprietor of the café was glaring down at them. 'Perhaps you'd like to pay now?'

Fitz offered to drive, but Isobel refused. She was used to the car and driving on the left, and the coffee had perked her up. He kept the map open on his lap, prepared to play navigator, but even that was hardly necessary, once they found the road that led out of town and onto the moor.

At first, high green hedges on either side of the narrow country lane hid whatever view there might have been, but as the road climbed higher it emerged into an empty, rocky landscape offering inspiring, if bleak, open vistas.

Here, England seemed a much larger, more ancient place, no longer cosy. The treeless space of the moor was interrupted by oddly shaped jutting rocks called tors. It was very different from the misty green watercolour scenes they had gone through earlier. If this land belonged to a fairy tale, it was one of the darker, more disturbing ones.

Fitz consulted the directions the solicitor had given Isobel and kept an eye out for the unmarked turning, a smaller road that wound down from the higher altitude into a valley. They crossed a rippling, rocky stream over an old stone bridge, and soon afterwards he spotted the wooden sign for Trescott Farm, pointing down an unpaved track.

Trescott Farm was where the neighbours lived, and Fitz was reminded of something the solicitor had said, about who had 'found the body'. 'How did your aunt die?'

'She killed herself. Pills, I think.'

His heart gave an unpleasant lurch, and he remembered Isobel's tear-stained face when she had said her mother blamed her. He had imagined a long, slow decline and a hospital bed. He had been thinking of Isobel's aunt as an old woman, like his father's older sister, but Isobel's aunt was her mother's twin, probably not out of her forties.

'Why didn't you tell me?'

'You didn't ask.' She gave a small cry. 'Look! There it is.'

The witch's house: a small, whitewashed, thatched cottage with windows staring like hooded eyes. Miss Ward had been dead little more than a week, but the house looked as if it had been abandoned long before. The land in front of it was neither lawn nor garden, but had been colonized by a wide variety of shrubs, brambles and nettles. He saw no flowers, nothing that appeared to have been planted on purpose and cultivated. At the back, the land rose sharply up towards the moor. Beside the house, on the left, was a small wood of twisted, stunted trees. Between the wood and the house was a roughly pebbled area that might have served as both driveway and parking space, and Isobel, after a pause to stare and take it all in, pulled off the track and drove slowly towards the house. Fitz thought he caught a glimpse of someone running away through the trees, but when he turned his head to look again, with all the branches and the shifting light, it was impossible to know if there had been anything.

He shrugged off a feeling of unease. 'So, is this the place you remember?'

'I don't remember,' she said sharply. 'I told you. But – yeah, somehow, I recognize it. I'm sorry.' She turned and reached for him. 'I don't mean to snap. I'm on edge, is all. I still don't know if coming here was a good idea. It could be the stupidest thing I've ever done. Stay with me, all right? Don't leave me.' She buried her face in his chest and held him tightly.

'You've got me for as long as you want me,' he said. After a moment she reached up and they shared a long, tender kiss.

They walked hand in hand around the house to the front door. It was painted black and Fitz had to seize the handle and give it several sharp tugs before it opened. Inside, the air was chilly and smelled of damp and something else he couldn't place.

Isobel made a small sound. 'I know that smell,' she whispered, clutching his hand.

The first room as they entered had a low ceiling, but it was a good size and felt spacious, with white walls and pale carpeting. The furnishings were simple and modern, tending towards pale wood and bright, printed fabrics. Everything was neat and tidy. There was a wood-burning stove, and bookcases ... but Isobel tugged him away before he had a chance to see their contents.

'This was her bedroom,' she said, opening another door.

In this room, the furniture was older, perhaps inherited. A high, narrow four-poster bed, small bedside table, a double-doored wardrobe, large chest of drawers, a dressing table, and, next to the window, a rocking chair. All were made of the same dark, polished, reddish wood. A boldly striped bedspread, yellow and red and grey, matched the curtains and the colours of an Indian rug on the floor. The walls were white but rather dingy. A few small pictures in heavy frames hung on the wall. Isobel released his hand and walked towards the dressing table. Fitz took this as permission to move nearer to one of the pictures, which turned out to be a portrait of a young woman. It looked very old, and was vaguely familiar, although he couldn't think what it reminded him of. The subject had a high forehead revealed by the elaborate peaked head-dress covering her hair, and wore a pale blue high-necked dress studded with pearls. Her face was pretty, but with something disturbing about it. Her slanting grey eyes reminded him of Isobel, but not the tiny mouth that was pursed in a way that made him think she might be about to bite with vampire fangs. Then he noticed she was holding something in her lap, just visible above the frame. Leaning closer, he saw it was some sort of ugly little animal. It might have been a lap dog, but surely not with such a boneless-looking body.

He frowned and turned away. Isobel was staring into the age-spotted mirror on the dressing table. She was very pale, her eyes wide and fixed as if she could not believe what she was seeing. He went up behind her, put his hands on her shoulders, and looked into the mirror at his face next to hers.

With a gasp, she shut her eyes and fell back against him. 'Oh, Fitz, she's not dead, I can feel it! She's been waiting for me all this time!'

He pulled her away from the mirror and into an embrace. 'Of course she's dead. You don't think old Solicitor Suit would be party to such a deception? There must have been an autopsy, to confirm the cause of death. She died and she was buried.'

Isobel muttered, 'Maybe her *body* was buried.'

'Is it her ghost you're worried about now? You think this house is haunted? Maybe her spirit is trapped in the mirror?'

She muttered against his neck, 'It's me who's haunted.'

'Want me to break the mirror?'

'No!' She looked up at him, frowning. 'Don't you start. I need you to stay sane and pull me back when I get crazy.'

'Yes, ma'am. How about we put a sheet over it? That's the tradition in some places when someone has died.'

She shuddered and shook her head, pulling away from him. 'Let's just get out of here. Come on. My room was upstairs.'

The staircase turned out to be hidden behind another door in the main room. The unpainted wooden steps were not easy to climb, being steep and narrow as they curved around, but they did not have far to go before they came to a small landing and three doors. 'That one is the bathroom. This one was mine.' She opened the door to reveal a bedroom furnished with twin beds, a dresser, writing table and chair, small wardrobe, and a bookcase. It was slightly crowded with all that furniture, but bright and cheerful, and the window with a view down to the green valley let in plenty of light.

'She didn't change a thing,' Isobel said in a wondering tone. 'Ten years later it's exactly the same, even the books she bought for twelve-year-old me.'

'What's in the other room?'

'Nothing.' She leaned towards the bookcase, tilting her head to read the titles, pulling at his hand until she released it. 'Go see if you want.'

He did. It was dark inside the room, but he could see enough to be sure that there was nothing in it: bare floorboards, bare white walls, and not even a window. That he found disturbing, and stepped back onto the landing and closed the door.

'I'm surprised she didn't use it for storage, at least.'

'Maybe she didn't have anything to store.'

'Most people –'

'Most people aren't as messy and don't accumulate stuff like you do, Fitz.' She smiled and cuddled up to him, removing any possible sting from her words.

'Feeling better?'

'I was happy in this room. I remember that much.'

He moved to kiss her. She broke it off before he could make more of it. 'Come on, I haven't shown you the kitchen, and we need to get our bags from the car.'

The kitchen was the largest room in the house, and it felt like the oldest, the least touched by individual tastes or the passage of time. There was not a trace of the damp smell from the other rooms, and it was warm. The big, solid-fuel-burning stove gave off a steady heat.

A note on the table from Mrs Teggs said she had lit the fire and left fresh milk, a box of eggs, butter and cheese for them.

'Oh, wasn't that nice of her!'

Fitz was not so sure. How had she known they were coming? Maybe the solicitor had told her. She obviously had her own key. He looked at the stove. It could have been fifty years old. He didn't know anything about such things but maybe it was better to keep them going than to let them go out, like some primitive version of a nuclear reactor. Not that he knew anything about nuclear reactors.

Isobel was exploring the cupboards. 'I don't know about you, but I'm starving. I could make a cheese omelette.'

'Sounds good. Any chance the sainted Mrs Teggs left us a nice bottle of wine?'

She wrinkled her nose at him, and he was put in mind of Samantha, the television witch who did magic by twitching her nose. 'No such luck. I don't know if Aunt Margaret was a drinker. I didn't see any in the pantry.'

'I guess we'll have to rough it,' he said. 'Can I do anything?'

'Just sit, keep me company.'

It didn't take her long to make a large omelette, but he almost dozed off while waiting, and by the time they'd finished eating, they were both yawning, eager for bed, happy to leave the dishes unwashed.

Getting their bags up the stairs was a bit of a struggle, but there was no question about where they intended to sleep. Fitz pushed the twin beds together, and then they undressed and climbed in between the sheets, shivering a little at their coolness after the warmth of the kitchen. They cuddled and kissed, and despite his weariness, Fitz was aroused, but seconds later he realized that Isobel was asleep. Before he had time to feel sorry, he had fallen asleep.

He woke in darkness, to the delicious feeling of Isobel's naked body pressed urgently against his, her hand stroking his cock. When he reached for her, she caught his hand and pulled it between her legs. She was very wet and knew what she wanted, guiding him with the pressure of her own fingers against his. This assertiveness was new and exciting. He wondered if she was really awake. He was still half asleep himself and let her take control. She had plenty of energy, changing position, gliding over him, rubbing against his unresisting body. Eventually she mounted him and rode him to some private, demanding rhythm of her own. As he fondled her breasts and felt the muscles flexing in her stomach and thighs his only regret was that the darkness meant he could not see her. But the sound that she made when she came was evocative enough to bring back a week's worth of erotic memories, and triggered his own orgasm.

She raised herself off him and got out of bed. Fitz made a small noise of protest, but already he was falling back to sleep.

A shrill scream jolted him awake.

'Isobel?'

Heart pounding, with no idea where the light switch could be, Fitz got up into darkness, stiff and uncoordinated as he shuffled forward with hands outstretched until he found the half-open door and saw a narrow band of light from beneath the door he remembered belonged to the bathroom.

'Isobel? Can I come in?'

Still no reply, but she had screamed; she might need his help. He opened the door.

Isobel was standing there, naked and streaked with blood. A large mirror hung on the wall above the bathtub, and she was staring at her reflection in horror. Her hands were crimson; her thighs, stomach, breasts all daubed with blood; there were even streaks of it on her face.

Shocked and queasy, Fitz caught his hand in his mouth and realized that it, too, was dark with dried blood. Looking down he saw the blood on his own thighs, matting his pubic hair, staining his penis, and breathed more easily as he understood what had happened.

'Sweetie, wake up, it's only your period.' He touched her shoulder.

She cried out and flinched away, still staring at her reflection. 'The blood!'

'Yes, but it's all right, nobody's hurt, it's only your period. Um, you're not hurt, are you? You are having your period?'

'It's happened before,' she said hopelessly. 'I remember now.'

'What?'

'It was her, all covered in blood. She was with my father.' She shut her eyes. 'Just now, when I looked, I saw her. I look just like her. All that blood! It wasn't mine.' Shuddering, she rubbed hard at her face.

'Let me clean you off.' He took a hand towel and wet it at the sink, then began to wipe her face.

Isobel kept her eyes shut. 'She might be my real mother, you know. That would explain why I look so much like her. And why my mother is so cold to me, if I'm not really hers. And why they both wanted me to come here.'

'I thought they were twins. Weren't they identical?'

'I can tell the difference. So could he, I bet.'

He decided to ignore that, and after finishing wiping her breasts, knelt on the cold floor and cleaned the blood from her stomach, her thighs and her legs. By then he was feeling sick. So much blood, everywhere. Even though he knew it was normal, no cause for alarm, he was disgusted. How could she let herself . . . why wasn't she embarrassed? How did women stand it? But they had to; he did not. He turned back to the sink and used another towel to clean himself of her blood. He wished they could both take a shower, but there was only the bathtub. He imagined how quickly the water would turn red, how she would appear to be wallowing in blood – her own, someone else's, what difference?

The next time he looked at Isobel her eyes were open. She was staring again at her reflection. Her skin looked unusually pink, but the worst of the blood was gone. Then he saw a fresh trickle run down her leg.

'Isobel, for goodness sake.' He grasped her by the arms and made her look at him. 'Have you got a tampax? Or do you want a bath first? I wouldn't mind one myself.'

She looked surprised. 'What happened?'

He sighed heavily. 'We had sex. Your period came on. You bled all over the both of us, and then you freaked out about it.'

'I mean what did I say? When I looked in the mirror? I remembered something – what was it?'

She was wide awake and desperate.

He sighed wearily. 'It didn't make a lot of sense. You must have been half asleep. I think you said you saw your aunt with your father. And that there was blood all over her. Or him. You said you looked just like her, and you thought that meant your aunt was your real mother. And then I said I thought your mothers were twins. Weren't they identical?'

'Identical twins, yes.'

He shook his head wearily. 'Then it doesn't make any sense – '

'Sometimes when I look in the mirror, I see her face coming through. But what did I say?'

'Just what I've told you. Don't you remember?'

'No.'

★

The black notebook

I don't have to stay. Nobody made me come here, and nobody can make me stay. Fitz would love to take me away, and it's tempting. But if I go, I will never remember what happened ten years ago. I will never understand, and my past will be as blank as my future. I'd be a mystery to myself forever.

Maybe it's dangerous, but if you don't take risks you might as well be dead. I want to *know*.

It's like sex. I used to be so afraid of sex. I thought it would be the end of me, somehow. I used to think there was a curse on me, a mark like the ring that my aunt had put on me to keep me a virgin and keep me safe. I was so afraid of what might happen if I ever gave myself to a man that I did not dare.

Now I can't imagine a life without sex. Sex is power, like knowledge. It could destroy me, but I won't let it. I will learn how to use it.

★

Fitz was eager to leave the next day, to set off to see more of the country. They could go down to Cornwall or back to London. He fancied Stonehenge . . .

But Isobel would not leave.

'This is what I came for. I want to find out who I am. Where my mother came from. What happened to my father. If the answers aren't here, then they might be inside me – being here will help me remember. I'm sure of it. But you can go if you like,' she said, with a hurt, sideways look. 'I won't stop you. You can even take the car.'

'And leave you stuck here all alone? No way! I came here to be with you. You stay, I stay.' He embraced her, and for a moment she relaxed into him, but when he slipped a hand underneath her T-shirt to caress her bare back she shrugged him off.

'Not now. We should go over to the farm and thank Mrs Teggs before it gets any later.'

They went out into the sunlit morning. The air smelled fresh and green with an earthy undertone. Holding Isobel's hand, walking along the empty road, hearing nothing but birdsong and the sound of leaves rustling in the breeze, Fitz thought he didn't need anything else.

But there was still a serpent in this garden of Eden, and he couldn't ignore it. Isobel had remembered something last night, and then quickly repressed it. Even when he had told her what she'd said, about seeing her aunt and her father together, covered in blood just as she'd seen herself in the mirror, she seemed incapable of making the obvious connection. The adults would have had to come upstairs to clean themselves – the only bathroom in the house was located directly opposite Isobel's bedroom. It wasn't exactly what Freud had called the primal scene, but it was bad enough. Had they threatened Isobel to keep quiet? Or flatly denied it? Or maybe they hadn't even seen her. Unable to cope with keeping this secret from her mother, Isobel had protected herself by forgetting it and everything connected to that summer in England.

Well, if she was going to remember, she'd have to do it herself. It was no good trying to force her.

As they approached the broken-down gate beside a white metal sign for Trescott Farm he became aware of a horrible stench.

'It's the pigs,' said Isobel, sounding excited. 'I remember them. The big ones were kind of scary, but the babies were so cute, I wished I could have one. I remember! Aunt Margaret said that if I stayed here with her I could. But I couldn't take it back to Tennessee, so that was that.'

'Bless the smelly pigs,' said Fitz, grinning.

'Why?'

'It's brought back a memory.'

She stopped where she was and gazed at him, then began to smile. 'You're right. And *I* was right. It's all going to come back to me.' She flung her arms around him and gave him a quick, hard hug before hurrying on into the yard.

There was the farmhouse, a big wooden house, painted green, with a pitched slate roof. A girl in a dirty yellow sweater and flowered skirt was sitting on the steps.

At the sight of her, for no reason he could understand, Fitz felt the hairs rise on the back of his neck. He had occasionally reacted negatively to strangers, but seldom with so much immediate antipathy. He tried to put a protective arm around Isobel, but she was already ahead of him, calling out.

'Donna? Are you Donna? You won't remember me – I think you were only about five years old the last time I was here.'

The girl rose to her feet. She had an expressionless, flat, freckled face. 'I know you, you're Isobel.' Turning towards the house she yelled, 'Mum! She's here.'

Then, to Isobel: 'I stayed home from school on purpose. Mum says, will you come in and have a cuppa?'

'Thank you. This is my friend, Fitz.'

Donna took no notice. She went up the steps to open the door. Isobel started after, until Fitz caught her arm.

'I don't want to go in there,' he said, low-voiced.

She looked at him in disbelief. 'What?'

There was no way he could explain. 'It's a feeling – I don't like it.'

'You can stay outside if you want.'

There was nothing to do but to follow her in.

The big farmhouse kitchen smelled of hot grease and fried bacon. Mrs. Teggs was a plump, plain woman. She embraced Isobel and exclaimed over how long it had been and how much she had grown and how sad it was that she had not been able to come while Maggie was still alive. Introduced to Fitz, she smiled and nodded vaguely, not meeting his eye. He wondered if she sensed his antipathy to her daughter – if, perhaps, this was not unusual. More than anything, Fitz was uneasily aware of the girl. There was nothing overtly threatening or uncanny about her; she was just a rather slatternly-looking teen who took no interest in the adults in the room, but Fitz would not have turned his back on her.

Mrs. Teggs offered them 'a good cooked breakfast', and, to Fitz's dismay, Isobel accepted, with every sign of pleasure. It was true that they'd had nothing but toast that morning, but he had no desire to extend their visit beyond the polite minimum.

'Nothing for me, thanks.'

'Nothing at all? You sure? Just tea, then.'

'I'd prefer coffee.'

She looked as affronted as if he'd asked for a shot of whisky. 'I don't have none of that.'

'Tea then, thank you.'

The drink was served to him in a cup with a film of grease on the rim and half full of milk. He wished he hadn't bothered.

Mrs Teggs got busy at the stove, chatting to Isobel while she cooked, answering her questions about her aunt with a flood of platitudes that avoided anything that felt real or individual. Soon, she served up a plate of fried food: sausage, bacon, eggs, even bread fried in bacon grease.

'Wow, this is great, thank you,' Isobel exclaimed before digging in with what appeared to be genuine appetite. For a brief while there was silence, but eventually Isobel asked her question: 'Do you know what happened to my father?'

'How d'you mean?'

'Was he at the funeral?'

'Oh, no, dear. It was a private funeral, just as she wanted.'

'Didn't he – wasn't he living with her?'

'Oh, no. Our Maggie was a single lady. She never married. She lived by herself ever since her mother died.' She gave Isobel an odd look. 'Whatever made you think your father – Maggie's brother-in-law – would be there?'

'He was here – he came with me.'

'Ten years ago. Why would you think he'd come back?'

Isobel frowned down at her plate. 'I thought he'd stayed with her.'

Mrs Teggs said nothing. Isobel sighed. 'So I was wrong. I got the wrong idea.' She pushed her plate aside. 'Thank you, that was very nice.'

'Oh, my dear, you haven't even finished your eggs, or touched the sausage. Didn't you like it?'

'It's all good, just too much for me. I'm not used to eating so much in the morning. Do you mind if I use your bathroom?'

'Of course, love. Donna, show Isobel where it is. More tea, Mr Fitz?'

'No thanks.' He asked the question he had hoped Isobel would bring up, bluntly, before he lost his nerve: 'Why did Margaret kill herself?'

Mrs Teggs made a *tsk*ing sound and looked down at the flowered oilcloth table covering as she replied: 'It was the cancer. She knew she was dying, and she couldn't stand the thought of being helpless, and ending her days in hospital. It was her choice.'

Fitz frowned. 'Her timing could have been better, don't you think? She had invited Isobel to visit, and if everything had gone according to plan, Izzy would have arrived to find her aunt had just died, and she would have had to take care of all the arrangements –'

'No, Mr Fitz, you are wrong about that. Maggie always knew she could trust me to take care of everything.'

'Still it would have been an awful shock. Not a nice thing to do to your only niece, was it?'

'I wouldn't presume to judge the poor dear departed soul, and nor should you.'

Nothing more was said until Isobel and Donna came back.

Fitz stood up, to forestall the possibility of staying longer. Isobel bent and kissed Mrs Teggs on the cheek. 'Thank you for everything. You must have been the most wonderful friend to Aunt Margaret. I'm very grateful.'

'I'm here for you now, dear; and Donna as well. You must let me know if there's anything at all we can do for you.'

They walked away from the house in silence. Only when they reached the old gate did Fitz feel free of the baleful influence of the two women who lived there. Isobel spoke first, her voice low and angry:

'What is wrong with you today?'

'With me?'

'The way you sat there. Glaring at poor Donna, acting like nothing Mrs Teggs could offer you would be good enough – you didn't even drink your tea. What's the matter, did you think she'd put poison in it? You couldn't have made it more clear that you wanted to be somewhere else. So rude! It was embarrassing.'

'I'm sorry.'

'Maybe they're not smart and sophisticated like people in New York City, but they were Aunt Margaret's friends, and I need to be on good terms with them.'

'Only if you're planning on staying.'

'Oh, really? That's the only reason to be polite? You were acting like a jealous dog, growling whenever anybody so much as looks at me.'

This was so true he could not deny it. He knew he had over-reacted, based on a physical aversion to the girl, her mother, the smell of the place, but he tried to defend himself. 'Look, I've said I'm sorry. I didn't mean to embarrass you. But those people ... we don't really know anything about them. Sure, they were your aunt's nearest neighbours, and maybe they were more than that, maybe Mrs Teggs was her best friend, but we only have her word, we don't know –'

'Quit saying "we" all the time. I know they were good to Aunt Margaret, and they were good to me, and they've been nothing but nice to us both.'

'I'm sorry. I'm only trying to – I only want to keep you safe.'

'Oh, for – ' She shot him a furious look. 'Can't you ever shut up and leave me alone for five minutes?' She did not wait for a reply but broke into a run.

He managed to stop himself from running after her, knowing it would only make matters worse, but once she was out of sight, the effort of restraining himself and walking at a steady pace made him nearly ill with anxiety. When he got back to the house he did not call out, and although a wave of relief rushed over him at the sight of her curled up on the couch with a book, he left her alone and went to the kitchen, longing for a cup of coffee.

But there was no coffee to be found, not even a jar of instant. He was going through all the shelves a second time, to make sure, when Isobel came up behind him and wrapped her arms around his waist.

'Sorry,' she muttered.

He shut his eyes, almost dizzy with relief. 'No, I'm sorry. You didn't do anything wrong; I'm the idiot. Can you forgive me?'

She kissed him in answer, and he began to caress her, the urge for caffeine forgotten. 'Let's go back to bed.'

'Not now.'

'Why not? Is there somewhere else you need to be?'

'Of course not.' Her reply came so sharply that it felt like a lie, and he had the crazy thought that she'd made some secret plan with Donna. Before he could put his foot in it again, she said with a sigh, 'Not while I'm – you know. It's too messy. I don't want to have to wash any more sheets and towels. The others aren't even dry.'

He winced, and gave her a gentle kiss. 'Sure. Sorry, I just got carried away. Well – shall we go out? I could murder a cup of coffee.'

'You go. I'm feeling a little . . .' she made a wavy motion with her hand.

'I don't mind staying with you.'

'There's no point. I'm just going to take a couple of aspirin and lie down with a hot-water bottle. Anyway, you need to get your coffee. And you could pick up something for dinner. Unless you're worried about driving.'

He bristled at that. 'Just because I don't own a car doesn't mean I can't drive. I learned to drive when I was fifteen. I grew up in the suburbs –'

'Yeah, but it's a strange car in a different country, it's OK to be nervous –'

'I'm not nervous, not in the least. Now, are you going to give me a shopping list, or will you trust me to buy what we need?'

He was out of the house and away, more than a mile down the road before the thought came to him that he had been played. She had *wanted* him out and tricked him into leaving her there alone.

His shoulders slumped. Well, of course she did. He was a pest, and she knew that if he was around, he'd start up with her again. Of course he would. Not that he'd ever force a woman, but he knew she'd enjoy herself again if she could forget her squeamishness about the mess. Good sex was messy. Orgasm was the best cure for cramps. Some women were even more responsive when they were on their periods . . . he remembered how she'd been last night, in the dark, urgent with desire, and it was all he could do not to turn around and go back. Only the narrowness of the road, enclosed by hedges on either side, made it impossible, and by the time he reached the first turning place, he'd had time to calm down. He wasn't going to be that pest. She'd wanted some time to herself, and he would give her that, in expectation of a warmer welcome when he returned.

★

The black notebook

The cave is where it happened.

As soon as Donna told me where she found Margaret's body, I knew. I almost remembered what happened there the last time I was here. Me and my aunt and my father went to the cave. And she went back there, in the end.

I should have been here for her. Or maybe she knew better and acted before I could arrive – to save me. I'm not scared anymore.

Fitz just went out, so I can go meet Donna. She said she'd show me the cave.

I'm going to find out what the dragon means.

★

Fitz returned, laden with goodies: steaks and spinach (both full of iron, and that was good for Isobel), also potatoes, two bottles of wine and a box of chocolates. Stepping through the door he called out, 'Home is the hunter.'

The still, silent air of the house seemed to muffle and then absorb his words. He knew immediately that Isobel wasn't there, but he called her name anyway; went through to the kitchen to deposit his shopping bags on the table, and then back into the sitting room and up the narrow, enclosed staircase.

'Isobel?'

Disturbed by the thought that she might be hiding from him, he even looked under the bed and inside the wardrobe, and into the empty room.

He trudged back downstairs. He imagined another quarrel brewing, her angry face if he went and found her at the farm, hearing her shouting at him: 'Can't I even go out for a walk? Do I have to ask your permission to talk to the neighbours?'

He was being ridiculously suspicious and overprotective. There was no reason to imagine Isobel was in any danger – and yet every nerve in his body was screaming that she was, and he must find her, save her, before it was too late.

The black notebook he'd seen Isobel writing in was lying splayed open on the couch, between the blanket and the pillow where she'd been nesting. He picked it up, caught sight of his name, and read the last entry.

He was shaking when he put it down. How long had she been gone? What if she got stuck in a narrow passage, or injured in a rock-fall? Presumably Donna knew all about it, but he couldn't trust that bitch to keep her safe. Isobel was such an innocent; it would never occur to her that those two witches at Trescott Farm might have been plotting against her all along.

He had no idea where the cave might be, but it was most likely up on the moor and not far away, so he went behind the house and saw a narrow path that led up onto the moor. When he got there, he saw something yellow, like a marking flag, and began to run towards it.

It was Donna in her yellow sweater. As soon as he was near enough, he shouted, his fury erupting into words: 'Where is she? Where did she go? What have you done?'

The girl gaped at him, her face flat and stupid. He grabbed her by the arm. 'Tell me! Where's Isobel?'

She let herself fall against him. He was very aware of her small, soft breasts beneath the sweater, and the warmth and pressure of her thighs beneath a thin skirt. His involuntary erection made him even angrier, and he held both of her arms with bruising force, holding her away from him as he shouted. 'Don't pretend you don't know! I'm not a fool. I know you know. Tell me where she is. Show me the cave!'

She nodded and made an effort to take his hand, her fingers pulling weakly at his. Because he still had hold of her other arm, Fitz allowed her to loosen his grasp, and let her take his hand, thinking she meant to lead him to the cave. He was taken by surprise when she suddenly thrust herself at him again and tugged his hand to her crotch.

He pushed her off so violently that she fell. Her skirt rode up. She was naked beneath her skirt. She had sparse, reddish pubic hair. She made no move to get up or to cover herself. Instead, she opened her legs wide.

Fitz was violently, horribly aroused. He wanted to throw himself on top of her. He wanted to hurt her. He wanted to rape her. Would it be rape when she was inviting it?

With an effort, he looked away. 'Get up,' he said. His voice sounded strange to him. 'For God's sake, get up.'

Her hand was on his ankle. He held himself very still, forcing himself not to move as she pulled herself up, and said, 'Donna, you must take me to Isobel. Please help me find her.'

She rubbed herself against him like an animal. She had found his erection and swiftly, skilfully, undid his pants to set it free. He did not stop her. He could not. Now her mouth was on him and he was in an agony of pleasure. He grabbed her hair, but only to pull it back from her face, the better to see her sucking on him. He didn't know how much longer his legs would hold him up. He thought of how she had sprawled on the ground, opening her legs to his gaze, showing him everything, and he wanted to see her like that again.

'Take your clothes off.'

As she moved away from him he saw her face, blank and round as the moon, and he hated her. He wanted to hurt her. As she took her sweater off, arms crossed in front of her breasts, temporarily helpless, he attacked. Shoving her onto the ground, Fitz pushed her skirt up, brutally parted her legs, and thrust into her.

She let out a thin, high scream, like a rabbit caught in a trap. He was fiercely glad he had hurt her, but her pain triggered his pleasure. He managed only a few, short, savage strokes inside her and then he was coming, helpless to stop or prolong the final moment.

He pulled out as soon as he was finished. Her clammy flesh sickened him. He wanted to be away. There was blood on her thighs, blood on his cock, he saw, as he wiped himself with his handkerchief. He threw the soiled cloth on top of her and left, not waiting to see what she would do. He wished he could forget what had happened and knew he never would.

He had to find Isobel. If he was too late, if something had happened to her, he would never forgive Donna – or himself. He was the only one responsible. What sort of hero was he, to rape a virgin when he should have been saving his own princess from the dragon?

'Isobel!' His voice was high and desperate, carried away on the wind. He began to run, although he had no idea where he was going.

Then he saw it: a rocky outcrop, the dark entrance to a cave. He stopped just outside, a sudden dread keeping him from entering. 'Isobel? Are you inside? Can you hear me?'

He had no light, not so much as a matchbook. But he had no choice. He had to find her, and that meant he must go inside, to follow the tunnel wherever it led. There had never been any other option from the moment he had set eyes on her than to follow and stay as close as she would allow. He breathed deeply, trying to calm himself, then dropped to his hands and knees. He had never had any particular fear of enclosed spaces or of the dark, but now, together, the prospect was terrifying.

'Isobel, I'm coming in.' He pushed himself, head-first, through the narrow entrance. His shoulders cleared the sides easily. Dry leaves crumbled to ash beneath his hands and knees. Inside, the darkness was profound. He closed his eyes in despair and saw no difference when he opened them.

'Isobel?' He spoke quietly, but the air seemed to vibrate around the name. For the first time he had some sense of the space, and thought it was not large, probably half the size of his own apartment.

He was about to speak again when he caught another sound.

Something moved, and he knew he was not alone in the cave.

It was not Isobel. Whatever moved was nothing human. The sound was of something moving without legs, something coiling and uncoiling, something writhing on the ground. Despite the utter darkness he thought he could see it: a gigantic worm stirring in its corner, roused to wakefulness by his voice.

Terror throttled him. He told himself not to let his imagination run away with him. Only the thought of Isobel kept him from scrambling backwards to get away as fast as he could. But Isobel must be here, too – probably unconscious, since she had not responded to his voice, and certainly in even greater danger than he was. He had come here to save her and he would, even if it had to be with his bare hands. How he wished he had thought to bring some sort of weapon: a knife, even a big stick, and – more practically – something to light his way. Still almost sick with fear, Fitz forced himself to move towards the sound, to take one crouching step forward, hand outstretched – and so he found Isobel.

She was lying on her back and did not respond when he ran his hands over her body. He was shocked to find her naked, but as far as he could tell by touch alone, uninjured. She breathed, slow and steady, and her heart was beating. He kissed her and felt the pulse in her neck. He wondered if she was concussed. Had she banged her head crawling in here? Or, like her aunt, had she taken some pills?

He had to get her out. When she did not respond to his gentle shaking and muttered pleas, he took hold of her shoulders and dragged her as best he could to the exit, wincing at the thought of unseen rocks and grit bruising or scraping her tender flesh. He clambered out first and then pulled her through, his heart beating madly with the fear that someone or something in the dark below would seize hold and pull her back again.

Once in the daylight, he saw no obvious injuries, no lumps or wounds to her head. The sweat was drying on him, making him shiver, and he knew he had to get Isobel inside and warm. In the meantime, he stripped off his shirt and put it on her, then, staggering under her dead weight, and stopping frequently to rest, he carried her down to the house.

He wanted to call for a doctor, but there was no telephone.

He couldn't remember if he had noticed that before. Surely there was one at the farm, but he wasn't going back there ever again. He imagined Mrs Teggs waiting for him with a shotgun. She might even turn up here. The obvious, the only, thing to do was to get Isobel out of here. There was bound to be a hospital in Plymouth.

First he had to get her dressed. He went for the easiest option and got her into some tracksuit bottoms, then finished buttoning the shirt he'd put on her earlier. He found a clean shirt for himself, then packed up everything else he could find and put the luggage into the trunk, and settled Isobel onto the back seat as best he could before getting behind the wheel.

The car would not start. The ignition made a clicking sound and there was no response from the engine. Fitz got out and had what he knew would be a pointless look under the hood. Everything looked normal; there were no dangling wires or pools of oil underneath. He guessed the problem might be with the battery, and that could be dealt with easily enough – but only if you had the right equipment, and help from someone with a car that worked.

He tried a few more times to get it to start, but each failure made him feel more desperate, until at last he had to give up.

He carried Isobel back into the house and put her to bed in her aunt's old room rather than try to negotiate the stairs. Then he searched the house. He found no first aid kit or medical texts, no shortwave radio, and no pills or drugs of any kind. He wondered how Isobel's aunt had killed herself. If Isobel had taken sleeping pills, she must have left the bottle in the cave. There were no prescription medicines, nothing but some aspirin, in her toiletry bag.

She looked and sounded peaceful, as if in normal sleep. Maybe she would wake up after a few hours and be fine. And maybe she wouldn't. She might be dying right now, regardless of appearances. He had no way of knowing. He had to get help.

How long would it take him to walk to Taviton? An hour? But he might be able to hitch a ride, or meet someone who would send for a doctor. Anyway, since he did not dare go to the farm, there was no alternative.

Walking away from the house, leaving her there alone, was agony. What if she died? Or if she woke and needed help? He imagined Donna spying on the house, seeing him go, and taking her chance to finish what she had started – but why should Donna want to kill Isobel? Why would anyone want to end her brief, blameless life?

By the time he reached the road, Fitz couldn't bear the uncertainty and fear. He turned and ran back to the house.

Isobel was still asleep in her aunt's bed. He gazed at her for what seemed a long time, his heart breaking with helpless love for her. It was even harder to walk away from her that time, but he knew he must. Doing nothing could mean her death. She needed a doctor.

This time, he decided, he would not try to walk to Taviton, but would wait to flag down the first car that came past and get them to take him to a doctor. Or maybe tell them to get a doctor, while he went back to watch over Isobel. He looked at his watch every few seconds, but it was not working. He had no idea how much time went by while he waited in vain for any vehicle, but it seemed to him that he had waited a very long time – he might have been halfway to Taviton if he had not made up his mind to wait for a car — when his nerve broke, and he ran back to check on Isobel.

He knew then that he would not leave her again. He would take care of her as best he could. Maybe, if he was really lucky, Donna or Mrs Teggs would have reported him to the police, and he could expect a visit very soon. He didn't care if he wound up in jail, if only Isobel was saved.

He heated some milk, added a lot of sugar to it, and propped Isobel up in bed, trying to get her to take some of it, but she slept on, unresponsive as he soaked a cloth in the warm, sweet drink and dabbed it on her lips.

He chafed her hands between his own, rubbed her feet, and piled on more blankets to keep her warm. He stared out the window and strained his ears for the sound of other people or any vehicles approaching. Nothing happened. Nobody came. It seemed like they were all alone in the world, and Isobel slept on.

Later, he cooked the steak and ate it along with half a bottle of wine. He was comfortably woozy by the time it was dark, and he lay down on the floor beside the bed and listened to the soft, steady music of her breathing, expecting to be awake all night.

This time, when he went to the cave, he took a light and a sword. The first thing he saw was a four-poster bed. Isobel was lying on top of the covers, naked. Her eyes were closed but she was not sleeping. She lay on her back with her legs spread wide and her arms thrown above her head. Her face was flushed and on it was that look of abandonment, of sheer appetite, that he had seen before. She was moving slowly and rhythmically, yet she was alone and not even touching herself. Fitz shone his light along her body and caught a glistening motion in her pubic hair. He leaned closer, steadying the beam, and froze in horror as he saw a snake moving rapidly in and out of her vagina.

If he tried to kill it, he would hurt her. Yet to leave the snake where it was, alive and unharmed, was unthinkable. The sight horrified and disgusted him. He could not permit it to continue. Dropping the sword, he reached out barehanded and grabbed the snake as it emerged, and he pulled it from her body. As he did, he heard Isobel cry out, and the snake sank its fangs into his hand.

Fitz woke. The throbbing in his hand faded and vanished: it was only a dream pain. He was disoriented for a moment, then he remembered where he was and sat up. He couldn't hear Isobel breathing.

He held his breath, listening harder, and heard something moving.

It was the sound he had heard in the cave, a boneless, limbless sound of some huge creature moving like a worm or snake. The monster from the cave was in the room with them.

Fitz tried to remember where the nearest light was, and the door, but he couldn't even tell from what corner of the small dark room the sound had come.

He got up and climbed onto the bed. He bent his head until his lips encountered Isobel's head on the pillow. He felt her smooth hair, her soft cheek, and then the fluttering of her eyelashes against his face. Awake!

'Izzy – '

Her mouth met his, her tongue flickered against his lips, and he forgot his fear in the rush of warmth as they kissed. Maybe everything before, everything but this, had been a dream.

She raised her arms to embrace him, and the covers slipped down. Although he remembered he had dressed her before putting her to bed, she was naked now. He felt her bare arms and rounded breasts, and they glowed with heat. He kissed her more passionately.

Outside, a cloud drifted away, and the silvery light of the full moon shone in through the window. Isobel's face was mysterious and beautiful in that light, and the gleam in her eyes thrilled him. He remembered how she had looked in his dream, as she was sexually pleasured by a snake, and it seemed to him that her face wore that same greedy smile now.

'Let me in,' he said, tugging the blanket. Her smile widened and she slipped to one side, away from him, and drew back the covers to welcome him in.

He gathered her in his arms and stretched his legs to catch hers, wanting to embrace her with his whole body.

But where her legs should have been was the smooth scaly body of a gigantic snake, two feet across at least, impossible but unmistakable. The monster was in bed with them.

Fitz shouted. The thing coiled itself about his legs, trapping him. He struggled to break free, but it was too powerful. And still

Isobel held him in her arms, smiling as if nothing was wrong.

'Isobel,' he begged. Helplessly, terrified, he wet himself. He was crying, understanding that it was Isobel herself who was wrapped about him, holding his legs in what could become a deadly, crushing trap; he knew that, and yet he couldn't believe it. 'Please. Let me go. I love you.'

'Make love to me.'

He wanted to, still, and was horrified to find that he could desire and fear her at the same time. 'Let me go.'

'No, Fitz, I'm never going to let you go.' Her lower half gave him a squeeze that made him scream; he felt a bone break in one of his legs.

At last the instinct for survival won out over the desperate, needy love she had inspired in him, and he fought for his life. His hands were free, so he grabbed hold of her throat and began to strangle her, not in play or holding back, but with serious intent.

The smile on her face did not change, but her neck did. The soft, warm skin became cool and slickly scaled, expanding in his grasp. As her neck lengthened, it began to become her whole body, the face still that of Isobel. He felt her breasts flattening against his chest and her arms shrinking away to nothing, and the moonlight showed him still more that he did not want to see. Her eyes went on watching him with undiminished intelligence, undiminished desire, as she squeezed him harder and harder with her powerful serpent's body. Her smile widened until her lips vanished. He didn't know if he heard his own bones cracking, or if that was the sound her jaws made as they opened before his eyes, dislocating. Her mouth was bigger than his face, bigger than his head, and he felt the heat of her breath, smelled the interior of her body, as he screamed for the last time into her mouth, down her endless throat, as it closed finally over his head.

★

The black notebook

There wasn't much of him left, but I buried his bones at the back of the cave, beside the bones of my father.